San Bruno Public Library
W9-AVO-134

SUNBORN RISING

Beneath The Fall

The World of Sunborn Rising

Book 1 - Beneath the Fall

Book 2 - coming soon

More at

www.sunbornrising.com

Other books by Aaron Safronoff

Evening Breezes

Spire

Fallen Spire

Sunborn Rising

Beneath the Fall

by Aaron Safronoff

Neoglyphic Entertainment
California

Sunborn Rising: Beneath the Fall

Published in the United States by Neoglyphic Entertainment, Inc.
www.neoglyphic.com

Story by
Dane Glasgow and Aaron Safronoff

Art Direction by
Christopher Danger Chamberlain

Produced by
Dane Glasgow, David Ramadge, & Kylie Kiel

Cover and Internal Artwork by
Neoglyphic Entertainment & Artwoork Studio

Edited by Rebecca Steelman and Yellow Bird Editors
Copy Edited by Dominion Editorial

For information on bulk purchases, please contact Neoglyphic Entertainment
contact@neoglyphic.com

First Edition
Printed in PRC

ISBN-13-: 978-1-944606-01-5

To Dane:

You sifted through a hundred pages of random ideas
and picked out the only paragraph that mattered and seeded Cerulean.

To Everyone at Neoglyphic Entertainment:

Your creativity and dedication are endless sources of inspiration,
and none of this would have been possible without each of you.

To the Original Six:

All those late nights reading chapters of Beneath the Fall
we were actually writing the story of us.
Excited for the sequel.

To Kylie:

You've changed my life in a thousand ways, supported my writing and
my madness, and despite my daily, "How many cats?"
you've never once asked me, "How many gnomes?"

For all of Neoglyphic's Children.

Contents

Chapter 1

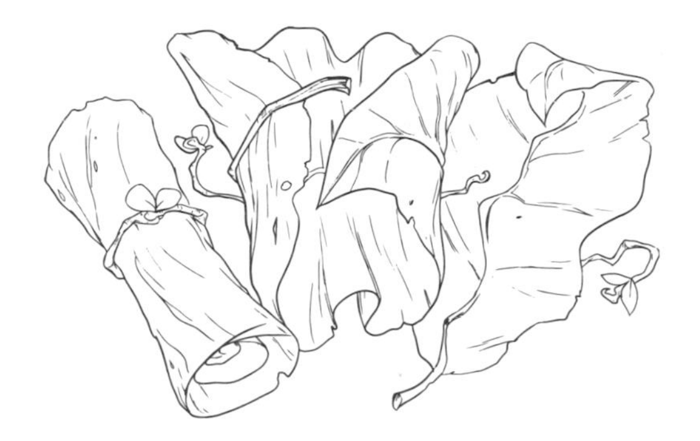

The Secret Remains

Barra's mother had never said that Barra *wasn't* allowed in her father's study. Maybe because she'd never asked. She hesitated at the threshold, feeling her mother's disapproving eyes even though she wasn't home yet. But Barra was determined, and she crossed into the dusty room.

The urge to know about her father was overwhelming, and her mother's memories weren't enough anymore. Barra wanted something all her own, a unique connection, and searching the rest of the den had turned up nothing. Even her mother's room with its keepsakes and journals had revealed little Barra didn't already know. She clung to the hope that some missed trinket remained in the old unexplored study. All she had to do to avoid disappointing her mother was not get caught.

The Secret Remains

Stalking around the study on all fours with her claws retracted and her long tail in the air, Barra was careful to disturb as little as possible. Her efforts were probably unnecessary, as the room had grown wild. The living boughs of wood that composed the floor, curved walls, and domed ceiling had been left untended for more than ten rings, and time had twisted the room's shape, shifting and obscuring its contents.

Few of her father's possessions remained. Barra's mother had cleared the room of any personal or important items long ago, preparing the study to be reclaimed by the trees. The lingering knickknacks were not at all what Barra had hoped to find. Still, she felt closer to him simply being in his room. There was a desk, the smoothed surface of a large braid of wood, arching up out of the floor against the far wall, and she was drawn to it. She thought about her father spending hours at that desk, and wondered if he'd ever held her there while working.

Barra spied a curious deformity, a recess, in the wall behind the desk. A withered cover hung to the side, its texture and markings meant to match the wall, concealing itself and the recess behind—and whatever was held within. Barra saw several sheaves of leaves rolled and tied into tight bundles deep within the hidden cubbyhole.

The rhythm of Barra's heart became a brief rapid staccato like an urgent knock at the door. Barra didn't hesitate. She answered. Reaching inside the cubbyhole, she pulled the sheaves out one at a time.

Laying the sheaves down side-by-side on the floor, Barra gathered seven bundles before the cubby was empty. Each was numbered, and she eagerly undid the braided-willow twine that secured the first. She unfurled the wax-thickened outermost page.

The inner pages of leaves were old and thin, but treated with resin to prevent them turning brittle. Etched into the middle of the top leaf was a symbol. Barra recognized it from the archives as the symbol for Cerulean: a spiraling ball of fire with a ring around it. The fire represented the sun, the space around it the ocean, and the ring was the canopy of the Great Forest.

Barra knew her father had written many journals, but her mother kept all of those in her room, on display. Her mother used to read aloud from them to help Barra sleep at night. *These* sheaves were something new. Something even her mother didn't know about.

Unfamiliar emotions surged through Barra, pressure building in her head as tears welled in her eyes. Laid out before her were her father's private thoughts, and Barra might be the first to ever know them. As though from a distance, Barra watched her own trembling hand grasp the edge of the top leaf and turn it over. She began reading:

> *As I sit down to these leaves, I can't help but wonder about what I'm doing, and why. I need an honest record somewhere. I don't feel safe sharing more with Brace. She probably knows too much already, and there's no reason to distract her right now. This is harder to do than I thought...*
>
> *My recent presentation to the Elders did not tell the whole story of what I discovered in the Middens. I withheld information at Jerrun's request. He said he spoke for the entire Elder*

Council. Maybe he did, I still don't know for sure. I believed him when he said my early observations of the Creepervine were dangerous, and might cause a panic. So, I presented my findings with no hint of the threat growing at our feet. I lied.

Watching myself write that out? Feels so strange. I guess I thought I'd feel relief, but instead I feel judged and I'm the only one here. But in my defense, I was sure my research would continue! I was sure my silence was for the greater good. I mean, I didn't have enough evidence to pass my own scrutiny. I only had my suspicions, a handful of observations, and a few archival anecdotes—but I'm lying to myself. I had seen the Creepervine with my own eyes, and still I allowed the Council to convince me otherwise. There are no excuses. I lied, and now I'm trying to make it right.

The Council has redirected me to taking nectar samples in the Reach for the rest of the ring, and that's no coincidence. It's only been a few days since my presentation. When I asked for an explanation, and stressed that we needed to continue looking to the Middens, Jerrun pretended like we'd never even talked! He put it back to me that there was, "nothing more to see in the

Middens," according to my research. To challenge him openly then would have been to discredit my work and my name forever! He trapped me in my own cowardice. I can't understand his motivations. But he underestimated me. I'm continuing the research alone.

Barra looked up from the loosely scrawled text. Goosebumps turned up the flesh beneath her fur, and she shivered. She felt like she'd summoned the ghost of her father, but it spoke with a voice she didn't recognize. Her father wasn't a liar. The words couldn't be trusted.

She found herself fussing over her tail, nervously tapping the mementos she'd woven into the Thread coiled around it. The Thread held memories, the story of her life told through a collection of baubles. She cared for it meticulously, but had a bad habit of scratching at it whenever she was anxious. Catching herself, she noted—not for the first time—the painful absence of any curios for her father. Other bups had many mementos for both parents, and Barra felt like her Thread looked empty by comparison, only half what it should be. She shook off the thought, stopped fussing with her Thread, and continued reading:

I wish I could talk to someone instead of just writing all this down. Brace knows something of my work of course, but I never told her about the conversation with Jerrun or that I altered my presentation. Better she doesn't know too much in case that old Rattlebark comes sniffing around the den. It bothers me not telling her everything, but it's not only paranoia about Jerrun that holds my tongue. I can't have her suspicious, wondering where I'm going at night, if I want to continue the research. She has to believe everything is normal. I'm lucky she's so busy preparing for Barra's arrival—whenever she asks about my strange behavior, I just say I'm anxious about our first. She'd try to stop me if she knew I was planning to explore the Middens alone. I have to lie to her. I can't see any other way.

I'm going to prove my theory about the Creepervine, or prove myself wrong, and either way, put an end to this need for secrecy. For now, the burden belongs to me and these pages, and I just have to look forward to the day that I look back on all of this, laughing at my silly paranoia.

The last portion of the leaf was empty. Barra slouched onto her hind legs, thinking. This side of her father was completely unknown to her. She'd never imagined him as anything other than a fearless explorer. Barra couldn't understand why her father would hide from anything or anyone. She sat forward again, flipped the leaf, and read:

To understand this world, our home, Cerulean, we must first understand the basic organization of its parts and how they interact. Having established this understanding, we can then make meaningful assertions about its health, its balms and its banes. We need to be the caretakers of the Great Forest in order to ensure that we Arboreals can thrive among its boughs. From the archives, Cerulean comprises a star at the center of a vast ocean covered by flotillas of Great Trees woven together by their roots. Those roots carry water and light all the way up the trunks and into everything that lives and grows in our world. All the flowers and berries, all the wood and leaves, everything we see—even us—it's all the result of the relationship of star, sea, and tree. But something is wrong with that relationship. We are in almost perpetual twilight in the Loft, while the archives are full of bright descriptions. I believe that we've been in the dark for so long, and no one questions it...

Barra's tail swept the air as she looked beyond the body of the text. There were notes in the margins, her father annotating the changes he was making to his presentation. This was the original. The words weren't always legible, and often seemed nothing more than rambling anecdotes. Barra flipped ahead, hastily. She was running out of time. Her mother had to be close to home, Barra was sure of it.

Quickly skimming the pages, she tried to digest as much as she could. Her eyes flew over the words, picking fragments from each of the leaves. There were sketches of insects, flowers, and funguses. Charts were drawn on a few pages showing the flow of water and "relative luminescence"—whatever that meant—over time. She stopped on a leaf that was obviously outside of the formal ordering of the pages:

> *The archives are either too disorganized, or sheaves are missing, or both. I've been trying to investigate without raising suspicion, but the Council is everywhere, and with Jerrun as the Head now, I'm not sure I can do much more there. I better avoid the archives for a bit...*
>
> *I've had dreams lately, like I'm living in the Cerulean of the archives. But the dreams all end the same way—scared and alone in the darkness. I discover the tendrils of the Creepervine in the dream, just like I did in reality, but in the dream the vine is writhing and reaching for something. The Creepervine grows in long, jagged black lines over everything I see, capturing the light and strangling the flow of water. My once vibrant dream is eaten whole, swallowed by the shadows, and I wake up each time in a cold sweat. Brace*

knows there's something wrong, something more than nerves. But I'm close to t he answers, I can feel it. If I could only get a sample to live long enough to examine it away from the Middens, but severed portions shrivel and die in a matter of moments. I'm overworked, filling in my normal time in the Reach and my spare time below. I cut myself exploring tonight. It was a careless mistake. The wound already looks nasty, and now I have one more thing to hide from Brace...

Barra turned over the odd leaf and saw a drawing. It was a menacing, curvy fang, or so she thought until she saw the label that read *Creepervine Thorn.* Barra turned the page back over and read it again. The change in tone of her father's writing bothered her. He sounded confident in his research, but that confidence in the margins faltered, and broke completely on the loose page she held.

Each of the seven sheaves was full of more leaves than Barra cared to count, and there was no time to even look at them all, much less read them all. She'd have to come back—but she couldn't tear herself away, not yet. She pointed her ears and listened closely to be sure; her mother still wasn't home. Barra opened the next sheave, and the next, parting the stacks in half, taking them in at a glance. There were more inserted leaves, and she picked one out to read:

I don't know if I'm any closer to understanding, and I'm frustrated. Every time I go down into the

Middens, I think I'll come back with answers, but I only have more questions. I've skipped some of my days assigned to the Reach to sneak down into the Middens. I think the vine recedes during the day? But that seems impossible, because I've marked only increasing encroachment since I started. And it seems like it would only be wasted energy to hide? So many questions. If I go by my nightbloom measurements, the vine could be growing all the way into the Nest in less than a dozen rings! And lately, I feel like I'm...

"Barra? Honey, where are you?" her mother called out from the kitchen.

The young Listlespur whipped her body around instinctively and knocked a loose seed free from a nearby weed. Barra snatched it from the air in a flash, and tucked it into her cheek to add to her Thread later. It wouldn't exactly commemorate a moment *with* her father, but it was pretty close. She scooped up the sheaves and placed them haphazardly on top of the desk preparing to tuck them back into the cubbyhole, but a quick glance around the study convinced Barra the effort would be wasted. There was no disguising that she'd been there. She stopped fussing with the sheaves, and then crept to the window and slid out into the treescape.

There were branches and dimly illumined foliage in every direction. Barra's fur bristled as she climbed onto the roof of her father's study. She padded onto the adjoining roof of her mother's nestroom, and then stepped—she hoped, silently—onto the kitchen roof. There was a porthole in the center of the roof, and Barra sat down beside it. She began grooming herself as though she'd been sitting there all day.

"Barra!" Her mother called again, irritated.

"Up here!" Barra put her face through the porthole and smiled.

"Get down from there," her mother said. She sighed, shaking her head. "You know I don't like it when you dawdle on the roof. You're like a thief skulking about up there." She continued with a raised eyebrow, "Couldn't you at least *try* to be *somewhat* civilized? For me?"

"Sure. I can *try*," Barra said as she dropped through the porthole. She landed lightly, arched her back, and stretched her tail up. Then she stood and faced her mother only to be greeted by a familiar look of disapproval.

Her mother opened her mouth to speak, but just then her soft pink nose began twitching. She sniffed the air suspiciously. "Where have you been? And *what* have you gotten into? Smells, hmmm, old and dirty." Barra's mom squinted at her and waited for an explanation.

"Nowhere." Barra shrugged. She wanted to tell her mother about the journal, but at the same time she wanted to keep it to herself. If she was silent about her discovery now, she could always tell her mother later.

"The Middens again?" her mother guessed.

"Aww, Mom. It's not dangerous," Barra said. She *had* been in the Middens, so why not go with it?

"Well, go wash up. Dinner soon." Barra was off the hook, and she scampered off before her mom could identify any other scents.

Brace shook her head and began washing berries for dinner. Of course, she'd recognized the smell immediately; Gammel was never far from her thoughts. She was okay with her daughter exploring the old study. Brace was even okay that her daughter didn't tell her about it. It was good for a young bup, especially her Barra, to find her own limits. Besides, there wasn't anything dangerous in the study. Just a bunch of old, crazy dreams.

Alone in the kitchen, Brace said, "She's your daughter, Gammel."

Chapter 2

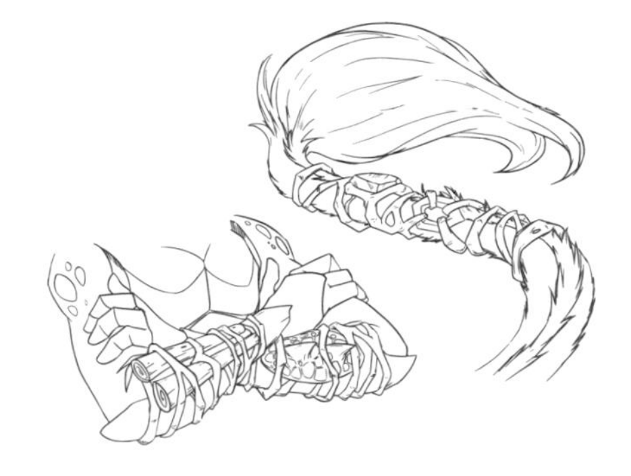

Stretched Thin

Flicks approached from upwind, and though Barra couldn't see him yet, she could smell him. She could tell he was steadily closing in on her.

Barra was strong and lean, fast. Confident she could outrun most Listlespurs, she knew she could outrun a Kolalabat. For this game though, she had to hide. Barra found a tightly knit web of branches and climbed into it. The plush of short, slick furs that covered her body made her difficult to catch and hold, and also, difficult to see. Settling into position, she flexed the fine muscles beneath her skin that adjusted her fur. The follicles bent and shifted in a fluid cascade that tricked the light. Barra blended into the branches and leaves. When the hypnotic movement of her fur stopped, she was almost invisible. Her ears stuck out, but they passed for the pink petals of a lily. She tucked her limbs to cover her less furry hands and feet, and wrapped her long, striking tail around and beneath her body to conceal the braid full of colorful mementos which was wrapped around the end. Her Thread served many purposes but not one was stealth.

Certain she'd taken care of any tell-tale signs, Barra sat statue and listened through the pulse in her ears for any movement from Plicks. She waited. He advanced.

There was a rustling through the thicket, Plicks' approach suddenly clumsy. Barra still couldn't see him. She peered through the close foliage, her large emerald green eyes open wide, gathering light from the dim wood. For a moment, she wondered what it would be like if the flowers and radiant mosses shined as brightly as her father described, but the thought ended abruptly. Plicks was close. She snapped her eyes shut, not wanting to risk their reflections giving her away.

It seemed a great deal of time passed without another sound or any hint of Plicks' movement. Barra had to fight off the urge to open her eyes. Plicks was so close that she couldn't imagine why he would have stopped. He definitely hadn't passed by her. She tried to count to one hundred, but gave up at thirty-three—she hated sitting still. Opening her eyes only a slit, she strained to see her furry friend. She saw nothing. Stretching one hand out from behind her cover, she started to climb down, but a sudden crash of breaking branches froze her solid.

When the leaves settled, Plicks' small defeated voice called out, "Barra? Barra, I'm stuck."

Barra hesitated. She remembered Plicks and Tory whispering conspiratorially before the game, and wondered if they were trying to flush her out of her hiding place with a trick. But it only took Barra a moment to dismiss the idea. Plicks just wasn't a trickster. Good-natured, hopelessly clumsy, and maybe a little gullible—definitely not capable of deceit. And now that she thought about it, he *was* frequently stuck.

Graceful as a feather falling, she lowered herself down to the pathwood. This particular pathwood had been abandoned long ago, along with the rest of the Middens though at one time the wide bough must have seen hundreds of travelling Arboreals a day. The bark of the thoroughfare was petrified, ancient and worn. Barra couldn't sink her claws into the pathwood, it was so tough. She did her best to pad softly in the direction of Plicks' voice.

"Barra? Help! *Barra!*" Plicks cried out.

Barra pushed through some large ferns, and there he was. The Kolalabat dangled from above, suspended in a hammock of his own furry skin. Plicks' scruffs, the two large flaps of stretchy skin growing from his back, had snagged on some brambles overhead, and he must have tripped and gotten all wrapped up in them on the way down. Plicks' purple and gray fur stood on end all over his body, thick and puffy-looking.

Plicks struggled as Barra finally announced herself. "Hey, hey, *relax*. I'm right here," she said as she scrutinized the tangle.

"Oh! Hello!" Plicks tried to sound cheerful. "I don't know what happened. I thought I had you for sure! But then... then *this*," he added with a little wriggle that must have been a shrug.

Barra was irritated that the game had ended without a clear winner, but she went to work at the new game of Untangle-the-

Kolalabat. Her mind kept wandering to her father, and though she pulled and swung Plicks around vigorously, she wasn't getting very far.

"So, uh, how bad is it?" Plicks asked.

Barra imagined he was nervously chewing away at his lip or clicking his talons together within the bundle of fur. She teased, "Well, I'm pretty good, but even I might not be able to get you out of this one."

Plicks' fur was accented sporadically by long, bright-violet whiskers. Usually, the whiskers helped him sense subtle shifts in air currents, but they were also effective indicators of his mood, and now they bristled in agitation. He was becoming frustrated. "Can you get me out?" he pleaded. "Where's Tory?"

Splashing through the thick leaves overhead, Tory appeared as if on cue. He jumped down, landing with ease. He stood up. A head taller than Barra, with arms as long and almost as strong as his legs, he might have been intimidating if not for the casual way he held himself. He grinned, and asked, "Hey, hey. What's goin' on?" Then he added, whispering out of the corner of his mouth, "That's five to four. I win." *He* didn't care, but he knew Barra would.

Barra scoffed at him, "No way. Uh-uh. This game doesn't count."

Tory kept on grinning, irritating her even more. Barra couldn't always tell when the young Rugosic was teasing her. He didn't have fur or whiskers, or a tail, or anything like a Listlespur that she could understand as body language. Instead, Tory was covered in a flexible layer of minerals bonded to his otherwise fragile skin. The tough second skin was thicker in some places, thinner in others, and it was cracked all over like the wrinkles in the palm of a hand. Barra'd had to learn to read the cracks, and sometimes, the translation was difficult and annoying. In particular, she'd been anxious all day about her father's journal, so she had even less patience than usual. She still hadn't told her friends anything about what she'd found. She wasn't sure what they'd think about it, what they'd say about her father.

She held up one finger, extending a sharp claw from its tip, and pointed it at Tory. "It's a draw if it's anything," she said.

Through his scruffs, Plicks said sarcastically, "It's a *tough* decision. Really. It was such an *important* game for both of you—I'm such a *worthy* adversary. How can we ever settle this? Maybe whichever one of you helps me down first? Hmm? Maybe?"

Barra glared at Tory, waiting for his agreement, but he wouldn't admit the draw. He shrugged off her annoyed look and slid over to Plicks. Without warning, he lifted Plicks up and flipped him over once, starting a reaction that unwound the Kolalabat completely. His scruffs tugged free from the brambles, and he fell to the ground in a heap.

Plicks stood up, long whiskers twitching to either side of his wide, stubby nose. He was only a little more than half Barra's height. He began carefully gathering up his scruffs, flexing the muscles in his back that bunched them closer to his body. Out of habit, he reached into his pouch and inspected his Thread to help him concentrate. When Plicks noticed his friends staring, he tucked his Thread away in a hurry. But the nervous energy had to go somewhere, and he tapped his talons on the pathwood.

Tory said, "Hey buddy, don't be embarrassed."

Plicks shrugged. He was the youngest of eleven brothers and sisters and their persistent teasing had given him a thick skin, an armor of his own, so to speak. The armor worked well against

overt ridicule, but offered no protection when he disappointed his friends. Tory and Barra were always careful not to hurt his feelings, but somehow that only made it harder to take. He wanted to impress them, not be consoled by them. He slouched and was glad the game was over.

Jerking a thumb at Barra, Tory added, "We all get tripped up sometimes. Even the *perfectly balanced* one over here."

Barra's mind had wandered, and she didn't notice the verbal jab. She surveyed the treescape the way she imagined her father would have, and wondered what other secrets were in the journal. She found herself edging away from her friends, wanting to go home to read more.

"Whoa, whoa. Where're you going?" Tory asked her.

"I was just...," Barra tried to think of an excuse to leave. It was getting late... it *was* getting late. She demanded, "What time is it?!" while looking around frantically for a dayflower. She scrambled up a bough and pulled a large urn-shaped flower into view. Through the translucent leaves, she could see the thick fluid inside had risen almost to the bottom of a dark mark. She didn't need an excuse, after all. "Oh no. I gotta go!" she said, but didn't move.

Speaking over the top of one another, Tory and Plicks said, "Well, get going!" and, "Better hurry!"

Barra's eyes grew wide. "Right!" She bounded along the pathwood, her tail flicking after her.

Barra jumped up and out of sight. The tip of her tail seemed to linger like it was reluctant to leave, but the slack ran out and it was dragged away. Plicks watched her go, and asked, full of hope, "Do you think she'll make it?"

"She's fast, but… I don't know. Maybe?" Tory said with a devil-may-care grin. Neither was in a hurry, so they started walking along the pathwood in the general direction of the Umberwood Nest. Tory may not have been concerned about Barra getting home, but something else was nagging at him and he asked, "Did you notice how out of it she was today? I wonder what's bothering her."

Plicks thought about it, and said, "I noticed, but I guess I think she just gets like that sometimes." He shrugged.

Tory nodded, but he thought there was more to it than that. He changed subjects anyway, and asked, "Been adding to your Thread?"

"Yeah. My weaving skills need some work," Plicks said. His Thread was ragged, the baubles loose.

Tory pointed out, "Well, it's not just your weaving, right? Your Thread is supposed to hold the most important moments together, not *every* moment." Tory held up his right forearm where his Thread was wrapped clean and tight. There were baubles and trinkets tastefully woven into the tough braid. "Each one is special to me," he said. He was distracted by one for a moment, his eyes shimmering. He shook his head and went on. "Anyway, what're all those?" he indicated Plicks' Thread.

Frowning, Plicks defended his misshapen Thread and the haphazard mementos it held. "Look, when you have as big a family as I have, there's lots to remember. Their story is my story too you know." He frowned at his misshapen Thread, "I just have to, erm, find a better way to weave it all in."

Tory seemed to accept the explanation, and they continued along the pathwood without saying more about it. Even though he spent a lot of time in the Middens, it was still new and wondrous to him whenever he took a moment to look around. The abandoned treescape was within the Loft proper, the bottom of it actually, though it often felt a world apart. The unique dens found throughout were mysterious, ancient, and warped, stretched by gravity over many rings. Each den gradually imposed on its neighbors, and they crushed together into a tangled mess. The Middens was entirely unlike the bustling Loft where the majority of the Arboreals lived, and sometimes it felt like a private space reserved only for the adventurous.

Different and exciting an area as it was, Tory rarely went to the Middens alone. The top few tiers were safe enough and that's where they spent most of their time—they could even see through to populated pathwoods, they stayed so close—but any deeper was risky. The deepest tiers were thin, boughs uncertain, and beneath the lowest bough was the Fall. He didn't like to think about the endless emptiness, branchless and frightening as it was, and it was easier not to think about it with his friends around.

Tory squinted, spotting a clear shot through the branches overhead. He challenged Plicks, "Seed throw?"

Plicks was dubious. "You can make that throw?"

"Are you kidding?" The confident Rugosic didn't wait for an answer. He knelt down and picked up Plicks. "Get ready," he said.

Plicks hurriedly gathered his scruffs for the throw.

Tory tucked and rolled backwards, head over heels three times, and then stood up all at once, launching Plicks through the air. The Kolalabat went soaring up out of the Middens and into the Loft.

At the peak of his flight, Plicks reached out and dug the talons of all four paws into a mossy stretch of wood. "Wooooo!" he cried out, triumphant until he saw how narrowly he'd missed a large thicket of brambles. The blood left his face, and his whiskers hung limply.

Tory nodded. "See? Told you."

A cool tingle shot up Plicks' spine and he shook all over. Wincing, he said, "Yeah. Of course."

They said goodbye and Tory started on his way home. Plicks took a moment to get his bearings. Then he plucked a pea-sized black fruit from the bramble bush that had almost gotten him. He popped it in his mouth and chewed on it to remove the bitter casing. Once he'd removed it all, he dropped it onto his paw to examine his work. It was a disc of swirled brown and orange. Exactly what he needed for his Thread. And with that, he scuttled off toward home.

Chapter 3

Buckling Down

Barra dashed home, her long tail rippling behind her as her claws chewed bark.

Her family's den was in the Nest area of the Loft with the many other families of Arboreals in the Umberwood. The Nest radiated out from the trunk, with dens spread wide from the center, and also above and below one another. The large area described a shape roughly similar to a squashed pumpkin. There was no hard boundary between the Nest and the rest of the Loft; like the Umberwood, it grew and changed. Barra and her mother lived on the outskirts, closer to the Middens than the older families deep in the Nest. Even so, from where Barra and her friends were playing, she had quite the distance to run. She went fast, maybe faster than ever before, but she was late as she slid inside.

Barra's mother stood at the waterfull flower in the kitchen facing away from the entrance. Two woven satchels were slung low across her hips. She removed a fruit from one satchel, dunked it into the waterfull, washed it carefully—rubbing it meticulously with both hands—rinsed it, and then placed it in her other satchel.

Brace Swiftspur was considered an imposing presence among other Listlespurs, she carried herself so confidently. Her Thread was a tough, variegated braid wrapped in fine coils over the entire length of her tail. She'd already begun overlapping. Still, standing there methodically washing fruit, she seemed incapable of a harsh thought. Barra knew better. Her mother rarely acted in anger, but she wielded disappointment like a weapon, and she was a master. Barra dreaded seeing that disappointment directed at her. Sometimes she thought she'd prefer her mother to be flat out angry once in a while—seemed easier than guilt.

Signs of aging had appeared prematurely in her mother: thinning fur and fading whiskers that were turning gray at the tips. Barra knew it didn't make sense, but she felt at least partially responsible for the early weathering.

Hoping her mother hadn't noticed the time—even though their dayflower grew right over the waterfull—Barra tried to stealth by unseen. Just when she thought she'd made it past, her mother leaned down and glared at her.

Yep. She was displeased.

Without releasing her daughter from her disapproving gaze, Brace pulled down the drainpetal on the back of the waterfull. Dirty water ran out over the lip and down into a little garden at her feet. "Where have you been, dear?" her mother asked pointedly.

Brace released the thick, waxy drainpetal, and it slowly folded up and back into its neighboring petals. The drainpetal excreted a sticky resin to create a watertight seal, and the deep bowl of the waterfull flower began filling again with fresh water.

Barra looked around like she was going to find an excuse floating in the air. Finally, she stammered, "Well, you know, where I told you I'd be, out playing with Tory and Plicks. The two nicest boys—that's what you always call them. Responsible friends, I think you said? Well, I was with them." She paused, gaining confidence, and went on, "Right after Coppice, exactly as we agreed. No dawdling or loitering about. Like. I. Promised." Stepping toward her mother, she reached into the clean bag of fruits and selected a blue one, "Indigobblyberries? My favorite!" She held it up to her nose. "Thank you, Mom!" Barra gave her a big hug.

Barra's mom wasn't fooled by her daughter's affectionate misdirection, and she did not return the hug. Instead, she asked, "*Where* were you playing with your nice and responsible friends?"

"Uh, well, we weren't playing in the Reach," Barra offered quickly. "I know you don't like it when—"

"Barra." Her mother's patience was thin.

"Aw, mom." Barra backed away from her attempted hug. She was caught. She managed to look hurt about it too, but her mother only waited for admission.

Barra gave up. As she put the indigobblyberry back in her mother's satchel, she said, "We were in the Middens." Her mother seemed about to speak, so Barra interjected, "BUT, I was out of the Middens before nightbloom. There was at least a measure left of Watering. At least!"

Brace knelt down and looked her daughter in the eye, "That's not the point, Barra. The Middens is unsafe any time of day. Especially this late. You know better."

A little know-it-all look crept across Barra's face, and she couldn't help but utter, "That's a myth. It's the same at night as it is during the day—"

"So, *obviously* you've been there after Watering, huh?" Her mother stood up, agitated. "Wash up," she said as she turned away. "We're eating soon, and then I'm going to watch you do your homework, and then you're going to bed."

"Aw, Mom! Come on! I was just..." Barra stopped her plea short when she saw her mother's expression. There was no room for argument there.

Shoulders sagging, Barra walked toward her nestroom. She pulled aside the doorweave, but before leaving the kitchen, she turned back to her mother and said, "I'm sorry."

Barra's nestroom was small, but she had her own waterfull and a nectarsweet too. A weave of rare soft ferns covered the entire floor and grew various different flowers with the passing seasons—as the ring grows. The bedding was comforting, and she loved rolling around on it.

Washing up, Barra prepared herself for what she expected to be a long tense dinner. She knew that she'd gone too far, been late too many times. It was plain that her mother had had enough. Barra took a deep breath, shook herself dry, and then went back out to the kitchen.

Dinner was even more strained than expected. Mother and daughter exchanged pleasantries and said little otherwise. When they finished, they cleaned up together, and it seemed to Barra that her mother was distracted—distracted by more than just her daughter's disregard for the rules. Barra got up the courage to ask, "What's the matter?"

Brace scrutinized her daughter's face carefully, and said thoughtfully, "I visited a dozen of the best gardens today. The fruits were… well, what did you think of dinner?"

Barra wasn't sure what to say. Dinner was typical, she thought. She thought they'd had better, but she felt bad for even thinking it. She wouldn't have said dinner was flavorless exactly, but there wasn't much to it. "It was okay," she admitted.

Her mother was not offended, and nodded as though she'd expected that answer.

"I'm sure it wasn't anything you did, Mom," Barra shrugged and smiled wanly. "Sometimes the berries aren't any good."

"Yes, yes, you're probably right," Brace said, coming back to the conversation. Dismissing her thoughts on the subject, she went on, "Okay, enough chit chat. Homework and bed for you!" She added as though she'd been repeating it for rings, "And bathe properly! For the sake of the Olwones!"

Later that night, Barra didn't have to do her homework with her mother after all. She thought about bringing it up, but figured it was better to leave it alone and just be grateful. Besides, it gave her a chance to sneak back into her father's study.

The port in the ceiling of Barra's nestroom was difficult to reach, especially silently, but Barra was practiced, and knew the quiet holds by heart. She was out of her room and on top of the roof in no time. From there, she made her way back to the study.

Everything was exactly as she'd left it. She crept quietly over to the sheaves and leaves of the journal and sorted through them again. Reverently, she put everything back in order, and excepting the first sheave, she placed the rest in the cubbyhole behind the desk. She read from the beginning, savoring every word again. The voice behind the words still didn't match up with how she imagined her father, but she read on, hoping to know him better.

Barra lost herself in her father's descriptions of the Middens, and his seemingly random, desperate interstitials. There was no dayflower growing in the study, so she had no idea the day was ending until it was over, until the buckle began. The low rumble pulsed through the wood up into her bones, and even though it felt the same as it did every night, it took her several moments to comprehend what it meant.

Cerulean was buckling. The Umberwood was floating closer to its neighboring Great Trees, millions of branches intertwining and sliding around each other, closing the gaps in the canopy. The world was exhaling, the ocean shrinking toward the sun, and so the trees embraced one another.

The buckle didn't take long to bring everyone closer together, but it also isolated; thoroughfares were closed off, intersections blocked, windows shut, and ports sealed—including those opening into a young Listlespur's nestroom.

Barra palmed the next few leaves from the sheave, rolled them together, and placed the slender bundle in her mouth. She bit in gingerly, and shook her head to check the roll was secure, and it was. Not a moment too soon, she dashed out through the narrowing window.

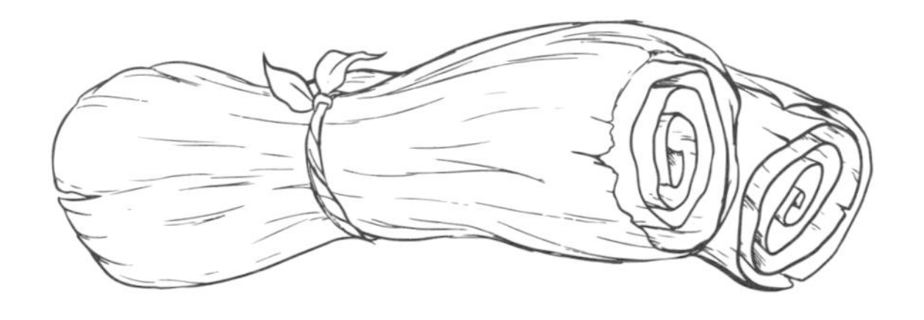

The rumbling continued. The entire treescape swayed. The wood was becoming unnavigable, twisting branches sliding into the open spaces. Barra only had to get back to her nestroom, but the roof was shifting beneath her feet. Her mother's nestroom roof was the fastest way across, and Barra decided to risk it. She snuck over her mother's roof, hoping she was still in the kitchen.

Barra saw her nestroom's port steadily closing. She moved faster, lost her balance, and then tumbled. If her mother hadn't heard that, she wouldn't hear anything, so Barra gave up trying to be quiet, took two leaps, and then dove into her room.

Landing louder than she'd wanted, Barra winced and waited for her mother to come barging in. But her mother didn't appear.

Barra released the leaves from her mouth and stretched her neck to gaze through the almost closed ceiling port. There wasn't much left of the dark purple sky, only patches, but she recognized the patterns of twinkling lights through them. Usually before bed, before the buckle, she snuck outside to gaze at those twinkling lights, but that night she caught only a glimpse before the small viewport shut completely for sleep.

Her nestroom swayed gently as the Umberwood Tree came to a stop. Several of her flowers were brighter after the buckle, and Barra brushed their petals so they would close for the night, saving one for reading. Only muted ambers and blues escaped the flowers after that.

Buckling Down

Cozy in her nestroom, she Barra thought about her father. She felt like she'd already read a lot, but she was only in the middle of the first sheave! So much more for her to learn about him. She didn't understand everything in leaves she'd brought back, and the drawings weren't always helpful either, but she loved how her father described exploring the Middens, the way it seemed to call to him. The old ruins had always called to her, too.

Exhausted, Barra tucked the leaves away, close but safe. She circled her bedding a few times, and then settled into the warmth reflected back by the downy ferns. She thought of adventures she hadn't had yet, and when she slept, she dreamt of a world that was familiar, but that she'd never seen. Its bright flowers dazzled, its colors danced, and she explored with her father.

The world's slow inhale after the buckle, the expansion of the Cerulean Ocean, was already beginning. Steadily, the trees were moving apart. By morning the Loft would be open again, and the Arboreals would wake up from their dreams to begin another dimly lit day.

Chapter 4

The Coppice

Confused and groggy, Barra had a hard time getting up that next morning. She'd woken up several times during the night and couldn't remember whether it was from dreams or nightmares. Calming herself had been difficult with her conscious mind spinning up thoughts about her father, and the Middens. She was so discombobulated on her way out of the den that she walked right out, passing her mother without saying a word.

Two steps away from the den, the cool air roused her and she turned around.

Poking her head into the kitchen, Barra said, "Morning, Mom!" She bounded over, stood up, put both arms around her mother's neck, and kissed her on the cheek. And then, grimacing, she asked for both forgiveness and permission to go, "Bye, Mom?"

Brace smiled warmly as she shooed her daughter out the door, "Hurry along now, Burbur. Have a good day."

Wincing at the nickname, Barra said, "Aw, Mom, don't call me that." Then she dropped to all fours and made her way back out again.

Following her daughter out the doorway, Brace teased, "Too old for Burbur? Really? Can't imagine. What with you running around on all fours like a two-ring old?"

Barra stood tall but did not turn around. "Love you, Mom," she tossed the words over her shoulder.

"Love you too, dear." Brace watched her leave for Coppice, making sure she was safe for as far as she could see. Even though she tried not to encourage it, she was proud of her daughter's willful attitude—reminded her of herself as a bup.

Suddenly realizing Barra was almost out of earshot, she yelled, "Be good! And *NO PLAYING IN THE MIDDENS!*"

Barra half-ran, half-walked on her hind legs until she was sure her mother couldn't see her, and then she gave up the pretense and ran. All fours wasn't the *civilized* way to travel, but she loved the way the wind felt through her fur, and the rush of the pulse in her veins. Besides, Barra mainly travelled the unpruned sidewoods, where no one would be offended by her behavior. She liked to avoid the thick foot traffic of the pathwood. The Arboreals bustling this way and that were fun obstacles to dodge, but too many of them knew her mother.

It wasn't long before Barra could see the Coppice ahead of her. The foliage was thinned out from regular pruning unlike the surrounding treescape and the approaching pathwoods were reflection smooth from the number of Arboreals who visited frequently. The Coppice was more than a place to play, it was where experience and youth collided. Aged Arboreals could be found engaged in hobbies and other interests, and often, they were willing to share their thoughts with anyone curious enough to ask a question. Many of the older tree-dwellers even played games, and in the Coppice, bups were included. Barra visited almost every day, but she only stayed around when Venress Starch was there.

The Coppice was large enough even on its fullest day that the Arboreals could spread out easily, so groups stood out. Barra spotted Plicks immediately where he sat among several others. They were chatting and asking questions of an elderly Kolalabat who was tending a small plot of lensleaf plants. Barra scampered over and arrived just as 'oohs' and 'ahhs' went up from the small crowd.

"Hey, Plicks," she announced herself. "What're you lookin' at?"

Startled, Plicks dug his talons deep into the bough beneath them. He released his tense-knuckled grip when he realized who it was, and said, "Barra! Don't sneak up on me like that!" He shook his head and turned his attention back to the old Kolalabat. Eyes full and bright, Plicks said, "Ven Tadafell has been tending this particular plant for more than a ring, and it's been growing leaves truer and larger than ever before! He pulled the first stem this morning, and... well, see for yourself!"

Leaning in, Barra caught a glimpse of the large disc-shaped leaf that Ven Tadafell was holding. Full of fluid, the lensleaf was perfectly clear, thicker at the center than the edges, and through it, everything was magnified. Ven Tadafell smiled broadly, and though he was eager to use the lensleaf himself, he proudly beckoned his friends closer so they could see too. Plicks

and Barra huddled in close, but after only a short time, Barra whispered, "Have fun."

As she started to walk away, Plicks said without looking, "Hunting Venress Starch again?" His voice curled up like his knowing smirk.

Barra raised a skeptical brow. "What about it?"

"She's here. I saw her arrive Nest-side, heading Reachward. Good luck," he said, and then scooted even closer to Ven Tadafell.

Barra whispered, "Thanks!" She bounded away, surveying the wood above for any sign of the sly Haggidon.

Venress Starch's body was covered in the same golden brown scales possessed by other Haggidons though age had stolen most of the iridescent shimmer from hers. Only the scales around her eyes remained vibrant. She was able to blend into her environment, and even with her ample belly, she was unexpectedly agile and silent when she moved. All great reasons for Barra to enjoy tracking her, but best of the lot was Venress Starch's uncanny skill to avoid detection; Barra loved the challenge.

Surveying the Coppice, Barra made her way carefully to the periphery, to the fuller branches where she could best hide her approach. She passed several other Arboreals including Tory who was working on some kind of binding project. Binding wasn't a skill Barra possessed, but Tory was adept and she stopped to watch him for a moment. Binders created structure from living wood, directing growth so that it was self-reinforcing, stronger with age. Tory was practicing with a group that was debating how to add a flourish to their work. The tight braids of wood looked like a common window to Barra; a hole in a half-finished wall.

She listened in, gathering that a spiral of nightblooming irises was to rise out of the window, but she didn't understand how. She moved on. Ascended toward the Reach as Plicks suggested. She saw no sign of Venress Starch.

High up and mostly isolated, Barra slouched down, disappointed. She began to wonder if Plicks had been mistaken. A fern brushed against Barra's fur, and she swiped at it. When she hit nothing but air, she realized too late that the irritating tickle wasn't from a fern.

Two thick tails tipped with sickle-shaped fangs were draped around either side of the young Listlespur. They coiled around Barra in a flash and she was snatched up into the air. Rolled over and held tight, she was suddenly belly up, face to face, with the fierce Venress Vallor Starch.

Vallor towered over Barra, even though she was small for a Haggidon. Horns grew in pairs along her spine, close together at her bottom, splitting as they went up her back to form a slender V-shape. The twin tails extending from the top pair were long enough to hold Barra, and still wave their fangs about freely.

Vallor strictly enunciated each word before beginning the next. "So busy looking ahead. No idea what was going on behind you." Vallor hesitated, sniffed at Barra and grimaced. "And you've been chewing grappabark."

Barra huffed a few times toward her own nose, and noticed the sweet dark smell, pungent and thick. Wrinkling her nose, she said, "But that could have been anyone."

Venress Starch raised a brow. "It was you." She smiled, lines of tiny sharp teeth exposed, and said, "Now what are you going to do?"

Abruptly, Barra fought back. She squirmed, pushed, and kicked, but the Haggidon only held her tighter. Barra's fur, slick as it was, couldn't slip her free from Vallor's grip. But then something new happened. The muscles that controlled Barra's fur for stealth were reacting instinctively, pushing against Venress Starch's hold.

Vallor pondered her captive, suspicious. She suddenly felt like she was trying to hold onto a water snake. The tighter she gripped, the more she thought the bup was going to squirt free. But Barra didn't recognize how close she was to escape, and she gave up. Vallor asked, "Well?"

"Please let me go?" Barra asked begrudgingly.

"Humph," Venress Starch grunted, disappointed. She released Barra without warning, and the bup fell a short distance before lashing out with her tail and pulling herself onto a branch below. Vallor dropped down beside her. "Well, at least your reactions have improved."

The two walked and climbed together for hours. Venress Starch identified shrubs and flowers and noted each one's utility. They examined some of the gardens, the plots that were chewed out of the boughs and filled with wood pulp in order to grow and feed special plants. Barra usually enjoyed her walks with Venress Starch, but she was having a hard time paying attention. She couldn't stop thinking about her father's journal.

"What's wrong?" the old Arboreal asked Barra with deep concern.

But Barra dodged the question. "Nothing, I'm just tired I guess."

Vallor knew there was more to it, but offered another excuse instead of pressing the matter. "Maybe hungry, too? Midday is long past."

Barra was astonished to hear the time. She hadn't even noticed the flowers of the Coppice changing over to their afternoon cycles. The middle of each day was marked with an exotic cascade as some plants closed and others opened, colors and shapes metamorphosing throughout the treescape. The display was especially beautiful in the Coppice because of the specialized flora that grew there.

"Why don't you go? Look for some food, and maybe I'll look for you, later." Vallor blinked slowly, respectfully, at the distraught Listlespur—her way of saying goodbye. Without further hesitation, she lifted herself up into the branches overhead and disappeared.

Barra couldn't find anything she wanted to eat, but the gurgling in her stomach won out, and she made her way to one of the many food gardens in the Coppice. Tory was there with another Rugosic named Juddol, and they were arguing about something.

Clearly happy to change subjects, Tory called out, "Barra! Hey, over here. Sit with us."

Barra clambered up to the two bups and sat between them. "Did you eat yet?" Tory offered a handful of spiderfruits. The nuts were gray sacs suspended in cushions of crunchy webbing made from a sweet resin. Barra was happy to take half and popped them into her mouth all at once.

Juddol rolled his eyes. "We were talking?"

"Sounded more like arguing," Barra muttered while chewing.

Without blinking, Juddol stared at Barra with the most emotionless, flat expression he could manage. Barra smiled widely back, making sure to show the contents of her mouth.

"That's attractive," Juddol said, wrinkling his face in disgust. Turning his attention to Tory, he promised, "We'll pick this up again later, Mafic." He stood up gracelessly and loped away.

Tory waved goodbye like he was in the New Ring Parade. Barra swallowed emphatically. "What was *that* all about?" she asked.

"Nothing," he said. After a moment, he went on, "He saw me helping Marley—you know, the Bellbottom from the Mangrove Tree? Her family is making a den near mine. Anyway, he saw me helping her with some bindings and—"

"And he's jealous?" Barra interrupted. Her face twisted up like she'd bitten into something rotten.

Tory replied with nonchalance, "I guess. I mean, he does have a point." Tory gestured to himself. He waited for a snarky response, but none came. The despondent Barra seemed to have mentally drifted away.

Tory was a little concerned, but he popped the rest of the spiderfruits into his mouth and waited patiently. When he decided he'd waited long enough, he spoke up, "What've you and Venress Starch been doing today?"

Barra blinked rapidly a few times, and said, "Not much. The usual."

"Are you, uh, okay?" Tory asked, skeptical.

"Oh yeah, definitely. I'm fine. You know, I think I'm still hungry. Where'd you get the spiderfruits?" she said as she stood up.

"I'll show you. Come on," Tory said.

As they walked together, Tory described the garden he was taking them to see. A spiderfruit bush required lots of water, and he'd helped create a base that could support one. He was proud of his work. Barra tried to show that she was impressed, but she wasn't able to muster much enthusiasm. She was too distracted.

At the garden, Barra ate her fill, and then after a short but strained silence, she said, "Tory?"

"Yeah?" he asked.

"Do you ever think about your mom?" Hearing her own words out loud, she shook her head immediately. She tried again, "I mean—of course you think about her—but like, how do you imagine—"

"Tory! Barra!" It was Plicks. He came shuffle-running up to the pair with something large in his hands. "I've been looking for you all over the place! Look what Ven Tadafell gave me!" He held up a large lensleaf, not as big around as the one Barra had seen that morning, but huge nonetheless.

Tory responded first. "Wow, that's great, Plicks!" He was genuinely impressed. Tory had a special affinity for bindings, but he had developed an interest in almost everything in the Coppice. Barra leaned in to inspect the lensleaf, and nodded emphatically.

Plicks was so excited he wasn't sure what to do next. He hadn't gotten the reaction he wanted from Barra, so he was frantically thinking of how to impress her. "Here. Here, let me *show* you," he said, and scuttled between his friends into the garden. He held the lensleaf by the edges between his small hands, careful to keep his talons from scratching the surface. Looking at one magnified plant after another, he kept shaking his head as though none of it was good enough.

"Oh, oh! Here! Look at *this!*" he exclaimed, and held the lensleaf steady while standing to the side.

The entire surface of the lensleaf had turned fiery orange. After a moment of confusion, Barra looked around to the see the subject regular-sized. Sitting on a broad, green leaf was a fiery orange insect. It had a narrow body and a long neck with an oblong head perpendicular to it. The insect was only slightly larger than Barra's nose!

The bups examined the magnified display closely. They could see every detail of the exoskeleton: its pores, segments, and pigmentation, even the veins in the folded wings.

Plicks explained proudly, "You are looking at the rare Aridifolia Tricopterus." Inspecting the subject closely, he nodded and said, "She's female. You can tell by the number of segments in the abdomen." After thinking for a moment, he added, "They're usually found deep in the Middens. Maybe she's here for the spiderfruit? It doesn't grow around here normally, right?"

"No. No, it doesn't," Tory confirmed, still mesmerized.

Barra gazed curiously into the lensleaf. "What's *that*?" she asked, pointing.

There was strange, dark webbing oozing out from beneath the insect's wings. The stuff was difficult to spot, even enlarged. Plicks tried to get a better view and Tory and Barra had to jockey for position to see around his furry head and large ears. "I don't know, I'm not sure." As Plicks spoke, the Aridifolia spread its wings. Threads of black ooze were revealed, gumming the wings to the body of the poor insect, grounding it.

"Barra, you know where the closest bellflower is, don't you?" Vallor had approached the bups from behind, undetected. She startled them all, seeming to appear out of nowhere. She was watching the insect carefully. Barra took only a moment to grasp her request, and she nodded and dashed away without a word.

"Where'd you come from? Uh... where's she going?" Tory asked of no one in particular, but Barra came back before anyone answered him.

Barra held a large bulb-shaped plant with her tail. The bellflower had thick translucent walls that were shaded peach and lined with thin green veins. The bellflower wasn't a flower at all, but a segment from the eponymous vine that grew it. Barra had already drained the bitter fluid from it so that it could be used as a container. Holding the bulb next to the insect, she pursed open the narrow stem. Venress Starch guided the insect into the bulb with gentle waves of her hand.

Plicks clutched his lensleaf close to his chest and asked, "Do you know what that sticky oozy stuff is?"

"I don't. I'm sure it's nothing to worry about, but I'll take her home and see if I can help. She certainly doesn't look well," Venress Starch said. She added confidently, "I know a thing or two about the Aridifolia Tricopterus. I'm sure she'll be fine." As Venress Starch spoke, Barra thought she was hiding something behind the dismissive attitude.

"You'll let us know?" Plicks asked. He rotated the lensleaf in his hands anxiously.

"Definitely. Barra knows how to find me," Vallor said as she pulled herself up with her tails, and then she swung away.

The three friends stood together, somewhat stunned. Tory was the first to speak up, "That was *odd*."

Barra squinted and nodded as she said, "Suspicious, you mean."

"Well, that's not what I meant. But, sure, yeah, suspicious," Tory said. He didn't know what to make of it all, but he could tell Barra had some idea.

Plicks could see the idea taking shape in his friend's mind; he knew her too well. Looking back and forth between Barra and Tory, he hoped he was wrong. Instead, he saw Barra raise her eyebrows to Tory, and the Rugosic smiled back slyly.

"Aw, come on..." Plicks said, but the deal was done. He heaved a sigh. "Okay, but I've got to stash my new lensleaf at home first."

Vallor stood alone in her den contemplating the bellflower. She held the container carefully with both tails assuring there was no escape for the insect. Shuffling over to her garden plot, she looked over her wyrmwood. The thick stump of a plant had a few stubby branches, but was otherwise a leaning cylinder. It had a sheath of rich brown papery bark covered with dark-purple buds. She nudged one. Sluggishly, the petals of the bud unwrapped, revealing they were actually wings. The creature rolled down the side of the wyrmwood, and then flew up in a sudden, agitated flash. It was a Rush, furry and round with a button nose, deep-violet eyes, and ring-shaped ears. It flew around the den in quick, short bursts. Eventually it settled, hovering steadily at eye level with Vallor. Many ribbon-like tails danced beneath it as three sets of rapidly beating wings kept it afloat.

Rushes are fast, their wings galvanized by unique nectars found in distinctive flowers throughout the Great Forest. They have to drink often, so they instinctively keep a perfect map of the flowers they sample. But their favorite and most potent fuel is the cultivated sap of the wyrmwood. Most Arboreals keep one well-tended in their dens.

"I have a message for Doctor Fenroar," Vallor began.

"Fenroar? Fenroar. Yeah. Got it. Know exactly where he is. Exactly. Don't you worry." The Rush flitted around the den in a blur.

She held up the bellflower. "Tell him I need this insect tested right away."

"Yep. Need it tested right away. Got it," the Rush confirmed, talking fast and blinking even faster. He flew around the bellflower, sizing up the package from several angles. "Yep, yep. I got it. Totally can do. Yep." He licked his lips between words with flicks of an extraordinarily long tubular tongue.

"You sure?" Vallor was dubious.

The Rush stopped a paw's width from her face. He hovered there, perfectly still except for the flashing of his wings. He narrowed his deeply saturated violet eyes. "I got it," he said, miffed.

The Rush landed on the bellflower and steadied himself expertly as he tested the surface with his glassy, needle-like claws. Satisfied, he buried his claws deep, flexed to secure his grip, and then displayed his wings broadly. They were iridescent underneath and spanned a length greater than the distance from his nose to the bottom of his tails. In an instant they vanished, flapping faster than the eye could see. Vallor released the bellflower, and the Rush floated up, then down, and then back up again, straining.

"I got it, I got it," he said to the once again dubious Vallor. Righting himself, the Rush licked his lips, and then flew from the den.

Venress Starch shuffled into her kitchen, turning her back to the doorway, and Barra slid down from where she'd been hiding, stealthed. She snuck back out unnoticed. She met up with Plicks and Tory a short distance down the pathwood where they were waiting for her.

"Did you have to go back in there?" Plicks clicked his talons together as he spoke.

"Relax. She didn't see me. Besides, it was worth the risk," Barra hinted.

Plicks waited, but Barra didn't continued, and he finally asked, "Well?"

"She's not keeping the Aridifolia with her tonight," Barra reported, wide-eyed. "She Rushed it to Doctor Fenroar's!"

Plicks considered a moment, and then gave up and asked the obvious, "Why'd she do that?"

"I don't know," Barra said, clear she thought it was a very good question indeed.

"Who's Doctor Fenroar?" Tory asked.

"I don't know." Barra's eyebrows were raised, leading.

"What're we gonna do?" Plicks was frustrated.

Barra let her excitement out all at once, "Wanna go spy on Doctor Fenroar?!"

Plicks was exasperated. "Why do you always want to get us in trouble? Tory?"

But Tory wasn't worried. "Sounds fun," he said with a wink

"Great!" Barra said, "Let's go!"

Chapter 5

The Rush

The three bups walked along the pathwood as quickly as they could without drawing unwanted attention. As they went, Barra shared the discovery of her father's journal; there were too many similarities between the descriptions she'd read and the black sticky strands that plagued the Tricopterus for her to hold back any longer. Her friends listened intently while they tried to keep up with the Rush. Luckily, the little messenger was slowed by the weight of the bellflower and stopped frequently for nectar. Whenever they lost sight of him, Barra would raise her nose to the air to find the wyrmwood scent that marked his trail, and so they travelled deeper and deeper into the Umberwood Nest.

The oldest dens of the Nest were closest to the trunk. As families aged they often migrated into the homes of their lineage leaving the ever-shifting outer boundary of the Nest for the young. Barra had never met Doctor Fenroar but she could tell he was old; they were deeper into the Nest than she'd ever gone. There were no other bups in sight, no one even close to her age. The trio hurried along with affected purpose trying to look like they belonged.

Tory hung back from the others after hearing about the journal. He wanted to be happy for Barra—he *was* happy for her—but he was also frustrated. It wasn't the first time she'd kept secrets. He wondered if she'd ever trust him. Sure, Barra hadn't said anything to her own mother either, but Tory didn't know what to make of that. He struggled with his feelings in silence.

The quiet blanket of Tory's reticence went unnoticed though as Plicks kicked it off with his excitement. The Kolalabat asked question after question wanting to know every detail. He jumped at the opportunity to share and connect with Barra about her father, a topic he'd deliberately avoided in the past. His relief came out in a flood of words that Barra worked to stay above, pausing more often than necessary to find the Rush's scent.

They were travelling slower than the messenger. Sometimes the Rush crossed paths with another, and choosing the right one to follow was tricky. There were distractions too; sights, sounds, and smells that were different from the rest of the Loft tugging at Barra's nose. She found it difficult to keep up her part in the conversation and soon the trio was walking in silence. No one spoke a word again until Barra noticed Tory lagging.

She bound over to him and asked, "What? What is it?"

"The bindings used here are so different from anything I know," Tory said. All the experimental bindings in the Coppice and he'd never seen anything quite like these.

Barra rolled her eyes. "Come on, we gotta keep moving."

Tory didn't budge. "Look at that," he pointed at a den with intricate fountains on either side of its entrance. The bases were each made from a single branch which grew in consecutively smaller circles, the end rising up in a flourish from the center. The fountain on the left was a spiraling tower of rings, while the other was dominated by sharp angles with steps and platforms. Colorful cup-shaped flowers and jagged protective thorns grew all over both. Tory recognized the flowers and he explained, "Those spillpetals fill with water every measure, and tip over when they're full. The way they're growing the cascade must be beautiful. It took a lot of care and time to bind them like that."

As engrossing as his description was, Barra didn't have the knowledge of bindings to even guess at the mastery on display. She understood it was important to Tory, but didn't think they could stay any longer. She urged him, "Come on, the Rush is getting away."

Tory stared for another moment trying to absorb it all, and then he started moving again.

Plicks matched his pace and asked, "Think you'll bind like that someday?"

Tory shrugged.

Reminding Plicks of his older siblings when they just wanted to be left alone Plicks took the hint even though he thought the behavior was unusual for Tory. He tried not to worry about it.

Barra pushed them to keep moving, but that didn't stop Tory from taking a look back at the fountains before they passed out of view. An old squat Nectarbadger came outside to prune. He squeezed the claws that grew between his fingers together several times rapidly to sharpen them. *Thwick thwick thwwwiiick.*

He clipped at the fountains like he'd done it a thousand times. The jagged thorns didn't bother the Nectarbadger. He just kept trimming without a care.

They rounded a corner, and Tory tuned back into Barra, who was explaining the importance of being sneaky-quiet to Plicks. "It's the only way. We don't want to get caught, right?" She dashed away.

Plicks squinted at Barra's back as she sniffed the air. He tried to bolster himself, saying, "I can be sneaky. Even if I can't *stealth.*"

Tory leaned in toward Plicks and whispered, "Just do your thing. You'll be fine." The Kolalabat's stride perked right up.

Slyly, Barra popped up between the two and startled them. Through gritted teeth she whispered, "We're here." She pointed ahead, and the boys looked just in time to see a downy grey Leghund open his den to the Rush.

There were a few Arboreals meandering about, but none were paying any attention to the bups. Barra thought they could act without being noticed. "Okay," she said with a hushed voice as she leaned in toward her friends. "I'm going to the roof to see if I can find a way inside. You two wanna go around to the windows and see if you can find a good place to listen?"

The boys nodded. Tory was confident, Plicks apprehensive. Then all three ran and jumped from the pathwood.

Barra went lithely from branch to branch until she was positioned above the Fenroar den. Lowering herself down to the roof with her tail, she stealthed, camouflaging her fur to match her surroundings.

Plicks couldn't jump very far with his short legs, but he scurried pretty fast, regardless. He dove around and down to the claw-marked, unkempt underside of the pathwood. Soon he was hugging the bottom support bough of the Fenroar home. He found a ventilation hole and listened in.

Tory could have cleared the distance to the den in two jumps, but he had to move slowly to avoid drawing attention. He found the closest branch large enough to hold him and ran out onto it. The bough flexed down toward one of the Doctor's windows, and Tory swung himself underneath. Hand-over-hand, he moved right up to the window and hoped he hadn't been seen.

Inside the living room of the Fenroar's cultivated den grew many elegant displays of lighting and watering flowers. Elaborate watershelves lined the walls, and a silky exotic moss covered the floor; rich brown accented by sprouts of bright blue.

Darby Fenroar called out, "Yorg? Yorg!" The Leghund eyed the Rush he'd just let in with suspicion, his marbled nose twitching. Darby's great size and strength made him an imposing figure despite the downy softness of his light grey coat.

A Muskkat responded to the call, entering through one of the curtains of braided vines that separated the rooms. "Yes,

Darby?" Doctor Yorg Fenroar asked. The average-sized Muskkat was slinky-slender and short, so he was dwarfed by Darby. He was covered in glossy, dark brown fur, and had a long snout topped with two large blue eyes, and the wrinkles on his face accentuated his beguiling smile.

Darby explained, "From Vallor. It's for you."

Yorg stepped toward the hovering messenger and accepted the delivery.

"Thank you, thank you," the Rush said, releasing the bellflower. Having lost his ballast, he shot up toward the ceiling, bobbed for a bit, adjusted, and then floated back down. He spotted the wyrmwood across the room and dashed toward it.

Darby cut him off. "Whoa, what about the message?" he demanded. He didn't think the Rush had earned his keep yet.

"Right! Test the sample. That's what she said," the Rush answered, zipping side to side.

Darby moved away from the wyrmwood, and the Rush flashed by. He landed, buried his claws, folded his wings, and simple as that became almost indistinguishable from any other pod growing on the stump.

Yorg inspected the contents of the bellflower. He raised a single eyebrow, perplexed. "What do you think it is?"

Darby's response was dry enough to wilt a waterfull. "It's a bellflower containing a female specimen of Aridifolia Tricopterus," he said.

Yorg looked sideways at Darby, switched his raised eyebrow, and said, "Quite."

Darby rolled his eyes. "Well, you asked didn't you?" He shrugged and added with sincerity, "I don't know anything more about it than you do."

Yorg examined the sluggish insect and asked, "Are you still growing fuzzberries?"

"Sure I am. I know how much you like them," Darby said. "Wait. You mean for the bug."

"Yes. It looks hungry doesn't it?" Yorg held the bellflower up to emphasize the point. Ari dragged herself around in obvious strain.

"Right. I'll grab some seeds," Darby said, acquiescing.

Yorg peered in at the Tricopterus. She was drooping, and the tiny hook of her tongue was lolling out of her mouth. Yorg thought maybe she was thirsty, so he crossed over to the waterfull located on the other side of the denroom.

Arriving at the waterfull, a sudden sound of crashing of leaves whooshed in through the window located above it. The noise ended as abruptly as it started. Yorg examined the treescape, but didn't see anything other than a few swaying branches. Whatever it was, it was gone. The Doctor shrugged, and returned his attention to the Tricopterus. He dunked one hand into the waterfull, and then held it dripping over the bellflower which he pursed open with a gentle squeeze. Droplets fell inside and Ari walked over to one and drank. Pleased, Yorg placed the bottom stem of the bellflower into the waterfull to keep it from drying out as well.

Darby swept back into the room, one paw cupped by the other. Yorg nodded, and tipped the open end of the bellflower toward Darby. The Leghund cast the seeds out over the opening, as many falling out as in. Yorg glared at Darby and sighed. Darby just shrugged and smiled, head cocked comically to one side.

Both of the aged Arboreals watched and waited. The insect's burning orange color had paled since she was captured, but the

Fenroars didn't know that. She stretched up toward the seeds, and the black strands that gummed her arms to her body were revealed.

Darby stepped back, befuddled.

"That's... not... good," Yorg said haltingly as he inspected the insect. She tried to fly, but her wings couldn't get free from her body, and even more black threads were revealed.

Darby recovered from his initial shock, and said, "That's Creepervine fungus, isn't it?"

From where Barra was perched eavesdropping, she heard the word as clearly as if Darby had whispered it directly into her ear. The blood ran from her face as she recognized the newly familiar word.

Yorg hesitated, but then he responded gravely, "Vallor was right to send this to us. I'll have to do some tests."

There was another crash through the branches outside, drawing the attention of both Fenroars. They stretched their heads out the window, and although several branches were still swinging, there was nothing to see.

"What was...?" Yorg began, but hushed when he saw Darby holding a finger to his mouth.

Darby rose up and unfurled his ears into two large saucers. He walked softly around the living room, tuned into something that Yorg couldn't hear. Around the middle of the room Darby pointed down as though he found something. Then he looked up, incredulous. Domed like most dens, the ceiling at its center was high, twice as tall as the Leghund. With no warning, Darby leapt into the air. He punched his hands through the ceiling and grabbed onto something from the other side. He pulled it down with him as he fell in a burst of leaves and debris.

Yorg seemed amused.

"Hey, let me go!" Barra demanded. Even as she wriggled in Darby's huge hands, the ceiling was growing back together. There would be a thin spot for a few days, but no permanent damage.

"Calm down," Darby said, exasperated. He placed the tense Listlespur down on the floor gingerly, wrinkling his nose.

Barra eyed the window, the entrance, and the braided curtain separating the living room from the next.

Darby read her face and advised forcefully, "Don't get any ideas. You're not going anywhere."

Unflappable, Yorg asked, "I'm Doctor Yorg Fenroar. You've met Darby. And you are?"

Barra had trouble calming down, but she managed after a moment. She resented being a captive, but seeing no way out of it, she said bitingly, "Barra."

There was a knock on the door frame that sounded like it was apologizing for itself: *Hel-lo, hel-lo?* Darby looked in the direction of the knock in total disbelief. He scowled at Yorg, but the old Muskkat disarmed him with an innocent look. He said, "You can't seriously believe I had anything to do with all this," but his tone suggested he maybe wished he had.

Turning to Barra, Yorg asked, "Friends of yours?" He drew out the words slow and sweet like pouring honey.

Barra winced as she spoke, "Probably?"

Darby answered the door.

"Hi," Tory said. He was standing there with Plicks unsure how much trouble they might be in. "I'm Tory. This is Plicks. We're sorry for the disturbance, but," he spotted Barra and pointed, "we're looking for her."

"Right. Of course. Why else would you be here?" Darby said, breathing in and out of his nose exaggeratedly. Once he'd soothed his mounting frustration, he instructed Tory, "Please explain what exactly is going on."

Tory and Barra responded at once, but Plicks only clicked his talons while chewing his lower lip. The resulting explanation was a jumbled mess of noise. The Fenroars waited for it to be over; Yorg patiently, Darby rolling his eyes in exasperation.

When they stopped to breathe, Yorg asked, "Whose idea was it to spy instead of simply knocking?" Barra looked around the room for a place to hide. Yorg shook his head at her, but he was clearly entertained.

"So, did I gather correctly that you're all here for the Tricopterus?" Yorg tried to tie the threads together.

Barra spoke up, "We found her in the Coppice. There's something wrong with her. We just wanted to find out more, that's all."

Plicks wanted to jump in with his thoughts on the insect and the black strands that bound it, but he was unsure of himself. Agitated, he shifted his weight from side to side. Tory noticed, and tapped him on the shoulder to tell him to knock it off.

"Uh, huh," Yorg said, "Wait. Are you Brace's little girl?"

Barra stood up straight and tall, and poofed herself up. "I'm not little." She wasn't surprised they knew her mother, but she immediately felt the impulse to avoid conversations that could lead to a discussion about the journal.

Her father's journal. *Her* journal.

"Forgive me, not at all little," Yorg said acting impressed and even apologetic. "So, which Coppice was it?"

For a reason Tory couldn't figure, Barra didn't answer. Plicks shrank away as well, so Tory stepped up, "Evergreen. We were near the bottom, Loft-side. More Loft than Nest anyway."

Yorg nodded. "If I remember correctly, the bottom of Evergreen is practically in the Middens, right?" The three bups had never really thought about it, but it was true. The Coppice didn't cross into the ruins proper, but it was close. Yorg thought for a moment and then continued, "Have you seen the sticky stuff on her wings?"

"Yes," Plicks spoke, startling himself a bit.

"Any ideas what it might be?" Yorg was testing them. He wanted to know how much *they* knew before he gave anything away. Darby stood by him, watching their reactions.

Plicks said in a rush, "I don't know what it is. But she's already lost more color in her wings and abdomen. I think the stuff is keeping her from capturing food, from eating and drinking." He added, somewhat embarrassed, "I like insects."

Darby chuckled, warming for the first time since the bups had disturbed his den. Yorg smiled broadly and then knelt beside the timid Kolalabat, and said, "Excellent observations." Very seriously, he went on, "You can infer then, that the sticky stuff might be dangerous?"

Darby snorted in disapproval, but Yorg continued regardless, "Darby and I have an idea of what it could be." Yorg consulted Darby with a look, giving him a chance to stop the conversation. Darby consented with a shrug, paws open to the sky. Yorg then asked, "Can you keep a secret? Each of you?"

"Yes!" they responded in unison.

"Good," Yorg said, convinced. "Well, the sticky stuff may be a very dangerous fungus. But, *but*, it could also be a variety of innocuous ergot, or something new. We simply don't know by looking at it. So you have to keep what you know about it to yourselves until we know for sure. Okay?"

Tory shrugged. More secrets. He understood the reasons this time at least.

Plicks, as squished a Kolalabat as ever there was, managed to shrink from the weight of the request, but he nodded at Yorg anyway.

Barra nodded too, but her mind was already far away, an idea taking root.

"Excellent. Now, run along, interlopers!" Yorg directed. "Come back in a few days. We'll have results by then."

The trio left the den with their new secret, unsure if they really knew anything more than they did before busting in on the Fenroars. They travelled in relative silence back to the outer rings of the Nest.

Tory broached the silence as he said, "Well, I guess I'll see you both tomorrow?"

"For sure." Plicks thought it felt like a normal, everyday goodbye, and he found comfort in that until Barra said, "I'll bring some leaves from my father's journal to the Coppice tomorrow, and we can..." she trailed off.

"Ahem, 'we can' what, Barra?" Plicks asked.

"Oh? You can help me read through them. Find out what we can about the Creepervine." Her tail snapped the bark once with playful impatience. "Okay, I'm off. See you tomorrow," she said before bounding away and out of sight.

Tory turned to Plicks. “Why’s she in such a hurry?”

“Probably needs to get home,” Plicks offered. Hands open, he added, “She’s been in trouble a lot lately.”

“Yeah. I guess so…” Tory said, unconvinced. He looked as if he was going to say something more about it, but then shook it off, and instead he said, “Right. Well, see you tomorrow, bud.”

Plicks’ whole body sagged. Wishing their dens were closer he waved goodbye and headed off on his own. It suddenly occurred to him that Barra could have walked with him at least a little farther. He stopped and scratched his head, and twitched his nose. She’d gone in an odd direction to go home.

Chapter 6

Alone in the Dark

Barra let her friends believe she as headed home. After all, she *was* going home, just not yet. No need for them to worry about her travelling to the Middens first. Besides, if they didn't know where she was going, they wouldn't feel the need to back her story if her mother ever found out.

Barra descended through the Middens. She recognized a nearby ancient ramshackle den. The first ruin she'd ever explored. She didn't head toward it. Instead, she shimmied down a thick bough and headed deeper into less familiar woods. The darkness became oppressive, stifling her movements, causing hesitation with each step. Her breathing was labored, the thick, cold air seizing her chest. Barra persisted.

She wondered how close she was to the Fall.

She thought she shouldn't think about it.

The Middens were old, but how old no one really knew. Barra had heard the fables, and though they varied some, they all agreed the dens of the ruins were built by the Olwones when the Middens was young, and the Loft closer to the Root. From there the stories went their own ways: the Olwones vanished, and the untended Forest grew tall and wild, and tore apart the Middens as it reached for the sky; the Middens was left behind for lesser creatures while the Olwones live on at the Root in a paradise detached from the Trees; the Olwones are a myth and the Middens? The remains of an Arboreal Nest abandoned for the danger of living too close to the Fall.

Barra didn't know what to think of the stories. No one could ever tell her what an Olwone actually was, what one looked like, or where they came from in the first place. They were portrayed as colossal creatures shaping worlds! But the dens of the Middens were sized for creatures like Listlespurs and Rattlebarks, Kolalabats and Rugosics—not giants, Barra thought.

Legends about the Middens, the Olwones, and the Root, Barra had heard a lot of them. The only story Barra had never heard was one of someone returning from the Fall.

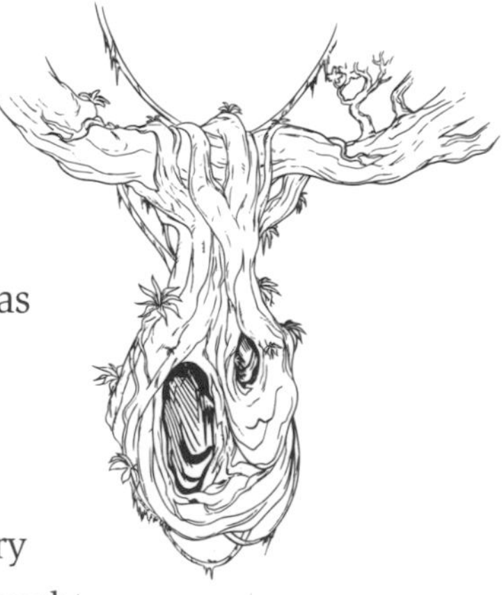

The Fall had no branches, no holds, only emptiness. The prospect was frightening enough to keep the even the boldest Arboreals away. Barra had a difficult time imagining a world without boughs, thin and thick, in every direction, and she had to admit the thought of it scared her too. So she tread carefully as she picked her way through the Middens, taking care not to delve too far, but the idea of finding the Creepervine drove her on.

Barra had never had a reason to go deeper with so much unexplored higher up. Looking around now she realized how much she'd been missing. Every branch was new and mysterious, each den strange. The homes were shaped from the boughs of course, but there were minerals, rocks, and metals imbedded as well—materials in far too short supply to use in the Loft. She thought of her father, noted everything she saw, and imagined adding her descriptions to his journal.

Farther and farther down, she went. The dens were even more stretched out and gnarled than those above. They'd been worn by time and gravity in a way that was disorienting. Barra felt like she was in another world. There were more distractions, but fewer branches. The odd gaps between boughs startled her more than once. If she stumbled, if she misjudged a step, she may not be able to catch herself; she could drop into the forever black.

Barra slowed. She stepped from branch to branch only when she was sure of her footing, and continued to scout for the sticky fungal residue of the Creepervine. She'd never seen anything like it in her previous adventures, but she might have missed it, not looking for it then as she was now. She wanted a sample because she was worried about poor Ari—the insect deserved to be free of the fungus—but also, knowing that her father was collecting a sample when he disappeared, she hoped somehow that she'd learn something about what happened to him.

Time passed without a sighting. Watering was coming soon, when the "evils" were rumored to wander the Middens.

Watering wasn't a big deal otherwise. According to Venress Starch, Watering used to refer to a surge of water that would burst from the flowers of the Loft twice a day. As long as Barra had been alive, Watering was a once a day trickle that she sometimes missed. Nevertheless, the disappointing event marked the beginning of the treescape's daily transition into night.

Inverted on a moss covered branch, Barra kneaded the brittle material, and it crunched beneath her paws—not a moss she recognized. Moving on, she hugged her belly to her spine to avoid the scratchy bits. She sniffed the air to gauge her surroundings in the waning light.

Not only was the light meager, but the number of sources was few. No bluebells or lemonlights or indiglows. No sparklenettles or lumenlichens or shimmerpollens. There were some starlights offering pricks of focused light, and a few radiantmosses softening the dark with a diffuse glow. Barra opened her eyes as wide as she could to gather the light.

There were irregular configurations of boughs making it difficult for Barra to orient herself. The bottoms of the dens looked like their tops, the branches growing with no purpose to shape them.

Barra wandered toward one of the dens. She wasn't entirely sure of finding her way back, but trusted her instinctual sense of up and down to get her there. Still, the unfamiliar treescape was unnerving. Out of habit, she ventured into a small hovel. There were tables and chairs made of wood that had petrified so that they were difficult to distinguish from the rocks used to shape them. Above her was webwork of stone woven into wood, rocks spliced into branches to bend them with their added weight. The bindings were strong, but the kitchen was still crushed side-to-side like everything in the Middens.

Stretching herself out, raking her claws against the floor, Barra wrung the jitters from her body. She stood upright and then sat down at the table in the kitchen as though she was preparing to eat. Imagining the room filled with a family of Listlespurs, she acted out sipping a teaflower daintily. She thought she could almost see the room come to life with all species of Arboreals talking and laughing, drinking and eating, enjoying themselves. But her moment of pretending didn't last long.

A prickly cold feeling grew like crystals in her blood. She felt the distance home, how far away she was from her mother. She wished she were somewhere else, somewhere safer than an isolated hovel deep in the Middens. Something moved in the corner of the room. Or maybe it was the corner that was moving.

Barra blinked several times to clear her vision. Still, the far wall was writhing. She froze and her heartbeat quickened. She felt blood push into her ears, and all the way to the tip of her tail. She sampled the air with several quick inhales through her nostrils.

The room seemed alive, but it wasn't. There was something else in the room with her.

Along the far wall, a sheet of black undulated like a doorweave waving in a breeze. The sheet grew wider as it moved, spreading outward from the center. It rippled and slid, covering up the wall and continuing up the ceiling, working its way around the room toward Barra.

The low light turned the sheet into a canvas where Barra's imagination painted nightmares. As the sheet grew closer, details resolved out of the darkness; it was a multitude of tiny creatures moving in unison. Barra caught glimpses of legs and antennae as the creatures flowed together and expanded along the wall. It didn't take long for them to cover every surface of the kitchen. She had no idea where they were coming from, or how many there were.

They were almost at her feet.

She stood, and the creatures stopped sharply.

The warped kitchen was trapped in stillness. Barra's heart was drumming the urge to run into her chest. She stole a quick glance over her shoulder to locate the way out, and when she looked back, the tapestry of creatures had closed the distance to her.

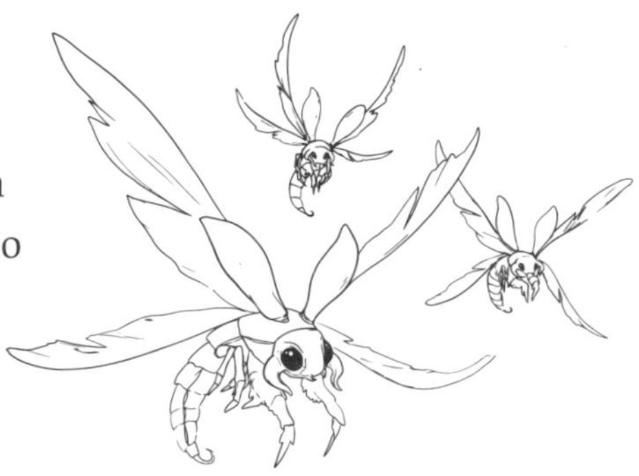

Eyes burning because she was afraid to blink, Barra backed up slowly.

The bugs moved. They matched her progress toward the doorway. She took another step backward. They narrowed the gap.

Barra felt her pulse in the quick of her claws. *Adolescent* claws her mother was always reminding her; fragile. Easily broken, easily repaired, Barra had argued. Suddenly, she wished she'd listened to her mother, and just tried to avoid danger. If she made it home, she would hug and kiss her mom, tell her how right she was, and promise to listen better. She had to make it home.

She felt the closeness of the insects, and the closeness of her escape.

She picked her moment. They picked the same.

Hundreds of pinprick lights turned on as the tiny creatures' eyes flashed open. Wings fluttered and clacked ominously. In unison, the insects faced Barra and swarmed like tendrils of smoke reaching for her. They billowed around Barra, a terrifying, rattling cloud. Barra coiled, and then in one swift motion, burst through the cloud and out the doorway. She flew into the open boughs of the Middens with the insects trailing after her.

Barra fled through the woods. The oily collection of insects accelerated. They flew together as one large predator. Barra cut through a thicket of brambles, but the insects were unfettered, flowing like liquid over the sharp thorns. The chase sent Barra winding around branches, through dense nettles, and over great gaps in the boughs, but she couldn't lose them.

Trying a new tactic, she jumped and spun herself around. She whipped out her tail, lassoed a branch, and pulled. Changing direction mid-flight, she headed up toward the Loft. But the insects were too fast. They swarmed and cut off her ascent.

Her pursuers flowed in and out of each other, eyes appearing and disappearing in a frightening miasma. Barra saw their eyes and felt chills—no warmth in those tiny lights, only predatory instinct. They were focused. They allowed her to turn any way but up, relentlessly driving her toward the Fall.

Barra dashed into a den. She bolted through distorted rooms and passages, found a window, and leapt back out. Her eyes were focused, seeing only the path ahead. She ran, but not at full speed. The shadows and boughs were dangerously interchangeable in the dark. Barra hesitated at turns and stumbled after jumps, all the while colliding with leaves and ferns she couldn't see.

A large clearing in the branches yawned open ahead of her. She couldn't mark the distance across, but all the way to the edge was clear. She went for it, increasing her speed to make the leap of her life… then realization skewered her like a broken branch through her chest. Her blood drained. Her lungs collapsed.

It was too far.

Digging in with all her strength, she tried desperately to stop. Her claws broke and cracked from the stress, but fear kept

her fingers braced through the pain. Searching for a hold, her tail thrashed like an angry snake behind her.

Barra stopped. A whisker's breadth from the edge, shaking, she inhaled. She didn't finish her breath before the mass of insects hit her like a tidal wave. They engulfed her and carried her over the edge.

As she struggled viciously against them, Barra realized that she wasn't falling, at least, not falling fast. The cloud of

tiny beasts was metamorphosing, becoming thick. Each insect clutched at the next, holding fast with their claws and jaws. Working together, they became a stretchy, writhing net.

Arms and legs frantic, Barra fought through the ever-thickening mesh like she was swimming upstream through sap. Finally, she splashed through the amalgam and burst out. The bough from which she'd just fallen was close. She reached for it. Pain shot through the tips of her shattered claws as she shredded bark before managing a grip.

Barra hauled herself back up onto the bough and was running again before she was even conscious of it. She glanced over her shoulder and saw the disentangling mesh of insects was slow to follow, unable to detach from one another quickly.

Barra went vertical, heading for the Loft while she had the chance. Hot blood in her veins, she ran and climbed like never before. She didn't look back again until she crossed into the Loft. Looking down through the dense branches, she was positive she spied the insects hiding in the shadows. But they didn't follow her. Cautiously, she waited. She stealthed, camouflaging herself with her specialized fur.

"*Why'd they stop?*" she thought as she paced, ready to run, but curious.

Snap!

It wasn't unusual for branches in the Loft to settle, creak, and crack, and sometimes for no obvious reason they snapped. That's probably all it was, that sound, but Barra was away in a flash.

Halfway home, Barra thought, "*At least I have a good excuse for being late.*"

Chapter 7

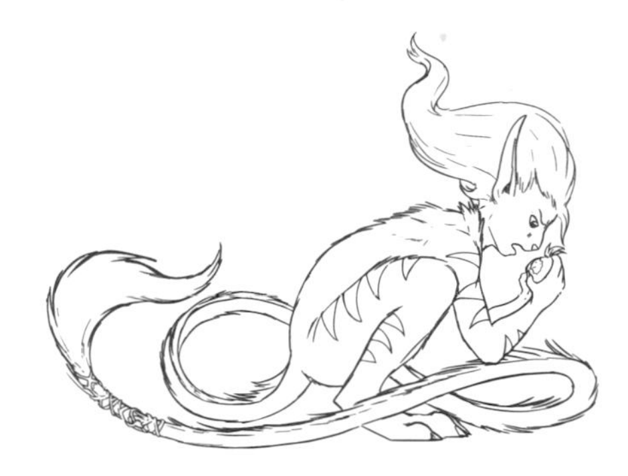

A Mother's Imperative

"Go to your room."

Barra had never experienced quiet anger before, and certainly not from her mother. The sound of it was potent and enervating, a disappointment strong enough to drain the very will from Barra. Her limbs felt weak and rubbery, and though she fought against it, her lips trembled. Her eyes stung with wet.

When Barra had rushed in through the front doorweave she'd been frantic. Her mother had calmed her down, hugged her and held her until her heart was steady and her mind clear. They'd opened milkweed pods together, and her mother added soothing herbs to the cloudy sweet contents. She'd broken fireseeds into the tonics too, to warm them, and as Barra had watched their tiny bubbles float to the surface, she'd sniffed the familiar aroma and felt safe again.

Barra had told her mother the story of her day, and when she finished, a silence had begun and endured until those words, "Go to your room," had marched from her mother's mouth. Go to her room?! It wasn't right! Barra sat there glaring with pools burgeoning in her eyes. Going to her room was the last thing she wanted to do! She *wanted* to stay right there in the kitchen with her mother forever.

Barra didn't budge. After another prolonged silence, her mother said, "You are very selfish, Barra."

Stunned, Barra sank away from her mother and that was enough for the welling tears to finally spill down her cheeks. Brace's eyes also began to shimmer. "Did you think of me when you ran off to the Middens?"

"I did!" Barra erupted, hurt and disbelieving.

The glare from her mother shut her up. "Really? You did? What do you think I would be doing tonight, if you didn't come home? How do you think I would feel with each passing buckle that I couldn't find you? Not knowing what happened?" Her mother paused, choking on her words, "You have your father's sense of adventure… and you have his selfishness." One tear rolled out of her mother's eye, over the gray fur just beneath, trailed quickly down the white of her cheek, and then fell to the plush grass floor where it landed without a sound.

Barra sat, stunned. She was crying without blinking.

Her mother took a deep breath. "Go to your nestroom, Barra," she said. There was an implied "please" in her tone as though she was too emotionally exhausted to continue.

Barra stood up, and mind-numb, walked out of the kitchen. She sat alone, and after a while her defiant nature returned. She stood up and roughly wiped away her tears. Pacing her room, she decided to confront her mother. Barra had done nothing wrong! She was exploring to protect their home, to find out what was out there! Her mother should've been proud! Her father *would* have been proud!

The conversation wasn't over. Dipping her paws into the waterfull in her nestroom, Barra carried a handful to her mouth, lapped at it twice, and then splashed the rest over her face. She repeated the ritual. She felt better, cooler, almost ready. She walked to the patch of drymoss she grew beside the entrance, and nuzzled her cheeks against it. As she finished up, fanning her whiskers, she overheard voices in the kitchen.

Barra listened in.

"... for Jerrun, the head of the Council of Elders." Her mother.

"He doesn't like to be disturbed. Nope. Nope." One of her mother's Rushes by the broken cadence of his speech. Barra didn't immediately recognize which one.

"I know my place. He'll receive a message from me without argument. I need you to be my fastest messenger tonight." Must be Neville, Barra thought. Her mother continued, "Can you do that for me?"

"Yes, yes. Ready." Neville gave up his doubts, and sounded so eager he bordered impatience.

"Assemble the Council for an emergency meeting. I will address them tomorrow night. No exceptions. Kudmoths attacked my daughter in the Middens today. The Creepervine has finally risen up out of the darkness, and it cannot be ignored any longer. Summon Venress Vallor Starch, and Vens Yorg and Darby Fenroar as well. Thank you, Jerrun."

"That's all? That's it?"

"Yes. And please, return to me when you've finished with Jerrun. I need to know that he *heard* me. He knows not to ignore me in these matters, but he may need persuading. Watch him for me, mark his attitude. I want to know how he reacts."

"Sure, sure. Got it."

"Go then," her mother sounded relieved. "And thank you."

Barra didn't expect more, but she listened for a while longer regardless. As her mother shuffled around the kitchen, Barra was too distracted to remember they were fighting. So much new information was buzzing around in her head, she felt like she couldn't keep track of it all. Another bout with her mother didn't seem relevant anymore.

Barra considered sneaking into her father's study again, but thought better of it as she imagined more quiet anger. Even as she thought about ways she could get in and out without being caught, her body instinctually prepared for sleep. She circled and picked at her bedding ferns, and then lay down. Her mind continued in a million directions, fighting her body's need for rest.

Eventually, her body won.

Throughout the night, Barra's sleep was disturbed by nightmares. Her room became liquid, tarry black, and she woke up drowning in it. She fell asleep again only to run from a darkness that chased her over an endless stretch of time and trees. When it finally suffocated her dreamscape, she woke gasping for breath.

Awake in the space between dreams, Barra stared into the shadowy corners of her nestroom, her imagination untethered from reality. She was sure the darkness was growing and moving, and morphing into something terrible.

By the time the soft light of morning poured out of the brightlumens around her nestroom, Barra was still tired, but glad the night was over. Barra could hear her mother working in the kitchen as she got up, stretched, and groomed herself. Her mother's words from the night before stayed unwelcome in her mind, and it was with considerable effort that she threw them out. She was hurt, angry with her mother, but she had to let it go. There were more important matters.

As far as Barra had known, her mother had always been a gardener. Now that Barra had the notion that her mother could assemble the Elder Council at will, her mind was flooded with questions. Also, she wanted to ask about the Creepervine and Kudmoths, but any discussion would be an admission of eavesdropping, and reveal that she'd found her father's journals. Both were trouble.

Finished preening, Barra extended her claws into the wall to sharpen them. Flinching from the soreness, she haltingly tried to put an edge back on the claws that remained. She arched and flexed her back, and cut thin shreds from the bark of the wall. Taking a deep breath, she left her nestroom and entered the kitchen. Her mother was at the opposite door with her back to Barra.

"Wait, from who? Jerrun?" Brace was distraught as she interrupted the odd-looking Rush mid-delivery. "Where's Nevel?" she interrogated the messenger. He had cataract-cloudy eyes and a twitchy smile. Completely distracted, Brace didn't notice Barra slinking into the room.

"I don't know any Nevel." The Rush rolled his eyes, making it clear for Brace exactly how little he cared. He asked, "Would you like to hear the message or not?"

Something happened to Nevel, Brace thought, and Jerrun knows about it. Why else would he send his own messenger? Suspicious, Brace gestured for the old Rush to continue.

"Where was I? Right. The Elders will convene this evening as you requested, but be advised, Brace, it is exactly this kind of request, if found frivolous, that will result in the loss of your inherited right to audience. See you tonight," the Rush concluded with a lick of his lips, expecting payment.

Brace was careful to say nothing about how she felt about Jerrun's thinly veiled threat. She had no doubt that Jerrun's Rush had the same instructions she'd sent with hers: wait and listen. She waved the Rush away, and said, "Thank you. I'm sorry, was there something else?"

"I'm a little hungry, actually." The Rush was incredulous.

"Oh, how terrible of me. Honestly, I'm embarrassed by the state of my wyrmwood, especially compared to what you must be used to, being in Jerrun's care and all. I really have nothing to offer. I'm sure you understand," Brace dared the messenger to challenge her.

The Rush weighed his response carefully, and then he spoke like the words were acid on his tongue, "I won't press you then, of course, but you should tend to your tree, Venress Swiftspur. It may be that's the reason your Nevel has gone missing." His face twitched as he feigned a smile. "Enjoy the rest of your day."

"You too," Brace responded contemptuously.

Barra eased out of the room before her mother turned back in. When Barra came in again, she announced herself with an obnoxious yawn. Her mother had already busied herself in the kitchen as though last night hadn't happened, as though she hadn't just confirmed an evening meeting with the Council. Barra felt awkward, not knowing what to say to broach the morning silence.

Fortunately, Barra didn't have to contemplate her opening words for long. Her mother, in a non-negotiable tone, said, "I'm going to be gone tonight when you get home. Please be here before nightbloom, though. I'll leave dinner on the table."

"Mom, I, uh…" Barra tried to stammer out an apology, but it wouldn't come. She wasn't sure she wanted to apologize.

Her mother stopped what she was doing at the waterfull, and then turned and stared calmly at her daughter. "I don't want to lose you," she said before returning to her work.

"I know, Mom," Barra sighed. She realized her run through the Middens hadn't just disappointed her mother. Barra had scared her. And something more serious had come from it too, maybe not her fault, but something her mother had to deal with. Barra said the only thing she could, "I'm sorry." An apology that came from her core. A sorry for every time she'd disobeyed.

Without looking up from washing fruit, her mother raised an eyebrow and said, "You'll understand someday." She shook her head, and explained, "That's what they used to tell me. But I didn't get it then, and I doubt you'll get it now." After a thoughtful moment, she stopped washing and faced her daughter. She said resolutely, "I *am* proud of you, Barra. You're willful and determined, the best kind of daughter I could ever hope for. Yesterday though? Yesterday, you showed poor judgment. You didn't have to go down there alone."

"But, Dad always went alone," Barra argued weakly.

Brace interrupted, one finger pointed sharply at her daughter, "Your father was fiercely, and irrationally, independent! It cost him... it cost us." She took a deep breath, and continued, "You don't have to emulate *everything* about him."

Brace reached out to her daughter. Without hesitation, Barra jumped up into her mother's outstretched arms. The warmth between them glowed, and Barra imagined she could see it.

They held each other a few beats longer than an everyday hug, until they surrendered to it. Brace had a shine in her eyes, as she examined her daughter. She was judging whether her daughter was presentable and ready to be out in the world. Really though, she wanted a little more time before letting her Burbur go for the day.

Barra wandered alone for a while. The treescape seemed different. Not scary, but not safe either. She was drawn to the Middens again, but not ready to return, she found herself headed to the Coppice. Venress Starch was seldom there two days in a row, and knowing she'd been summoned, Barra thought it unlikely today would be an exception. Still, Plicks and Tory would probably be around and at least she could talk to them. She wished Doctor Fenroar hadn't asked them to keep quiet.

Barra pictured the Elder Council meeting. She envisioned Venress Starch testifying with her mother and the Fenroars, and how strange it would be for them to be on the Dais together. She'd never been to a Council meeting, and thought of the Elders as spectral figures with overgrown claws, and icy, empty eyes. But that was ridiculous. She'd seen Jerrun before. She knew better. Still, she was haunted by the notion.

At last, she spotted her friends walking together. Barra rushed over to them. They were talking about Plicks' latest attempt to fly by his scruffs—he practiced frequently in an open area of the Coppice. She bounced around impatiently, waiting for them to finish up, and they pretended not to notice her. Finally, she couldn't hold back any longer. She grabbed them close and whispered, "My mom is going to an Elder Council meeting at the Dais tonight!"

The boys stared back blankly. As they eventually caught up to her words, they exchanged skeptical glances.

"I think she's got some weeds in her brain," Plicks whispered to Tory through the corner of his mouth.

Tory put his hand on her forehead for a quick check, and said, "She's feverish, maybe delusional."

Barra lowered her head and glared. "Yeah. That's right. Weeds in my brain. Delusional. Could be. Maybe? Or maybe, my *mom* is talking to the *Elders* tonight!" Before either of the boys

had a chance for a snarky retort, she added knowingly, "About the Creepervine and the Kudmoths."

Tory still thought she was a few seedlings shy of a garden. "I'm lost. The Creepervine again? What's a Kudmoth?"

"I don't know!" she said, eyes flashing enthusiastically. "But I was chased all the way out of the Middens last night by 'em!" she spoke in a loud whisper-tone, huddled in tight with her friends.

"You were in the Middens last night?" Plicks asked, taken aback. "I thought your mom banned you for like, well, forever?"

Tory added, "When you left us yesterday, didn't you tell us you were going home?"

"Aw, come on, Tory. I just didn't want you to worry. Either of you," Barra implored. She turned to Plicks hoping he would take her side. "Someone had to see what that stuff was that attacked the Tricopterus. Right?"

"Whoa, don't bring poor Ari into this," Plicks didn't have a lot of practice confronting Barra, but he knew when he was being manipulated, and he didn't like it.

Tory imposed himself between the two with his hands raised before they could start a real argument, and said, "Let's just try to figure this out. When you left us yesterday, what happened?"

Barra told the story, ending with how she overheard the message from Jerrun. At the conclusion of her tale there was a lengthy silence. Barra was impatient and prompted her friends, "So what do you think?"

"I think you're planning to crash the Elder Council tonight, so I'll save you the trouble of asking me to join you. I'm in," Tory said, eagerly. Then he asked the nervous Kolalabat, "Plicks?"

Plicks rubbed his face with both of his hands, squeezing and wrinkling the many folds of his skin into strange, inscrutable expressions. When he stopped, he had to blink several times before he could focus again. He was trying to come to terms with his anxiety. "What are the rules regarding the Elder Council?" he asked, hoping for an easy out.

Barra started, "We can just…"

Plicks stopped her short with a look.

Tory answered, "Elder Council is open to everyone." He stopped to think about it a moment longer, "But that doesn't mean they want a bunch of bups around either. We could watch from a distance, try not to draw attention." Shrugging and nodding his head nonchalantly, he added, "No reason not to try."

Plicks rubbed his face again, and though his voice was muffled, he said, "Fine."

They spent the rest of the day together. They didn't have any leaves from the journal to read, like Barra had hoped, but they had plenty to talk about regardless. They worked out the details for getting together later, and went their separate ways.

After dinner, they would meet again in the Reach.

Chapter 8

Harbingers

The den was cold and unadorned. Jerrun had few friends and no need for creature comforts. Whenever he entertained guests, either from within the Umberwood or abroad, he used the Council's official meeting chambers. The head of the Council wasn't in the habit of inviting Arboreals to his personal quarters, so tonight was unusual in that way.

A Rattlebark hunched over by the weight of the many rings he'd lived, Jerrun had huge, protruding eyes, and long flat fingers and toes. His pale, bald skin hung loose on his bones like a wrinkled sheet. A robe woven from blue-grey moss draped from his sagging shoulders, frayed where it dragged on the floor. The robe was a necessary second skin, his own failing to keep what little warmth he generated from escaping.

A gnarled leg of petrified wood served Jerrun as both a staff and a crutch. The wood had turned pale white over the rings, color drained from it like from its owner. On the top was a knot like a clenched fist worn to almost reflective smoothness. Below that was a band equally worn, and together they marked the habitual placement of Jerrun's clutching hands. The staff was heavy, and most of the time it was unclear who was carrying whom, but he was never seen without it.

Jerrun sat with his knees crossed in the center of his living room, his staff laid before him. The floor grew no moss, no grass, no fern. Petrified, rigid, and cold, it was about as forgiving as he was. His eyes were closed, but fluttered open to the sound of rapping at his door. Rising without surprise to greet the late visitor, he tapped his way to the entrance and whisked aside the doorweave.

A fluttering, jittering countenance appeared there. Jerrun recognized Brace Swiftspur's Rush immediately. She attracted and employed a quirky, rebellious sort that Jerrun detested. Still, it wasn't the visitor he'd expected. He looked at the hovering creature disdainfully and waited, wringing his staff.

"Message for you, for Jerrun—excuse me—for the Head of the Council of Elders. Sorry for the disturbance, sorry about that." Nevel flitted about anxiously.

Jerrun made a dramatic show of his irritation, tensing his grip on his staff and inhaling loudly. He turned and hobbled back into the center of the room. "Well?" he said, waving the messenger to follow, "What *is* the message?"

Nevel flew into the den and calmed down. He relayed the details of Brace's request.

"Interesting," Jerrun said at the conclusion. He pointed to the back of the room, offering some nectar to the lip-licking Rush. They exchanged a wordless tense regard for one another as Nevel drank. When he was done, Nevel returned to the Elder and waited for his response.

"Tell her that the request is denied. The Council will no longer be moved by requests from her family. If she still seeks my counsel she may see me in private. That is all." Jerrun rapped his way back to the entrance where he ushered the messenger out the door.

The Rush barely nodded farewell before darting away, but his flight was cut short. As Jerrun stood there watching, Nevel was snapped up mid-flight by the gaping mouth of a shrouded figure.

Jerrun raised an eyebrow, "Tell me you didn't just eat him." The Elder knew reality couldn't be undone, even if he demanded it, but he held to hope anyway.

The shrouded figure was virtually invisible in the darkness of the wood, though he stood in the open. He wore a cowl that hung low, obscuring most of his face and covering the rest in shadow. His lips parted in a smile, exposing bright, glistening teeth that seemed to glow by contrast. A feathery tuft stuck out pointedly from his mouth. The interloper strode forward lightly and let himself into the Elder's den without an invitation. He slid by Jerrun as easily as a shadow sliding on a wall.

Inside, Jerrun asked, "You were listening?" He was uncharacteristically uneasy with the intruder, but doing his best not to show it.

"Yes, I was listening," he said. His words were surrounded by soft whispers, echoes before and after like others were in the room advising him what to say and repeating him after he'd said it. Even in the relatively well-lit room the intruder remained cloaked in darkness, the details of his face obscured.

"Then you know also, that I shut down the request. Why kill the messenger?" Jerrun inquired, perturbed.

"Because you *will* have the meeting. Announce publicly that there is no reason to investigate. Remove curiosity. Nip it in the bud so to speak," the creature seemed satisfied, and nodded to himself.

Jerrun looked away from the creature as he argued, "You don't think that'll incite *more* interest? Brace is a powerful voice in the community. Compassion for her and her daughter since Gammel's untimely fall makes her a poor choice for an adversary. She could become a problem."

The odd Arboreal slowly nodded. "Precisely the point," he said. "This is an opportunity to defuse her completely. Show her to everyone as the *hysterical* mother. Give her sympathy, but eliminate her support."

After some consideration, Jerrun decided the idea had some merit. "And what of the lately dined-on messenger?"

To that, the cowled figure raised his head revealing the mottled, swirling fur on his face. Two bright amber eyes opened, and he said, "Messengers die sometimes."

So that was it, Jerrun thought. If Nevel was brought up, Jerrun would have to deal with it alone. He couldn't plead ignorance, because he was going to send his own Rush in reply. But there were lots of lies, small and large, that could explain why he wouldn't trust Nevel to take his response back to Brace.

Not ideal. But really, who would question him? Jerrun stopped considering it with a dismissive shake of his head. "The Kudmoths have been seen in the Middens. Do I have anything to worry about?"

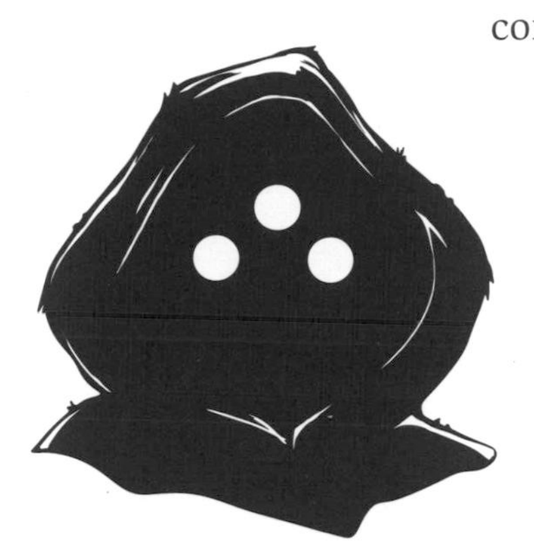

A third eye appeared above and between the other two, and the cloaked Arboreal said, "That's why I'm here."

CHAPTER 9

The Council's Reach

The trio met in the canopy of the Great Umberwood, the Reach. Tory was the last to show.

"You weren't waiting long were you?" Tory asked as he swung up.

"No," Barra said, "But we have to hurry to get there before the meeting starts."

From where the bups started the Elder Dais was difficult to see in detail. The large black platform rose from the trunk of the Umberwood like an enormous dark flower blooming into the purple sky. The Dais was created from ornate, complex bindings and was large enough to hold thirty Arboreals standing shoulder-to-shoulder. Polished with sappy varnish to an almost liquid sheen, the surface mirrored the lilies growing along the rim as well as the raised and gnarled Knot at its center.

The three took up positions close enough to the Dais to hear but not necessarily be seen, and waited. Barra noticed several makeshift vacant seats in the treescape. Seemed they were a little early after all.

They stared into the illumined sky where magenta shifted to purple between the bright points of light called the Wanderers. The young tree-dwellers were disoriented by the branchless expanse, by the seemingly unending depth of the sky, but the strength of the Umberwood Tree beneath made them steady.

"It's peaceful up here," whispered Plicks with reverence.

Tory said, "Yeah, it's nice. I used to come up here with my mom. Since she left the trees though… I don't know. My dad says the Reach is no place for us. He doesn't like it."

Barra never felt like she could relate to Tory's loss directly—he'd *known* his mother. Still, there was something about the way he talked about his mother that always pulled hard at her chest. Her eyes shimmered. Her mouth opened, but she found no words waiting.

Plicks didn't know what to say to Tory either. Maybe there was nothing that could be said. He gazed into the distance over the rolling canopy of the Reach, and hoped the undulating leaves said anything that needed to be said, everything that he couldn't.

There were many flowers lighting the Loft, but few grew in the Reach, and the Wanderers, as bright as they appeared, offered no light to travel by. The canopy itself was radiant but dim, and so the assembling Arboreals saw mainly by the glow of a magenta cloud billowing from the horizon and filling half the sky.

As time wore on, even the spectacular view wasn't enough to stave off Barra's impatience. She peered out over the Reach, focused only on the Dais, and waited for any indication that the meeting would begin.

"Is that the Starwood?" Plicks pointed far into the distance where one Great Tree's canopy shone brighter than the rest. The surrounding Lofts appeared pitch black by contrast.

Tory's distracted look washed away. "Yeah, that's the Starwood." Tory indicated the Loft between. "See there? Those branches pointing up into the sky instead of arching down? That's the Grove. Beside it—the dense grouping of thin branches and bramble thickets?—that's the Braidwood. So, yeah, that one? That's the Starwood."

There was sudden movement near the Elder Dais, and it stole Plicks' attention. He said, "They're here."

A Bellbottom flew up and around the Dais, and touched down on the far side from the bups. She sat down in one of the lilies on the rim with her tails behind her, up and over her head. One by one, the rest of the Council members arrived and found their respective seats. There were rustlings from the audience gathering beneath the Dais as the Head of the Council arrived.

A wake of quiet and stillness rolled out from him as he climbed onto the platform.

In addition to his usual robe, Jerrun wore the Elder Story loosely thrown around his neck like a scarf. The Elder Story was an intertwined braid of the Threads of the Elders that had passed before him. It was a monumental piece, and heavy with the legacy of the order. His personal Thread was not yet tied to his forebears, but it would be.

Jerrun's staff was with him, of course, and the rapping sound it made against the Dais was clear and sharp. He made his way to the center, and then stood solemnly near the raised Knot.

A young Rugosic, smaller than Tory, made her way onto the Dais and over to the Knot behind the head of the council. She placed her hands over the top of the Knot, and flashed her fingers in a well-practiced gesture. Once she felt ready, she placed her fingers comfortably, but purposefully into openings in the Knot. A rainbow of light passed through the openings, and the Rugosic used her hands masterfully to block and release the various colors. The attendant rested her hands a moment, and saw patterns in the spectrum that were caused by another attendant just like her, at another Knot, just like hers, far away on the Dais of another Great Tree.

Though the bups couldn't see what the Rugosic was doing, it was clear that Jerrun was waiting respectfully for her before continuing. After a moment, she nodded to Jerrun. He nodded back. He laid the staff down and gracefully sat on the floor of the Dais.

Jerrun greeted the Council, his voice rich and thick with age. He announced the members by name, giving each a deep nod and a few words of praise. There were scholars, poets, archivists, and more. Each brought a unique talent into the circle. Once he'd introduced them all, Jerrun addressed the Dais as a whole reciting a traditional segment about Aetherials. He concluded by saying, "May you find your Star."

The Elders responded together, "May your Star find you."

After a moment, Jerrun summoned Barra's mother. "Please welcome, Venress Brace Swiftspur to the Dais." The Rugosic attending the Knot went to work transcribing Jerrun's words for the Elder Councils of the other trees.

Barra's mother ascended one of the lead branches to the Dais, facing Jerrun. She walked into the circle, but remained several paws from the Head of the Council. She nodded to Jerrun and to the other Elders. Some nodded back. Barra noticed most did not. She tried to recall the introductions, to attach the names to the faces—Barra didn't like anyone who shunned her mother like that and she planned to remember each one of them.

"And please welcome her witnesses: Venress Vallor Starch, Doctor Yorg Fenroar, and Ven Darby Fenroar," Jerrun's thick voice carried clear and true all the way to Barra and her friends. Climbing up to the Dais, the witnesses appeared and then walked to Brace, where they stood slightly behind her.

"Please explain the purpose of your summons," Jerrun said, addressing Brace directly.

"Thank you, Jerrun." Brace's voice was full of respect. She composed herself, and then began, "My family, the legacy of the Swiftspurs, is well known on this hallowed Dais. For generations, we were the protectors of the Umberwood. We fought the drooling Maws during the Rot. We defended the Umberwood against the Barblites during Nihil's Conquest. We hunted the Lifedrinkers until no more could be found."

Brace paused dramatically. "It has been many generations since those feats of bravery preserved our way of life. Nevertheless, the Swiftspurs remain fiercely loyal to the growth of the Umberwood. Today, we protect the future by keeping the past close at hand." Brace looked deeply into the eyes of several Elders before continuing. "We left the Root. We left the Root because we were afraid. Afraid of the malignant growth we created. A growth that threatened to drown us all in darkness if we stayed. We retreated to the Loft. We didn't fight for the Root, we gave it away."

Stopping again for her words to carry the full weight of their meaning across the Dais and out into the audience, Barra's mother stood tall and confident. Barra was overwhelmed with pride as she watched her mother command the attention of her entire world.

"But we were wrong about the appetite of the Creepervine. Not only have we all seen the diminished light, the weakening water, and the softening of the boughs, but we know in our hearts that the Great Trees themselves are faltering. The sickness we left at the Root grows. The Creepervine has breached the Middens!" The attendant at the Knot moved her fingers in sync with Brace's words.

A murmuring wave of unrest radiated out into the audience. The reaction among the Elders was a mix of disbelief, suspicion, and fear.

Brace continued, "Only two buckles ago, a child found an insect in the Evergreen Coppice with Creepervine fungus growing between its wings." A din rose up from the attending Arboreals, which did not end until Jerrun struck his staff against the Dais.

Brace waved her hand to her witnesses. Venress Starch stepped forward and relayed her story to the Council. The Fenroars followed with their story and observations. At the conclusion of their presentation the attendant at the Knot spoke, "Elder Jerrun, the Starwood Council poses a question."

Jerrun nodded and said, "Please."

The Rugosic addressed the Fenroars, "The Starwood Elder Council would like to know where the afflicted Tricopterus is now?"

Passing each other a worrisome look, the Fenroars took a moment to respond, but eventually Yorg answered, "The specimen burrowed through the bellflower during the evening. She's gone."

Jerrun inquired, "What of your tests?"

"There wasn't enough of a sample from such a small specimen to generate conclusive results," Yorg said matter-of-factly. Then he looked at Darby, and continued, "We were planning to grow more—in a controlled environment of course—but as I said, the specimen was gone by morning."

"Are there other fungi that behave as you've described?" Jerrun asked, but he already knew the answer.

"Yes, but..."

Jerrun waved off Yorg mid-sentence. The Rugosic indicated there were follow up questions from the other Councils, but Jerrun only raised a hand to her. She removed her hands from the Knot.

"I assume then, that it is your *opinion*," Jerrun spoke the last word with particular distaste, "that it was the fungus of the Creepervine causing the ailment..."

Yorg, expecting a question, interrupted, "Yes, absolutely."

But Jerrun continued talking over the Muskkat, "… which is worth almost nothing to this Council." Jerrun leveled his gaze on Barra's mother. "I assume, Brace, that you wouldn't waste our time?"

Brace shot back, "I wouldn't ask for your time if I didn't need it. Respectfully, Jerrun, it's my job to raise the alarm…"

"*Not* your job, as I recall. You were discharged from that responsibility quite some time ago," Jerrun interjected.

Brace continued, undeterred, "*And* I stand before you as the only authority on the Creeper."

Jerrun flashed a patronizing smile, and said, "An authority? Brace, for the last—what has it been? Ten rings?—for the last ten rings, give or take, you've tried very hard to establish these theories of yours and failed. Even Gammel's work refutes—"

Brace broke in, "Gammel was in the middle of his research when he was reassigned by *you*!"

Jerrun would not be talked over. "*—refutes* the existence of the Creeper in the Middens. Gammel found nothing down there! His work will not be revisited yet again, nor will your conclusions about it be regarded as fact. He acted without regard for this Council, without regard for you, or his daughter. Who knows what he was doing down in the Middens? I certainly don't claim to know. Gammel fell and his Thread fell with him." Jerrun paused to collect himself, and then finished his thought out loud, "That was the end of his story."

The tension on the Dais was palpable. Even the bups felt it. Anger burned in Barra's belly, and the heat swelled through her body and poured out of her eyes.

Plicks saw the uncanny resemblance between mother and daughter in that moment and knew he'd never want to be on the wrong side of either Swiftspur.

Jerrun shook his head, and then sighed heavily. He gestured to the Rugosic at the Knot to begin again. "I sincerely hope you have more, Brace," he said, his compassion a show for the audience, like he was helping an old, wayward friend.

"My daughter was chased from the Middens yesterday by Kudmoths," Brace said, sending another disturbance through the crowd. Again, Jerrun had to strike his staff to quell them.

Unprompted, Brace continued, "Before you ask, I have no proof but my word, and the word of my daughter. Still, the archival record written by the Aetherial, Ren Argus, states that where there are Kudmoths there is Creepervine."

Jerrun seemed amused. He said, "The archives? A valuable resource true, but the archives also say Cerulean was created by an Olwone from the Outervoid. Should we take that literally?" There were pockets of laughter, some stifled, others too loud.

"The Creepervine is here, Jerrun! We should have fought it long ago, but we retreated! We've lived in the dark for too long!" Turning to the audience, Brace implored, "We gave the Creepervine our past and it's taking our future! It's been strangling the life from us since Argus created it!"

Jerrun returned coldly, "You speak of legends and myths as facts—"

Brace interrupted, "We have the Aetherial's sheaves and—"

Jerrun spoke over her, "Wrinkled and decaying artifacts of a time lost and forgotten."

"Not forgotten!" Brace lost her poise, her voice shaking. Jerrun raised an eyebrow, but remained silent for the moment.

Raging, Brace continued with fire on her lips, "You say you want facts, but so few have explored the Middens. We don't know what's down there. How are we to grow *up* if we don't know the nature of what's beneath us?!"

Jerrun shook his head like a disapproving father. After a moment, he addressed the Council, "I suggest we not waste any more time on this topic. Though I'm certain it was convened with the best intentions, I don't believe the matter warrants our action." Moving on, business-like, he said, "Instead, we might discuss other pressing matters, such as the improvement of trade routes—"

"Why are you being so obstinate!?" Brace's voice was full of vitriol.

An uncomfortable silence overflowed the Dais and reached out into the surrounding boughs. Poised, Jerrun said, "One matter I've been meaning to address is the ancient edict that requires us to respond to a summons from the Swiftspurs. The notion of any family gathering us on a whim..."

As Jerrun went on, Barra's mother remained on the Dais, defiant. Barra saw the shine in her mother's eyes and wanted to do something terrible to Jerrun. She watched as her mother looked to her witnesses for help, and saw they were unwilling to offer more than sympathy. Barra couldn't decide who she hated more in that moment. Clenching her fists, she tried to focus on what she needed to do next.

After an awkward measure on the Dais, Jerrun dismissed Barra's mother and her witnesses with a gesture, and they descended together.

Stunned and confused, the Tory and Plicks stayed where they were. When Barra eventually stood, the other two gathered themselves up and they began their walk back home. Seeming to have lost some of its magic, the Reach wasn't much of a distraction from what they'd all just seen.

Barra stopped them short. "I have to ask you both for a huge favor."

The boys nodded.

"Well, you said I should have asked for your help last time, and maybe you were right." She paused. "I know what we need to do to prove my mom is right about the Creepervine, and make Jerrun choke on his words."

Chapter 10

Kudmoth Traps

The trio began searching the Middens for Kudmoths the very next day. They found nothing, and it was the same every buckle for weeks.

Barra's mother was busy looking for support among the Arboreals, so it was easy for Barra to disappear for hours at a time and borrow whatever she needed from the abandoned study. She brought entire sheaves to the group, and the three pored over her father's reserach, learning what they could. They devised a plan for capturing the Kudmoths. Now, they only needed to find some.

As night after night passed without a sighting, Barra worried that Tory and Plicks doubted her story. There were lots of reasons why they hadn't found anything yet. Maybe the Kudmoths heard them coming, or only came out at specific times, and maybe they were in completely the wrong part of the Middens. It was hard to know.

Their plan for capture came from Plicks and Tory. They gathered trapwillow moss and arranged the strands into a net. Setting trapwillow into a mesh demanded patience and precision because the resin-sticky strands were difficult to manipulate once they were torn from the bunch. If the job was done well, the end result was a dense, almost invisible curtain with a hole in the middle. The hole was big enough for one of them to pass through unfettered, leaving any chasing Kudmoths stuck to the net. The plan was fine for everyone except the bup setting the trapwillow. That bup had to spend hours cleaning his or her fur, and the tacky resin tasted the way rotting bark smelled.

Plicks was the unlucky one this time, and he was licking at his fur like it was torture. Barra remembered the last time it was her turn and almost gagged. He looked miserable.

Barra realized it was getting late. She stared through her brushy hiding place to see how Tory was doing. They made eye contact. He was far away, on the other side of Plicks, but the shaking of his head was clear. Disappointed again, Barra started out from her hiding place to call off the hunt. But she saw movement beneath the preening Kolalabat, and froze.

She waited and watched, perfectly still. Plicks didn't notice the growing pool beneath him. Barra wondered if she'd been staring too long into the darkness and was only imagining things. But the shadow continued to grow, and she knew it was the Kudmoths. They moved like thick liquid spilling over the bark. She turned to signal Tory, but he'd already marked the threat. Plicks was in trouble. Undetected, the Kudmoths had gotten closer than the bups had planned. Tory was already moving and Barra joined, stealthing toward the growing mass of insects, her camouflage rippling as she moved. As scary as the Kudmoths were, Barra was overjoyed that she was no longer the only Arboreal who'd seen them.

The oily, thick pool spread fast, and Barra hastened her pace. She didn't have much of a plan, but she thought that she could at least distract the Kudmoths, maybe get them to chase her. She'd outrun the tiny terrors before and she was confident she could do it again.

Oblivious to the darkening branch below, Plicks was still busy cleaning himself when he saw Barra reveal herself. His face twisted up in confusion as he watched her arch her back, raise her tail, and recoil onto her haunches.

Baring her teeth, Barra hissed, and the slow-flowing Kudmoths became still all at once. Thrashing the nearby foliage with her tail, Barra created a threatening rush of noise ten times bigger than she was. She whip-snapped the bough twice, announcing a challenge. The Kudmoths clicked back at her in a cascade of flipping wings. Knowing she had their collective attention, she bolted through the hole in the trap and ran. The shadowy pool rapidly sublimated into a dark sentient cloud that followed after her.

Seeing the opening, Tory dropped down near Plicks. He grabbed the Kolalabat in one arm and leapt away. Free hand and feet interchangeable, Tory tore through the treescape like they were falling sideways. When he finally looked back to see if they were being followed, he saw only leaves and branches waving at them.

Barra swept up and down the boughs with fluid grace, a rush in her heart pushing her farther and deeper into the Middens. She started off so fast that she had to lag a bit to make sure the insects stayed on her trail. Confidence built up inside her as she went. Even when she stumbled or misjudged a jump she turned it to her advantage, taking the acceleration with her, racing onward.

Flashing through the treescape, Barra realized the Kudmoths could keep up with her every move. Suddenly fearful, she regretted bringing them in so close. She hoped she'd given Plicks and Tory enough time to escape.

She started back toward the trapwillow net, slinging herself around a branch with her tail. Barra charged headlong into the black cloud. The Kudmoths only had time enough to form a weak mesh, and Barra broke through easily. But the Kudmoths didn't give up. Instead, they were incensed by the closeness of their prey, and they flew even faster than before.

When Barra saw the trap area ahead, the muscles of her arms and legs were burning and tightening up. She'd run farther than she'd thought, and now, she was running rigid. She dashed toward the almost invisible mesh, spotted the hole, and jumped. But fatigue sapped the burst from her legs, and she didn't get the height she needed. She stretched out mid-air, trying to bend herself around the strands. She couldn't avoid them all. A portion of the net was ripped away with her, tangled in her fur. Landing awkwardly, her ankle twisted, and her chest listed forward. The roughness of the bark gripped and tore away tufts of her fur, but she kept running. Behind her, the cloud was thinner, but still intact and gaining.

Driving hard for a group of dwellings she knew well in the crush of dens, Barra pushed for a second wind. She was scared, and saw no sign of Tory or Plicks as she stole occasional, furtive glances into the treescape. She hoped they were out of harm's way, but still, seeing either would have given her some confidence. Not looking again, she decided she was alone and focused on the maze of dens ahead. A deformed roof porthole marked her usual entrance. The connections among the dens had formed from generations of collapse and regrowth, and Barra figured the Kudmoths couldn't know them as well as she did.

She dove in without hesitation. The Kudmoths followed.

The first den—like the rest in the crush of the Middens—was stretched, and strange, with thick and crooked branches growing up around everything. But Barra didn't stop to look around. Sliding beneath what must've once been a table, she slipped through an obscured hole into the next den. She wove in and out of the overgrown rooms, from den to den, as fast as she could. Her arms ached, and her legs burned, but she was a needle sewing a unique pattern into the fabric of the treescape. The Kudmoths didn't know the pattern, and she lost them.

Confident she was out of view, Barra reversed and jumped toward a high space over a doorway. Above the doorway was a collapsed portion of wall just large enough to hold her, and she reached for it in desperation. Barely clinging to the top of the frame, she peddled her legs in the empty air. Fear dumped one last flood of adrenaline into her veins, and she hauled herself up.

Heart pounding in her ears, she tried to focus. Slowing and deepening her breathing, she tested her stealth muscles. There was tightness in the action, but she gritted her teeth against it, and bore down. The Kudmoths were coming.

They entered the room in a flurry of clicks, red eyes flashing on and off. Out of the cloud, one pair of floating red points flew toward her, and as terrified as she was, Barra forced her eyes closed. She listened as the creature flew around her face. It came close enough that she could feel the breath from its small wings disturb her whiskers. Time stretched and her heart slowed. She didn't breathe. The Kudmoth hovered even closer.

She thought she was spotted for sure, and prepared to make another run for it. But the curious insect delayed only a moment longer, and then returned to the cloud. Barra listened. The entire cloud was moving away. She opened her eyes to slits and watched as the smoky insects were exhausted from the room.

Barra waited, and when no Kudmoths appeared, she waited some more. She was terrified of giving herself away by moving out too soon. Only when she'd waited much longer than her patience normally would have allowed did she crane her neck out to take a better look.

Maybe two measures passed, she wasn't sure. She hoped she was rested enough to make a run straight for the Loft. Sampling the air with a burst of quick inhalations, she detected nothing of the wet, fungal smell the dark bugs exuded. She swung down from her perch gingerly, but didn't let go. There was a sudden loud noise through the wall, and she retreated to her hiding place and stealthed again. Barra wasn't sure how much more tension she could take. The urge to run was almost irrepressible. A shadow appeared across the doorway—

—and Plicks entered the room.

"Barra!" he exclaimed in an excited whisper.

Tory ran in when he heard, and then followed Plicks' gaze up to Barra. "Well, that was an adventure," Tory said. His posture was nonchalant, but he couldn't hide his relief.

Barra let the tension fall out of her body as she jumped down. "I'm so glad to see you! What happened to the Kudmoths? They're gone?"

"Not entirely," said Plicks as he stepped forward, holding up a bellflower. Inside the container there were several swirling, agitated insects.

Barra inspected the contents. "You caught some!?"

Inside, the amorphous group of bugs congealed in a way, and became a simulacrum of a vicious animal that sneered at Barra. She peered closer, mesmerized. With her nose almost touching the container, the imitation bit at her and she fell back, startled.

Plicks said wryly, "We'll probably need to transfer them to something stronger."

"How'd you get 'em?" Barra asked, astonished as the insects returned to their shapeless, swirling flight.

"As soon as we realized they were following you, we went back to the trap," Tory said, beaming. "We knew you'd come back that way." He added, teasing, "Nice *jump* by the way." He reached out and touched one of the numerous strands that still clung to Barra's fur. He tugged at it, and Barra flinched away.

"Hey! Don't do that!" she said, wrinkling up her nose at him. "It'll take days to remove this stuff." She pulled at another sticky strand.

Plicks went on explaining, "As soon as you raced by, Tory and I checked the net, and all of these buggers were just stuck there like we thought they'd be! We dropped whole strands into the bulb because they were eating through them so fast. I mean, look, there's nothing left of the net in there now."

Tory added, trying to be funny, "Maybe the Kudmoths will clean you off if we ask them nicely."

As though gravity tripled in an instant, Barra felt her limbs become heavy and slow. Breathing was hard. Her stomach felt like it was in her feet. She wasn't strong enough to move.

Worried and confused by Barra's grave expression, Tory apologized, "I was only kidding."

Barra had forgotten his comment if she'd even heard it in the first place. Her tongue was thick and stuck to the roof of her mouth. "You *saw* me?" She rippled her stealth muscles. Looking down at herself, large patches of trapwillow entangled fur were not only visible, but emphasized by the rest of her body fading into the background.

The boys looked at each other, not grasping the situation. But they didn't need to understand to know they were in trouble, because every entrance to the room was outlined in black. They stared in disbelief.

"Run!" Barra commanded.

Plicks was slow to react, but Tory was already in motion. He scooped up the Kolalabat and tossed him through the porthole in the ceiling. Kudmoths swarmed away from the opening, and then billowed out after him. Tory's momentum carried him toward a window, and he jumped through it. A swarm of Kudmoths followed him as well, but there were many more. Insects flew into the room and blocked the exits.

Barra barged through the wall of Kudmoths and out the door. The swarm followed close, and Barra worked hard to stay out of reach. The miasmatic cloud drove her down, forcing her ever deeper into the Middens.

Barra panicked. She made bad choices. She missed her jumps. Instead of redirecting the acceleration like before, she fell haphazardly. Her ankle complained, but the pain was barely noticeable as the alarm in her head screamed for her to ascend. Out of control, Barra ran inexorably toward the big emptiness between the Middens and the Root, toward the Fall.

She saw a blur of purplish gray rolling through the thinning branches of her descent. It was Plicks. Looking up past him, she saw that Tory wasn't far behind. The bups were funneled down together. Barra was desperate to conceive of an escape, as their options disappeared with the branches into the ether.

She made her way closer to her friends. They saw her and tried to close the gap between them. They flowed around each other in a braid as they maneuvered away from the Kudmoths.

Barra bellowed, missing a branch. She was freefalling. Tory lunged at her and the collision sent her flailing toward a hold. She was safe for the moment, but Tory didn't make it to the branches. Quick to react, Barra lassoed the heavy Rugosic with her tail and pulled him over. Her claws dragged from his weight.

Plicks was tumbling by and Tory reached out to him. He caught the flailing Kolalabat. Her tail strained from the extra force, and her claws cut deeper into the slender branch. Sharp pain, and her eyes were tear-blind. She squeezed them shut, hard. They clung to each other frantically, trying not to think of what was beneath.

Barra held.

The branch did not.

Barra heard the snap-crack of the wood—not with her ears, but with her heart. Her eyes burst open and she watched the bottom of the Middens fly away.

The bups fell into the void with nothing to hold onto but each other.

Chapter 11

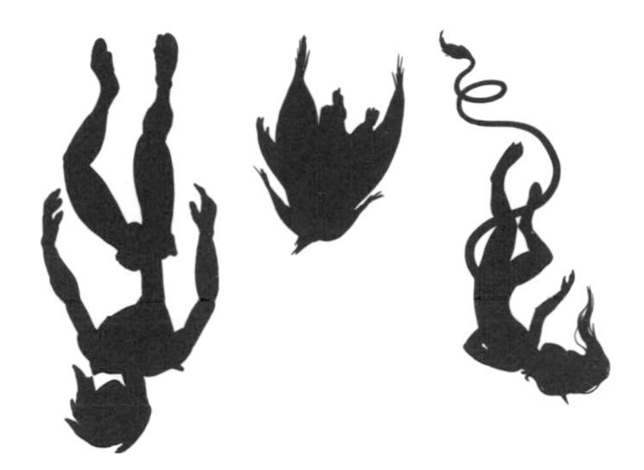

The Fall

The wind rushing past Barra took her breath away. Her skin rippled. Her eyes watered. She plummeted through the blind-black of the Fall, clutching her friends with no other thought than to hold onto them. The force of the wind threatened to rip them apart, but they were stronger, and they fell as one.

Barra thought they would fall faster and faster forever. She extended her arm, dragging it into the wind, and as she did they started spinning slowly. She tried to keep focus, but her eyes rolled and her stomach flipped, and she snatched her hand back. Accidentally snagging a claw on one of Plicks' scruffs, Barra realized the flaps of loose skin were pulled tight overhead, their tips snapping overhead.

There was hope.

Barra struggled with Plicks' scruff. Yelling out, she begged for help, but her voice was beaten away by the relentless wind. She couldn't even hear herself. They tumbled. Spinning faster, Barra felt another dizzy-sick punch in her gut, but she kept trying to wrangle the scruffs.

All the scratching and pulling got Plicks' attention. He understood what Barra was trying to do, and knew there was a chance. Determined, Plicks worked to reel in his wild scruffs. He dug his fierce talons into the stretched skin, pierced it, and pulled down. Inches at a time, hand over hand, he gathered.

Scared Plicks was taking too long, Barra cinched her tail around the boys and held tight. Hands and feet free, she bunched the scruffs down to Plicks one at a time. The reduced drag caused them to speed up, and the buffeting wind attacked the bundles.

Luckily, Plicks already hooked the ends and held one securely in each hand. He released the bundles. The scruffs blew up, mushrooming into two large arcs going from his back to his outstretched hands.

Nauseating deceleration overwhelmed them again. Barra, who had been holding on with her tail, slammed into Tory as the speed changed. She felt weak and lightheaded, but had the wherewithal to get a new grip and hug her friends close. The lack

of blood to her brain threatened to knock her unconsciousness. Even in the blackness of the Fall she could see the tunnel closing around her vision.

Barra swallowed hard. She took a few deep breaths and managed to push back the tunnel. Looking around, she noticed the light improving a little, and saw the silhouettes of impossibly tall columns in the distance. She guessed they were the trunks of the Great Trees, but she couldn't know for sure.

There was something else too. Something moving in the distance, falling with them. Barra saw it change direction abruptly many times, and realized it was flying, not falling, and it was getting closer. Two pairs of long, diamond-shaped wings swept out of the darkness. The creature was colossal, dark, agate red, and without eyes as far as Barra could see. It had four gigantic ears, a pair above and below its T-shaped head. Barra had never seen anything in her life to rival its sheer size. An intense sound, like a gale rushing through a hollow, erupted from each beat of the creature's wings. It flew straight at them.

Barra braced herself for impact. Instead, all she felt was a warm gust as the creature passed above them. Plicks' scruff sails collapsed from the pressure, and the three tumbled sideways until he was able to sort them again. Barra looked for the immense creature when they were under control again, but couldn't find it. She wondered how something that big could disappear.

"You okay?" Barra yelled as loudly as she could. The boys nodded.

They kept falling. They were doused in an eerie twilight. Barra saw drab, unfamiliar petals waving and rippling up and down the great columns in the improved light. Above them, a dome of darkness blocked out everything save a few bright

points. She wished she could ask her mother about the lights. "*If* we get back home again," she whispered. But she shoved the doubt firmly out of her way. "*When*," she corrected herself.

Below them was the surface of a gigantic lake of fog that radiated a soft, mantis green glow. The fog rolled in huge liquid waves. They were moments away from being engulfed by it, and on instinct Barra howled a raw screaming challenge against whatever would come next. The boys heard her defiant call and joined her, eyes and mouths wide to the fog, refusing to look away.

They passed painlessly into the moist, close air. Barra held her breath. Her senses told her she was floating, but she wasn't fooled. They were falling fast with no visibility. She felt trapped. All Barra could do was wait out the claustrophobic fog for whatever would come next.

She didn't have to wait long.

The veil of fog lifted all at once, revealing a strange, Loft-like wood. The branches curved and looped like tangles of ropes. The boughs were close-knit, and as they passed swiftly from empty space to thickets, Plicks was hard-pressed to avoid collisions. They were knocked around painfully, but Plicks' clever maneuvers kept them from serious injury.

Plicks yelled to Barra, "Let go!"

She felt him tug at his scruffs, and realized she'd unconsciously grabbed them for security at some point and was holding on, hindering his control. She let go and wrapped her arms around him doubly tight. With total influence over

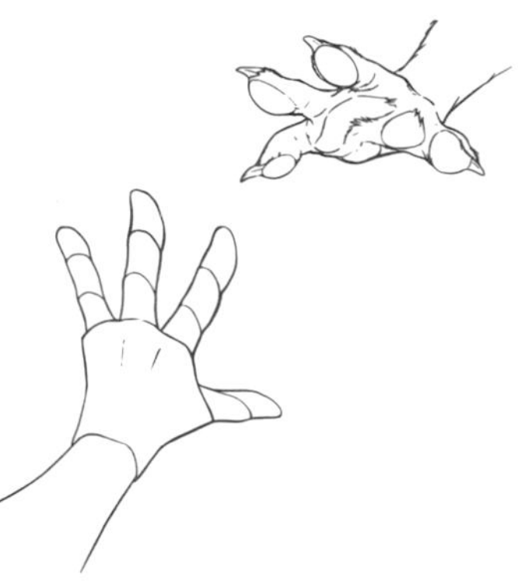

his scruffs, Plicks guided them into the open spaces between branches. Tory thought they were still going too fast to land safely, so he tapped Plicks and yelled something to him that Barra couldn't hear. Plicks nodded, and Tory jumped clear.

It was disorienting to watch him drop away because they slowed as he sped up. Barra was washed with vertigo again, and her stomach turned over. Her eyes lolled in her head; she'd had enough. Still, she managed to hold down the contents rising up from her belly.

Tory slid and grabbed the foreign boughs, slowing his fall. Plicks felt the relief of the reduced weight, and flew with even more control. Finally, Tory managed to stop ahead of them, and Plicks drifted over and touched down beside him.

They were alive beneath the Fall.

Chapter 12

Lost

The trio caught their breath atop a pathwood-sized bough. Tory's entire body heaved with his heartbeat, and Plicks' eyes were glazed over as he stared blankly. Barra was the first to move, and she crouched down to kiss the wood they were standing on. It smelled funny, but she was too relieved to care.

Her senses slowly returning, Barra jumped up. Cheering, laughing hysterically, she hugged Plicks, and exclaimed, "You saved us!" Tory was stunned a moment longer, and then he joined in. He was vibrating with exuberance, shaking as he lifted his friends into the air.

Plicks was listless, his chin bobbing up and down limply as they thanked him. When Tory finally set them down, Barra stepped away to look over the situation, but Plicks was rigid, both feet white-knuckled to the bough. The Kolalabat held his scruffs vice-like, as though they might fly away from him even though they were wrinkled up and motionless behind him. "Where are we?" he managed to ask timidly.

Tory didn't venture a guess. He knelt down and touched the bark. It was wet and cold, and the texture was like superfine fur. Rubbing his fingers together, he grimaced at the slippery quality.

Barra surveyed the tangle of branches surrounding them. There were scars the shape of eyelets rent into the woods, emitting the same green that tinted the fog overhead. The boughs in every direction were crisscrossed, dense, and overgrown similar to those less-travelled areas of the Loft, but otherwise unfamiliar. There were no flowers or ferns, and the branches themselves were gnarled and overrun with burls. The moist air created halos around every source of light, a rare thing to see in the Loft. Barra thought the halos were magical at home, but here they seemed ominous. She smelled damp mosses and rotting wood, salty traces in all of it. Where were they?

Eventually, Barra broke the silence, "Everyone alright?"

Tory shook his arms out and tested his legs. "I'm okay," he replied as he massaged his forearms.

Finally releasing his death grip from his scruffs, Plicks began gathering his loose skin into his arms. His face was drawn down, his chin quivering. Unable to concentrate enough to shrink his scruffs to his back properly, he stood there staring at his half-hearted bundle. There were wounds that needed cleaning in order to avoid an infection, but Plicks wasn't looking to them. Pools welled up beneath his big blue eyes as he said, "We're fallen—"

"No!" Barra cut him short. "We fell. We're not *fallen*." She limped over to the sagging Kolalabat. "Did you see those gigantic columns on the way down? They stretched all the way up to the Loft. Maybe the trunks of the Great Trees?"

Tory and Plicks didn't argue, but it was plain they weren't so sure.

Barra went on, her voice tight and too loud in the hollow silence, "It might be a long climb, but that's our way back to the Loft." It *was* a long climb. Before they'd hit the fog, Barra couldn't even see the bottom of the Middens anymore.

Peering around in the darkness, Barra tried to decide which direction to go. Everything looked so different, and visibility was meager. The eerie shades of green emitted from the scars did little to push back the darkness. Sitting with a decision was hard for Barra, so she picked a direction and started off. She turned back to her motionless friends and waited.

"Come on, Plicks," Tory said, and then walked toward Barra.

Plicks didn't blink. His normally expressive face was flat. He gathered in his scruffs and followed without a word.

In the branches behind the bups several green glowing eyes appeared. Different sizes and shapes, the sets belonged to more than one kind of creature. They moved. Like shadows hidden in the near-dark of dusk, they followed the trio.

The bups ascended through the branches without words, an oppressive dampness and isolation holding back their voices. Strange squeaks and unidentifiable, frightening noises filled the void and plagued their imaginations. The wood was filled with knots and dense nettles intertwined with one another, often blocking their progress. The obstacles sometimes forced them to back track, and the already climb-weary bups found it harder to keep going each time. The skin of the boughs was unlike other barks too. It peeled away in shreds with the slightest pressure, frustrating each step.

Lost

Each bup had to adapt to the strange treescape. Tory used controlled slides, and it didn't take him long to regain the confidence of his stance, even when branches fell away from him unexpectedly. Plicks climbed with his razor talons carving into the meat of a branches, through the unreliable bark. Barra had the most trouble, and had to work twice as hard to keep pace, and needed several breaks. The silence among them lingered.

Finally, Barra said, "I don't think we can get above this."

Tory said, "I was thinking the same—"

"What do you mean?" Plicks interrupted.

Tory explained, "We can't get above the fog. It's empty. Branchless. I guess I thought we'd be able to climb to a vantage of some kind, but look around. I can't see any better now than when we began climbing."

Barra watched Plicks' face waver as Tory spelled it out, vacillating between hysteria and despair. She extended her tail to hold him around the shoulders, but he flinched away.

Dumbfounded, Plicks barked a shaky question, "Well, you're not suggesting going back down?!"

There was a sharp sting in Barra's eyes as she watched Plicks tear up. She needed to say something encouraging, but fumbled the words and said nothing.

"The plan's the same," Tory offered sympathetically. "We get to the trunk of Great Tree and make the climb from there."

Barra joined in optimistically, "Exactly. Any trunk will do. Doesn't even have to be the Umberwood."

Plicks was in shock. He glared at Barra. He glared at Tory. Anger, sadness, frustration, and fear overcame him. The emotional load spiked, but instead of screaming or crying, Plicks smiled oddly. "Sure. Yeah. Okay."

"Plicks! You saved us!" Barra impressed on him. "We're alive! We can do this. It's just a little detour," she said, afraid it was obvious that she was trying to convince herself. She reached out to Plicks, but again he recoiled from her touch. Barra was disappointed. She wanted a hug as badly as she wanted to give one.

Apprehensive, Tory suggested they get going. Something was unnerving him, but he didn't say what. Barra didn't ask. She led the way back down. Inviting hues of blue became visible as they descended. Barra guided the trio toward those lights, kinder than the bilic greens around them.

Through the misty air, Barra eventually made out a great expanse of tightly interwoven boughs beneath them. The rolling stretch of continuous footing was like the bridges between Lofts. Thousands of bindings were used to create those enormous highways, but the surface they saw now was larger by far. There was no end to it in any direction. It had to be the Root.

They came upon strange dwellings similar to the dens in the Middens except they were squat and heavier looking. Their bindings were unrecognizable. Barra impulsively steered her friends toward one of the dens. As they approached, Barra could see the dwelling was much larger than she'd first thought, at least three times the size of anything she'd explored before. The outside was a tangle of petrified knots. There were giant misshapen fists of wood growing at irregular intervals along the walls, sometimes growing into twists larger than Tory. The den had identifiable windows and even a doorway. Tendrils of charcoal grey vines wove into and around the entire structure, sprouting bunches of glassy blue berries.

Barra was feeling her first hunger pangs, but she wasn't eager to eat anything growing from the menacing vine. On close inspection the berries were stuck together by black ooze that looked similar to the stuff they'd found on Ari. As they stepped up to the entrance, Barra could see that the vine had attached itself to the den with a combination of hooked thorns and tarry ooze—just like her father had described the Creepervine is his journal. She didn't want to frighten her friends, so she kept her thoughts to herself.

"What are we doing here?" Tory looked uncomfortable.

"Investigating?" Barra didn't sound sure, but she went with it, "There may be some clue inside, something to tell us where we are."

"Come on," Tory said, "We *know* where we are." He leaned into Barra, revealing what was on his mind, "I can't shake the feeling that we're being followed."

Plicks took in the environment with uncharacteristic calm. His attitude was irritating Barra because he looked more like he'd lost hope than gained confidence. He said matter-of-factly, "I don't see anything." He stepped between his friends and entered the den as he added, "Let's go in."

Barra didn't argue. She went in after him. Tory was reluctant to enter, but after one more suspicious look around, he joined them as well.

The interior of the den was unlike any other that Barra knew. If seats, beds, or tables had grown there before, they hadn't left much evidence of their existence. The high ceiling was domed in a familiar way, but instead of bindings as the bups knew them, there were jagged, stony shards holding the branches together. There were smooth, reflective shards too, embedded into the ceiling. Walking around the room caused a cascade of reflections that unnerved Barra.

There was a deep basin in the center of the floor made from spiraling branches big enough to fit all of Tory and more. A shallow, luminescent pool of water rested at the bottom.

Barra leaned way over the lip of the basin and sniffed at the water. After smelling from a few angles, she decided it was safe and lapped up a few tongues full. She sat up. "It tastes strange, but I think it's safe."

Tory and Plicks drank. After each had slaked his thirst, the basin was almost empty. In a couple of moments, the water began refilling slowly from the bared roots at the bottom.

Barra's fur was still matted from the trapwillow moss, and Tory pointed it out. "You might want to clean that off in case you need to stealth again."

Barra reached up with a paw and unceremoniously began ripping the thin strands from her fur. "Ow!" Barra stopped suddenly, and inspected her arm where a bright line of red appeared. She began licking at it, lapping up the blood that beaded up. Scrutinizing the sticky strands she held she saw a large thorn glued to one. It was small, but it had a nasty hooked point on it.

"You okay?" Tory asked. He was at a window keeping watch.

"It's only a scratch," Barra lied. It was deeper than a scratch, but it didn't look serious. "Watch out for the thorns on that black vine, they're really sharp." She finished pulling the last of the strands from her fur—more carefully than before—and cleaned up as best she could.

Tory paced from opening to opening, watching for anything dangerous that might come their way. His patrol was interrupted by a dense, low hum that began at his feet and travelled up his spine. The den swayed subtly, causing his vision to swim.

Tory lost his balance. "Whoa. Do you feel that?"

Plicks was shock-calm in the alien environment, staring at his feet where he dangled them into the watery basin. He was disconnected from their plight, detached from the world. He said nothing.

Barra felt the den moving. She experienced the same eerie disorientation as Tory, and echoed his thoughts, "What is it?"

The swaying and vibrating increased. The hum became a rumble and the floor of the den seemed to slide around beneath their feet. The pool lapped at Plicks' toes, startling him. He retreated from the lip of the basin like it was the salivating mouth of a hungry animal. Indeed, the opening of the basin narrowed. Plicks pointed and *erpped* repeatedly.

Barra and Tory followed Plicks' gaze and saw the basin closing. The narrowing opening created a conical light that was focused on the ceiling. Barra was the first to look up. The mirrored surfaces came together as the branches rearranged themselves. Barra yelled, "It's the buckle!"

The Great Trees were sliding together for the night. The floor was shrinking, the ceiling collapsing. The windows of the den were closing and Barra feared they'd be trapped inside. She raced to action. Dashing to the closest porthole, Barra leapt through. Outside, she turned around to see Tory and Plicks standing motionless, slow to react, apparently mesmerized. "Come on!" Barra screamed. The sound of the wild thicket weaving all around her was terrifying, hissing wet and sinister. The implications were havoc in her mind.

Tory and Plicks were still stuck in place. Barra scratched anxiously at the opening that wouldn't be for much longer. Glancing over her shoulder at the rootscape, she sighed. Inside the mysterious den or outside in the scary unknown; she'd rather be with her friends than alone.

Barra slipped back inside.

"What're you doing!?" Tory exclaimed as he and Plicks finally ran over to her.

"The window's already too small!" Barra pointed and yelled angrily.

Tory didn't blink. He only stared at her, unable to process everything that was happening.

The buckle eventually ended, and just like that, they were sealed off from the rest of the Root for the night. Trapped maybe, but also safe from the green eyes that lingered outside.

Chapter 13

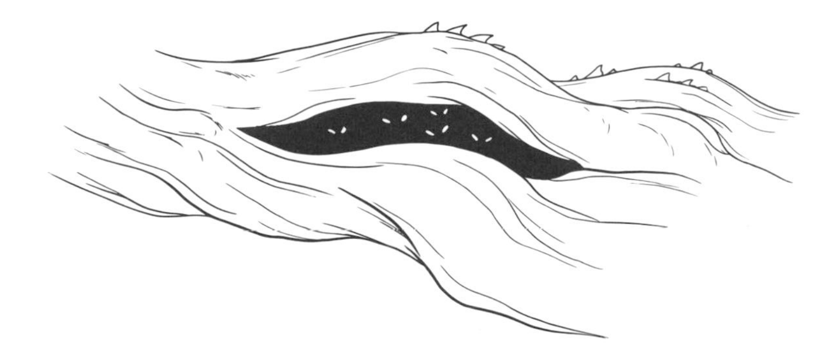

Reflection's End

The ancient den was well lit, the ceiling buckled into a mostly contiguous array of reflective surfaces where the shrunken basin focused a wavering blue light. The soothing nature of the curvy lines bouncing around the room did nothing to ease the bups' fear.

The trio searched for a way out. A few obvious doorways offered hope, but their bindings had erupted long ago, rendering them impassable. No escape, the trio instead found an alcove sprouting a few withering berries and sweet roots. The food only appeared meager, but was in fact potent. The strong flavors woke the bellies of the ravenous bups and they ate every bit.

Nothing left to explore and having found no exit, the three friends rested around the narrow basin. They watched the ceiling dance, and despite their circumstances, felt awe. The longer they looked, the deeper the reflection pulled them in.

After a while, Tory whispered, "What're we gonna do?"

Barra was preoccupied and Plicks still had a detached, glazed-over look in his eyes. Propping himself up, Tory reiterated, "No really, what's the plan?"

Barra was thinking about her father and the Root, trying to remember everything from the journal. She didn't appreciate the interruption. She glared at Tory and said, "Tonight? What do you want us to do? There's nothing we can do."

"We can't talk about it? Try to figure it out? We've got the time," Tory said, an edge of agitation in his voice. Of course, they were stuck. He knew they were stuck. He wanted to get unstuck. That was the idea.

Oblivious, Plicks said, "What do you think makes the light ripple like that?"

Tory threw his hands up, eyes rolling.

Barra scrutinized her fluffy friend, and wondered if he'd hit his head on the way down.

No one answered Plicks. No one said anything. Barra felt pressure to say something, to offer a plan, but her mind was swimming. The laceration from the thorn pricked for her attention, and she licked at it absentmindedly while she tried to think.

Tory walked his nervous energy off, circling the mouth of the water basin. After many tiny laps he knelt down beside Plicks. Tory waved his hand in front of Plicks' face. The Kolalabat wore an unflinching, unsettling expression and didn't react. Tory poked at him, "Hey. Hey, you gonna be alright?"

"Sure. I'm good," Plicks seemed surprised that Tory would think anything else. After an uncomfortable delay, as though he'd suddenly remembered something, he returned, "How are you?"

"I'm doin' okay," he said, evenly. Tory sat again, right beside his dazed friend. He tried to see what fascinated the Kolalabat so much about the ceiling. It was brilliantly architected—Tory couldn't imagine how the binders accomplished it all—but he thought Plicks saw more.

As Tory watched the beautiful play of light and shadow, he calmed down. His irritation with Barra subsided. He thought he could almost see through the ceiling into another world. Looking deep into the reflected image instead of at the surfaces that created it, he thought he saw something familiar.

He pointed and said, "I can almost make out some boughs. Reminds me of when my mom took me to the Mangrove Loft. We visited the wading pools with the other Rugosics, and left the deeper ones for the swimmers—Bellbottoms, you know? But I was curious, and I snuck off to look at the deep pools. There were branches grown into them, Arboreals darting in and out. Looked like fun. Anyway though, the water was green, but otherwise it looked a lot like this."

Barra wasn't interested in the ceiling. She sat up and said, "I think we had the right idea already. Find a Great Trunk and climb." Shrugging, she continued, "We found food, and I expect we'll find more in other dens like this. Nothing left to do tonight but rest. Tomorrow, we hop from den to den until we find the Umberwood."

Nodding, Tory said, "Yeah. Yeah, that could work. Maybe start thinking about saving some food too."

Grimacing, she recalled how poorly her last attempt at weaving had turned out; the satchel she'd made fell apart the first time she'd used it. She said, "Ermm, we'll have to figure that out I guess."

Plicks' legs jerked like he'd nodded off. He rolled onto his side and said, "Night."

Barra and Tory took the cue, exchanged goodnights, and tried to get comfortable.

Their sleep broke many times as the night opened to day. The foreign sounds of the rootscape agitated their dreams, and the uncomfortable floor of the den kept them tossing and turning.

Daytime in the Loft wasn't exactly bright, but the Root was worse—like the Loft wearing a shroud. There were few flowers, though some fungal blooms sprouted in the nooks where roots entangled or split. The mushrooms had shoots that sprung like hair from their caps and cast light from their tips, but not enough to see by. Instead, the bups' vision relied on the faint mist that soaked the air, which lit the perilous rootscape but also obscured it. Barra did her best to guide them.

As they travelled, the alarms in Tory's head kept going off. He was sure they were being followed, but whenever he looked, there was nothing. He suspected every shadow of hiding a threat. That wasn't all he had to worry about either. Plicks had apparently worsened overnight so that now he muttered nonsense from time to time without explanation. The Kolalabat startled easily too, which only fueled Tory's rampant imagination. The Rugosic kept a vigilant watch on his friend, and the wood.

The slimy boughs high above the floor of the Root were home to a variety of dens. None had a reflective ceiling like the first, though the woodwork of each did make unusual use of stones and metals. There were several food plants as well, but never in great quantity. Barra worried that when it came time to store some for the climb there wouldn't be enough, but she tried not to think about it. Besides, not one of the bups was experienced enough to weave any of the bark fibers they'd found so far into anything useful. Barra kept a look out, hoping to spot a familiar willow or anything she could make into a satchel.

The passage of time was difficult to track. They hadn't seen a dayflower, and couldn't guess the time by changes in light. Regardless, eventually all three were sure evening was coming. They began seeking a shelter that would offer more comfort than the last. Approaching one of the largest dens they'd seen, Plicks took off running. "I'll search this one!" he called back over his shoulder.

Barra and Tory raced after him and caught up to him inside the den. Barra scolded, "Don't do that! We have to stick together." She liked his attitude less and less, and wanted to snap him out of it. Everything she thought of saying just sounded mean, so she held her tongue.

The den they'd entered was large, with several doorways. Like everything else they'd seen at the Root, it was overgrown with vines, and the floor and walls were becoming unbound. Nevertheless, the den was accommodating.

Despite Barra's warning, Plicks bounded off through one of the doorways into an adjoining room. He yelled back, "I think it's a nestroom!"

Tory and Barra followed and found Plicks rolled up on some moss. Barra sniffed the air and said to Tory, "It doesn't smell worse here than anywhere else." She was tired after trekking all day, and willing to rest pretty much anywhere.

"I don't like it," Tory said while shaking his head slowly. "It's so big. Right now, I gotta admit I kinda want the security of a neatly bound space. If we stay here, we'll have to take turns keeping a look out."

Plicks whined, "This is the safest place we've found! We need a break."

Just as exhausted as everyone else, Tory said, "We just have to do some work to check it all out. That's all I'm sayin'."

"Great! I'll check the nestrooms!" Plicks got up and left in a bolt of nervous energy.

Barra shrugged, and gestured for Tory to follow her. She said, "Let's look around outside. See if we can guess how the bindings are going to work tonight. I don't really know what time it is. Might be better to stay here, regardless. You know? Rather than get caught outside?"

"Whoa, what about him? You really want to leave him alone in here?" Tory asked.

"No, I don't want to, but we have to talk… about him. We won't go far. He'll be okay," she said. She added, "It's not like there's been an Arboreal alive down here in a million rings."

Tory wasn't worried about other Arboreals. Still, they hadn't actually seen anything else to fear either. He followed her out, and they climbed the perimeter together. Tory called attention to several misshapen, obviously broken bindings, and guessed that several were missing, but saw nothing that worried him about the safety of the structure.

Certain they were out of Plicks' earshot, Tory began, "There's something wrong with him."

Barra said, "Yeah, definitely. We gotta help him, but I don't know what to do. He seems like he's already given up."

"He'll figure it out. We just have to stay positive, and… I don't know. He'll be okay. We're all going to be okay, right?" Tory asked.

"Hey, I'm scared too, but we gotta keep it together. We're…," she trailed off, distracted by something.

Tory thought Barra could use some help keeping it together, considering how she seemed just as edgy as the rest of them. He peered into the shadows trying to see whatever had distracted her.

Barra sniffed the air, and Tory could see her pupils grow so wide that the emerald of her irises disappeared.

"What is it?" Tory asked, but Barra was already running to the front of the den. He ran after her, but when he caught up she was already inside. He found her sniffing and dashing frenetically around the room. "Where's…?" Tory didn't finish the question.

Plicks was gone.

Chapter 14

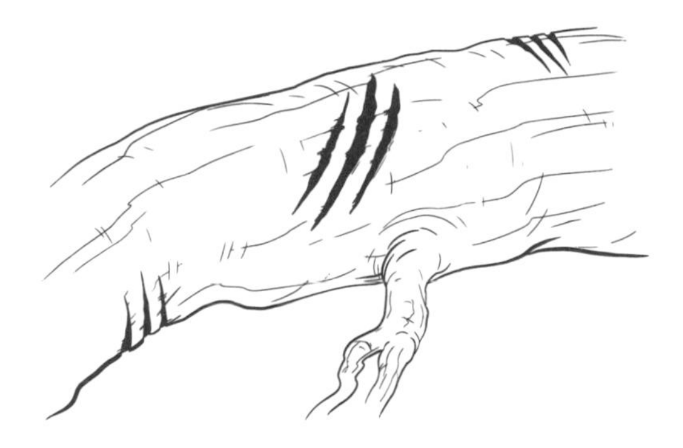

Extinguished

Fresh talon marks carved the floor, wood curling from the runs that ended at a far window. Tory leapt to the window and peered out, but saw nothing. Hanging half out the window he hissed to Barra, "Come on! Something dragged Plicks outta here! We gotta go after him!"

Barra's pupils were swallowed by her emerald irises. She didn't move. "There's something awful out there," she said. She sounded utterly lost.

Tory ran over to her. "That awful—whatever it is—has Plicks. We gotta go."

Barra didn't need to hear it from Tory. It didn't matter who or what took Plicks, they had to go after him. Her head was achy, her thoughts fuzzy. Barra was overcome with guilt.

Reading her face, Tory firmly said, "When we find Plicks, we can both tell him how sorry we are."

She nodded. Focusing, she sniffed the room one more time. Confident she'd identified the mingled scent of Plicks and his captors, she jumped out the window following the trail with Tory close behind.

They alternated between racing and crawling, and refused to rest. Barra's nostrils pulsed rapidly, into the air, along branches, hovering over any surface with a hint of Plicks' passage on it. She kept them going, and Tory stayed close and alert. As it turned out, the trail was more than distinctive, it was pungent. The stench was difficult to breathe, and after a short while, Barra became dizzy from the fumes. She had to stop frequently to keep from passing out. She started believing the trail was purposefully rank, as a deterrent. Sure, it was easy to follow, but who would want to?

Every time they stopped, Barra worried Plicks was slipping away from them. She couldn't let him disappear. They kept on his trail even though her body ached for rest. She tried to forget the stress wearing her down, but each passing measure of time was a painful reminder.

They found a grown-over, derelict pathwood and followed it down. All around them were empty dens, like an abandoned Nest. The dwellings seemed to sprawl endlessly in every direction. Barra thought the number of dens could support a greater population of Arboreals than any Loft she knew, even the Umberwood, and that made the emptiness and ruin even more unsettling.

Overgrowths of jagged, twisting brambles choked the pathwood they travelled into dangerous, narrow sections. They were careful to avoid the dark vine which seemed to grow everywhere, its flat, hooked thorns carving up the open spaces. Barra still hadn't told Tory that she suspected it was the Creepervine. He'd read the passage about her father's infected cut, and she didn't want him connecting the dots. Rescuing Plicks was all that mattered. The gash on Barra's arm was merely a throbbing reminder to stay far away from the thorns.

The pathwood eventually bottomed out, twisting into the intertwined boughs of the Root. The dens didn't continue down with them to the bottom. Instead, lattices of ropey, vertical boughs sprawled in every direction. The braids of wood supported the weight of the dens above, though Barra thought they looked more like tethers to keep the dens from flying away. Closer to the Root the lattice was a complex maze with hollows that felt like cages. Barra swallowed hard.

As they continued, Barra and Tory homed in on a not too distant blue glow. Barra sniffed at the damp air and tried to squint through the mist. She prowled up a branch to get a better view while Tory stood guard below. After a few moments of observation, she skulked back down. Standing beside Tory, Barra stretched and tested the strength of her ankle.

"We need to rest," Tory whispered, nodding to her injured ankle.

Barra nodded. Haggard and covered with brown and grey slime, Tory looked worn down. Besides, her second wind had come and gone. She'd passed the point of shaky muscles and carried herself on rubber-legs. If they'd found Plicks right then, she wouldn't have been much help to him.

She gestured into the distance and reported softly, "That blue glow looks like a big pool of water. We could wash and rest there?" Her body was coated in even more grime than Tory's. "There's an open area around it, lots of tangled vines, but nothing else really," she said, staying positive. "Pretty sure they're headed that way."

Nodding, Tory puffed himself up and set his sights on the blue haze.

They took turns climbing to survey the area as they approached. The narrow opening in the Root jagged back and forth a few times severely with a fine mist hanging over it. Waves lapped at the sides, the gentle sound amplified by the hollow space surrounding the pool. Warm currents drifted off the surface.

Tory's cheekbones cast austere shadows up his face, and Barra's eyes were lost in darkness. The light drew rolling ribbons of dark and light blue across their bodies.

The soothing rhythm of the waves stuttered. Something moved in the water, doming the surface, but never breaking the tension. Barra flicked her eyes at Tory and then up. Together they clambered for a better view. They hid behind a tangle of knots, and watched as whatever was in the water bobbed and circled. In time, the swimmer came to rest in the middle of the pool. Emerging from the surface came a single, dancing tentacle. It was glossy and tangerine-colored, and flicked around like a tongue tasting the air. Eventually, the tentacle rose up, folded back on itself, and then touched back down to the water. Another tentacle breached the surface, and another, until there were a dozen. They pushed down on the surface of the water, creating deep dimples. A bulbous form lifted into the air, the body rising among its tentacles. Barra thought it looked like the creature was turning inside out.

Completely above the water, the tentacles moved along the surface like they were swaying in an imaginary wind. The body bulged at the top and became narrow at its bottom. Water cascaded down over the creature's body, and droplets fell like sparks onto the surface of the pool.

Barra was awestruck. Tory was spellbound.

The creature changed shape, metamorphosing as it floated. The tentacles grew long and flat like ribbons and the body squished into a disc. The creature also pulsed subtly, light passing from its center outward as it rose into the air. Suddenly, Barra felt longing sadness. Her father had probably never seen anything like the tangerine creature. She wished he were with her. She imagined him taking notes, and knew that his sketch would have been awful. His words would have captured the moment even more beautifully than she saw it now. Her breath quivered as she choked back her tears.

A flourish of clicking and clacking sounds rained down, jolted Barra out of her daydream. Hundreds of Kudmoths beat their wings in a dark cloud that descended like a shroud over the watery creature. Shimmering brightly, the creature shifted back and forth like an orange blur burning the air. The short-distance bursts weren't enough to evade the insects. The Kudmoths interlocked, forming a loose net. They enveloped the creature, and tightened their grips to collapse the trap.

Barra flashed angry. She remembered being suffocated like that, swallowed by the darkness, and she needed it to stop. She couldn't just sit there and watch, no matter what the Kudmoths' purpose was.

Tory grabbed Barra. Recognizing the expression on her face, he whispered gently, but firmly, "No! There's nothing we can do! We don't know what that thing is!"

The net of Kudmoths shrank until there were no holes, no sign of the creature within, only a writhing ball of insects buzzing above the pool. That was all Barra could take. Her body was slinky, built for escape, and even with his tremendous strength, Tory couldn't hold her. She wriggled free and dashed from where they were hiding. Tory stumbled after her, grasping at nothing. He shook his head, exasperated, and then ran to catch up.

Charging up to the edge of the pool, Barra reared up and hissed savagely. Tory rushed up to her with his imposing, loping gait. He readied himself, arms and legs flexed, head low, eyes flashing. Barra tried to thunder her tail against the floor, but the resulting *thud* was dampened-weak, and the Kudmoths seemed unimpressed.

Tangerine liquid began oozing out through the Kudmoth ball. Tory took a few steps back, showed his teeth, and growled so deeply that his chest vibrated visibly. More of the liquid appeared and Tory decided that threats weren't working. He took two long strides, launched himself into the air, and crashed into the net, exploding through it.

The Kudmoth ball disintegrated in a burst of splintered carapaces and tangerine goo. Tory landed on the other side of the pool with splashes of the viscous fluid sliding through the grime

on his body. Gathering himself, he prepared to run away, but when he glanced back, the remaining Kudmoths were already gone. "What the...? Where'd they go?" he asked in a low voice.

Bewildered, Barra answered, "They just flew away."

Tory followed Barra's searching eyes but saw only the shadows of the rootscape. The water creature was gone. Tory rubbed some of the tangerine fluid between his fingers and the light within faded. The texture changed too, becoming tacky, and then turning into a fine, ashy powder. He shook his head uncertainly as he wiped his hands together and watched the dust fall from his arms.

Judging the distance across, he called back to Barra, "I don't know if I can make that jump again."

Barra was searching for signs of Kudmoths. They'd tricked her before and she didn't want to be fooled again. "I'll come

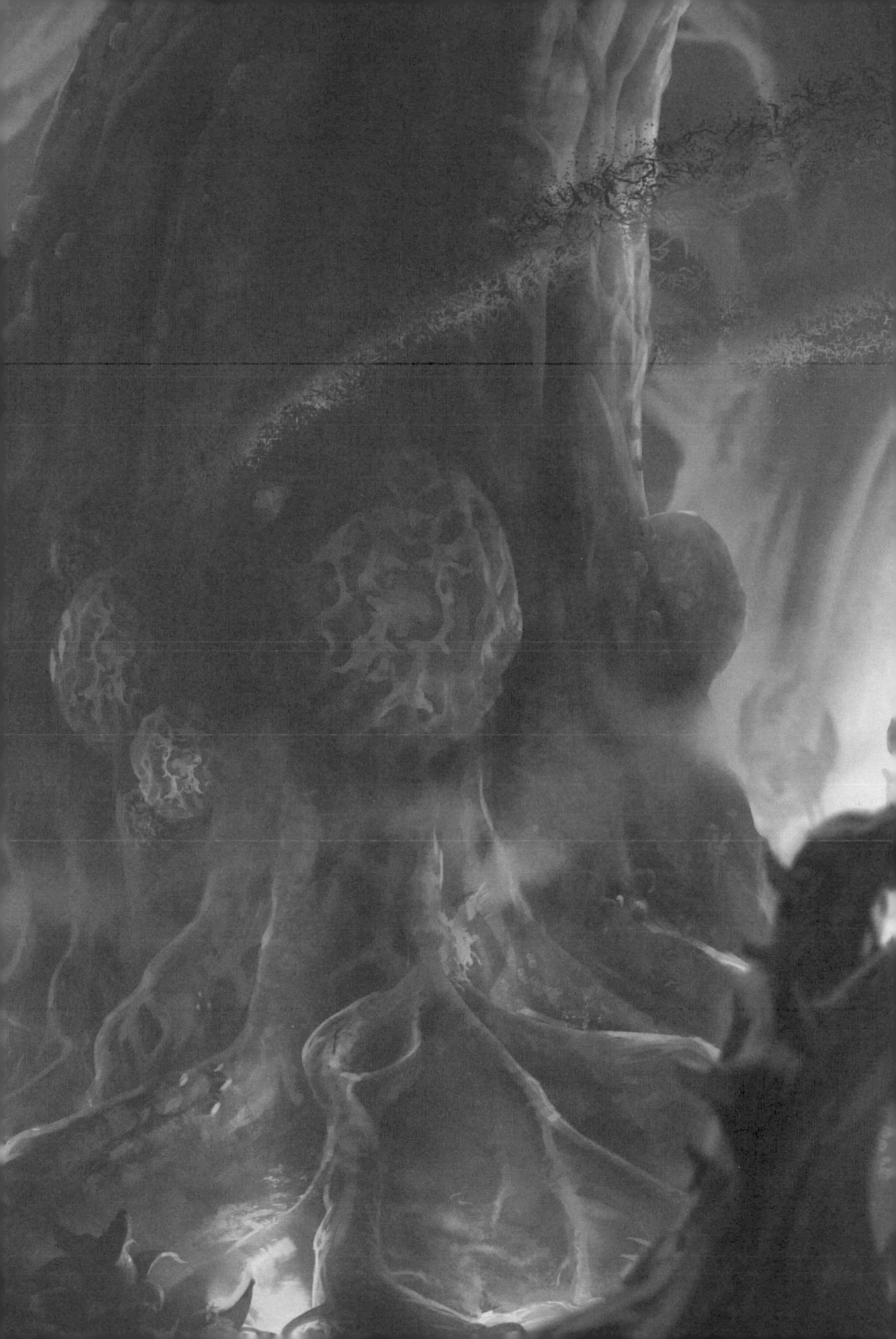

around," she said. She started walking, staring the darkness down as if a monster lurked behind each branch. She shrank away from the shadows, but she also had to take care around the ragged opening in the Root. Lined with sharp branches covered in slimy bark, Barra didn't know how she'd get out if she fell in.

Tory kept pace on the opposite side. He was worried about Barra. He didn't want to lose her the way they'd lost Plicks. They needed each other to get home, and he was going to make sure she stayed safe. Tory couldn't swim, but he was drawn to the edge regardless. He pictured himself sinking and shivered. "Hey, did you notice how deep..." Tory's voice trailed off as he tried to make sense of the bottomless reservoir. In the Loft, water pooled in natural or bound structures of wood and resin. Tory had never seen one so deep that the bottom vanished.

Gazing into the water, Barra couldn't fathom its depth, though her interest waned quickly. Her forearm throbbed, her head ached, and they lost Plicks more with each passing moment. Without explanation, Barra's stomach traded places with her lungs, or seemed to anyway, and she felt woozy. Not trusting her footing, she crouched away from the edge. Barra worried she was sick, but then realized her nausea was the result of the buckle catching her off guard again. The signs were different at the Root, and Barra still hadn't figured them out. The wood beneath her feet writhed. The rumble grew ever louder, and she dug in with her claws.

Vines and brambles reached toward Barra as the surrounding wood wove together. Tory had to dodge the thorns and boughs that swept slowly into his path. The water of the pool sloshed about tumultuously as the opening closed.

Tory gave up on the idea of going around. The vines were forcing him toward the water, and soon, he'd be able to simply step over the pool. But with the opening gone, the light would disappear too, and it was already too difficult for him to see Barra. Searching for her in the thorny blackness would be dangerous.

Tory waited, saw his moment, and jumped. The Root shifted beneath him, and his jump was clumsy. He landed off balance, but recovered fast and rushed over to Barra while he could still see her. Tory grabbed her paw up in his hand and held it firmly. "We're okay. The thorns aren't going to come much closer," he said, acting more certain than he was.

Barra knew Tory was right. There was room for both of them, even if only a small pocket. Safe from the thorns, she worried about Plicks. She was scared they might already be too late to help him, and there was nothing she could do about it.

The buckle ended, and the last breath of light was snuffed out.

Chapter 15

Blind

I can't see any way out," Barra said, her voice strained.

Tory thought he heard her swallow. In the complete darkness, her eyes were all he had to know she was there. Whenever she turned away to scout their surroundings, it was like she vanished, and Tory was alone.

Struggling to stay calm, Tory steadied his wobbly legs. His reliable, easygoing confidence was faltering—something that hadn't happened since his mother passed from the branches. He remembered when she'd gotten sick. He and his father had sat down with the doctor, and they were told she had time. But the illness moved faster than the predictions. The memory of his father explaining she was sick merged with the one of his father explaining she was gone. Tory'd had no response back then. He'd felt nothing except an awkward guilt for feeling nothing. The hurt came later.

Every achievement, every festival, and every birthday he spent without her was painful. Her absence had grown slowly, and he'd become disinterested in everything. He'd even started believing that he'd died with her, and wished he had sometimes. Tory had been angry with his father for getting over her before he did, and they fought once, just one time, about it.

Tory remembered the fight well. After he'd yelled his accusations, his father responded with severe calm: *I don't miss her any less than you. I don't grieve her loss any less than you. I just remember* her *instead of the moment she left.* It'd been hard to hear. Tory realized that he'd allowed her death to become more important than her life, and it bothered him that he'd let that happen. He wished he'd thanked his father for those words, but he hadn't yet, and now he was worried he'd never get the chance. Barra winked in and out of existence again, but he thought of his mother, and the fear of the pitch black receded, and he felt less alone.

Unfortunately, they really weren't alone.

Shivers went up Tory's spine as he thought he saw Barra's eyes change color. Then inexplicably, her eyes disappeared and reappeared in the distance, and he had to check that she was still beside him. Many sets of eyes blinked open in every direction. Tory felt fear, but courage too, and he silently thanked his mother for that, as the eyes closed in around them.

Whatever they were, they shambled oddly in the lightless after-buckle. They seemed almost clumsy, but then, their eyes opening and closing disguised both their number and their movement. Reaching out, Tory held Barra close, shielding her with his body.

Barra extended her claws and poised her arms to attack. She slashed viciously, promising pain to any creature daring to come near, but even with her highly effective night-vision, she saw only hints. Her depth perception failed too, and she swiped at nothing. She leaned back into Tory. She screamed out, and they turned together, but the creatures seemed to be everywhere and nowhere all at once. Suddenly, Tory's body went slack, and Barra felt his arms fall away. She flailed about, searching for him, but he was gone. Spinning around, sweeping her tail broadly, she prepared to strike. Several eyes opened at once, and she turned to face them, eager to get on with it. But the creatures hidden behind her had other ideas.

Powerful hands grabbed Barra's arms, legs, and tail simultaneously. They pulled her from her feet as she hissed and screamed and growled, but her struggle was futile. They were too tough, and too many. They bound her limbs and heaved her into the air. A large one slung her like a sack of berries over its shoulders, and just like that, carried her away.

Barra tried to see where they were going, but mostly, she saw the back of the creature carrying her. "Tory!" she yelled, but he didn't answer. It was like that for a while, call and no response. She was worried, but she didn't give up. She struggled with her restraints too, but the more she fought the tighter they became.

A repulsive, sickly-sweet scent of decay rose from her captor. She tried to wrinkle her nostrils closed but it wasn't enough to block out the stench. To make matters worse, the creature jumped, and when they landed together her face was plunged into the rot that covered its back. After the nausea and dizziness passed, she realized her sense of smell had burned out. She wasn't sure she'd ever smell anything again. She wasn't sure she'd want to.

Testing her restraints again, Barra tried to identify the material and thought the ropes felt like braided willow twine, but rougher. She faked unconsciousness, and when she thought the creature lowered his guard, she twisted violently. It didn't help. The caravan of creatures stopped, inspected the coils, tightened them and added more. There was nothing Barra could do but wait and watch for an opportunity to escape. She hissed and growled regardless—she would be free again and she wanted them to know it.

Know it, and fear it.

Barra worried about Plicks. She worried about Tory too, but Plicks? He could barely take care of himself on a good day. The sooner she found him the better. With any luck, these creatures were the same ones that took him—they certainly smelled the same.

The number of glowing, seeping scars increased as they travelled, providing improved light. Barra caught ephemeral glimpses of the rootscape. She was vigilant, looking for anything that could help her escape. There wasn't much to see. She noticed however, that some of the thorny vines slid back into place in their wake, obscuring the return path. The vines appeared to move out of their way, as though the will of the creatures compelled them.

The density of the scars continued to grow, and Barra was able to see that they weren't on the bottom of the Root any more, they'd climbed some. They were in another abandoned Loft-like city, except most of these dens were covered in tarry ooze, thick and abundant. The ooze existed wherever the Creepervine grew, and the Creepervine was everywhere. Her father's journal had been clear that the vine was always covered in a layer of slimy fungus, but what she saw before her was a plague. The wound in her forearm ached, and she tried to ignore it.

Barra howled Tory's name yet again, and again he didn't answer. The caravan continued. She screamed louder, but her captors went on unaffected. She redoubled her efforts to figure a way to break free.

A creature fell back to travel beside her. It was hunched over slightly, and covered with growths of twigs, molds, and flowers. The creature had Tory's proportions, with long limbs ending in huge hands and feet, and no claws Barra could see. Wrapped all over its body were vines that

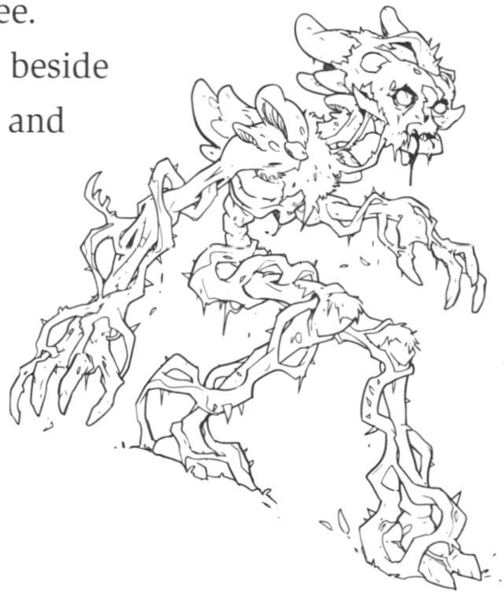

looked like exposed veins, and there was fuzz growing in layers on its shoulders and head. As the hunched creature moved its molds bunched and pulled like muscles while the vines slid like tendons. The movement disturbed, but also, captivated. Barra couldn't look away.

Slowly, the hunchback faced her. His large, pale-green saucer eyes locked with hers. Barra was terrified, but as she gaped at the creature, she thought there was something sad about him. Unexpected as it was, she felt sympathy toward him, and then even more surprising, she saw her sympathy reflected back. The creature's head bobbed gently, eyes never wavering from hers.

Barra whispered, "Help me. Help me, *please*."

The creature stared long enough for Barra to believe he understood, and then he looked away. He stared at his feet, his head bobbing weakly in time with his steps. Betrayed, Barra tore the air with a hiss until her lungs were exhausted. The fungus-covered puppet-monster seemed not to notice. The caravan kept going.

After a time, there was some commotion among the creatures. Barra was jostled and thrown around. She saw Tory and relief rushed through her body. He was draped, limp, around the shoulders of a serpentine creature covered with furry molds, flowers, and roots like the other fungal-puppets. This particular monster's flowers were unusual though, flat black with edges sharpened by poisonous lines of color. The

creature had arms but no legs, and there were small beads of eyes all over its head. Two of the creatures approached Tory and lassoed his wrists before Barra was hauled to the ground and lost sight of him.

The creatures changed the bindings on Barra's arms and legs, tying them with her tail behind her. They laid her down on her belly, where she received another face full of slime from the damp wood. She heard the persistent motion of her captors, their shuffling feet and slithering vines. After a short time she was lifted, and then set back down on her side. She faced away from the terrible creatures. Their commotion ceased, the air was still, and the silence poked her skin like needles.

After a bit, another creature crept into her view. It had tall wings that were wrapped and tied around its slender body. Its arms—tucked under its wings—were restricted, and they twitched as the creature bent closer to observe Barra. She braced herself, not knowing what to expect. The winged creature's mouth opened as though to speak, but its snout only moved up and down wordlessly. One twitching hand reached for her, and Barra shrank away. She parted her fur using her stealth muscles. Laying her fur flat to avoid the touch, something she'd never even thought of doing before. The moldy creature tilted its head left, then slowly right, and then smiled. It nodded at her, its snout moving again without a sound, and then it sauntered away.

Barra's vision floated and her head spun. Without realizing it, she'd begun hyperventilating. Claustrophobia struck her hard. Again, she struggled against the ropes. The friction melted wrist hairs, and burned her skin. She growled until her throat was ragged and her face blood-hot.

Her momentary fit eventually broke, and she took a shuddering breath. She tried to focus on a happy thought, and with her eyes shut, she imagined she was in her nestroom, her mother humming while stroking her fur, and she felt a little calmer. Barra wondered what her father would do, how he would handle the situation. She pictured him conserving his energy and maintaining his wits, so she tried to do the same. Thinking it over, the fungal-puppets could have harmed her already, but they hadn't. Barra took some comfort from the thought, not much, but some.

Barra tested the ropes again. More relaxed this time, she experimented and decided they weren't at tight as she'd first thought. The muscles that manipulated her fur for stealth tingled for her attention, and she rippled them. She felt the ropes—the texture, number of loops, and the kind of braid—through her fur. Shifting weight onto her shoulder, she lifted her arms a bit off the floor and found she could move the ropes a little. Her first attempts were clumsy, but she learned quickly, and soon she was able to cascade her fur in a concerted effort to lift and push the ropes around. Keeping her hands lax to provide slack, she began shifting the loops down over her wrists.

Barra was elated when the first loop fell to the tips of her claws. The entire rope loosened with it, too. No celebrations though. She had to be cautious. She had to be patient. The fungal-puppets were near, and they'd only tie her up again, tighter than before, if they suspected she was free. She pretended her hands were still bound and began working on her legs.

Meanwhile, she wriggled around trying to get a better view. She snuck a careful peek over her shoulder. Glowing sap seeped out from long gashes in the boughs. It seemed like the whole place was rotting from the inside out. Barra saw a dozen creatures: some standing, others kneeling, all facing away from her. She couldn't understand what occupied their attention—they might have been sleeping. The floor between Barra and the host of fungal-puppets was open and flat, but with no clear exit through the Creeper-infested bramble walls.

There was a grunt beside her, barely audible. The grunt turned into a groan and a few of the standing creatures turned to look. Barra rolled back over to avoid drawing attention. The groaning sounded like Tory. She knew it was him a breath later when he tried to speak. His tongue sounded fat, like it was filling his mouth, so she couldn't make out the words, but it was definitely him.

Barra stole a glance over her shoulder again, and noted that the creatures had lost interest. They were unbothered by Tory regaining consciousness, so she assumed he was tied up the same as she was. She figured she could get away with a whisper of her own, "Tory. Tory, hey, it's me. Are you okay?"

"Why are...?" He was groggy, not quite remembering what had happened. "I can't move my... What the!?" he started, frustrated and angry as he discovered he was tied up.

"Shhh! You'll draw them over here!" Barra shushed him as quietly as she could. She kept her voice low, "These creepy things ambushed us, and brought us here. I'm not sure..."

"Tory? Barra, is that you?" Plicks called out weakly from the other side of Tory.

Discouraged, but not without a sense of humor, Tory said, "Not much of a rescue, huh? You okay?"

"I'm okay. Just scrapes and bruises. You both tied up, too?" Plicks asked, expecting the worst, but full of hope anyway.

Reunited, the three exchanged whispers for a bit, gathering what they could from each other. Barra kept a watch over her shoulder, expecting their captors to break up the conversation. Occasionally one would take a look, but that was all.

From what they could determine, Barra, Tory, and Plicks were lying down along the outer edge of a large, open platform similar to an Elder Dais. The platform was bounded by rigid and jagged nettles, and a tall, concave wall at the far side that created a kind of half-ceiling overhead. There were long twists of Creepervine as well, dangling down from above like disembodied tongues.

There was no obvious way to escape. Plicks could see the wall from his vantage, and described what might be an opening carved into it. It wasn't obvious where it would lead. Even if it was a way out, many of the fungal-puppets were huddled there, blocking it. Barra worked her restraints loose while they talked, and was finally free. She wanted to tell her friends, but maybe the creatures were listening after all. She didn't want to risk it.

Their conversation dwindled as each tried to suss a way out, and after a short time, Tory said, "I think I can break these ropes..." He tested them. "Mmm... maybe?" he added uncertainly. The ropes were sturdy, but he believed a swift pull with all his might could snap them.

A sap-thick voice growled through the air. "What have you brought me?" it asked. The voice was as deep and slimy as the scars all around them.

The tall, winged creature that had visited Barra earlier stood up and walked toward her again. The creature's eyes were forlorn and distant, and though it stared at her, it seemed not to see her at all. Standing near Barra, the creature turned toward the voice, and spoke without emotion, "Three survivors from above, Argus." The winged creature's voice was higher and silkier than Barra expected.

"Survivors? It's been so very long..." the voice said with an odd cadence, the pauses as long as the words. The owner of the voice hid behind the huddled fungal-puppets and none of the bups could make him out. He might have been there all along or just arrived, there was no way to know for sure. "Is that a Kolalabat?" he asked hungrily, followed by a sound like he was sniffing the air.

The bups were afraid to answer.

Several moments passed, and then the unseen thing laughed. What started as a chuckle soon developed into a heavy bass that seemed to crush the platform as it rolled over it. When the laughter ended, the thing sighed. He growled something to his fungal-puppets that none of the bups could understand, and the minions began bustling around again. They shambled toward the captives. Barra twisted around and counted at least a dozen, their vines slithering sadly with each step.

"Let me go!" Plicks screamed. One of the creatures grabbed him by the trusses and began dragging him away.

Barra rolled over, dug in, and steadied herself, giving up her ruse. The fetid minions were staggered at the far end of the platform. A tall, lithe figure stood near the wall, or really, writhed *within* the wall like a body entombed in sap. Around him was a thick membrane of rippling, dark ooze. There were hollow voids where his eyes should have been, and he was naked, soot-colored, and furless. His toothless maw gaped, saliva dripping down from his chin.

Six fungal-puppets were closing on Tory, and Barra dashed between, thrashing her tail. The minions watched her, but kept moving toward the tied up Rugosic. The hideous, eyeless creature partially emerged from the wall, his body shifting in the ooze. The dark membrane wrinkled and stretched. He leaned out, and Barra could feel him *see* her with his empty sockets.

She yelled to Tory, "Break those ropes! Let's go!"

He wrestled with the restraints, but they only grew tighter. "I… I can't!" He yelled back through gritted teeth, his circulation to his hands cut off.

Barra bounded over to him and slashed at the braided vines. She didn't cut clean through them, but they shriveled and opened up anyway. Wrenching his arms, Tory tried again, and the ropes snapped, spraying green fluid from the broken ends. Hands freed, Tory went to work on the ropes around his ankles. The creatures watched, stunned. Barra bolted to the fungal-puppet holding Plicks, leapt onto its back, and then began hacking furiously at it. Sweeping arcs, bright and jagged cuts, carved the creature's layers of fungus. The gashes didn't seem to cause the creature any pain, but with its vine-like tendons severed, Plicks fell in a heap at the monster's feet. The creature began bucking and jerking violently, trying to throw Barra from its back.

Ripping the last of the ties from his ankles, Tory hurried over to Plicks. The stunned minions began to move, but not fast enough to interrupt Tory. He freed Plicks and then the fungal-puppets were on top of them. Plicks scrambled around the grasping creatures, Tory dodged. They weren't captives, but with nowhere to go Tory didn't think that would last. "Barra!" he howled, "We have to get out of here!"

Barra needed to get clear of the wild monster that was still tossing her around. She wrapped her tail around the oozing beast and squeezed hard. Its flailing arms were cinched to its sides. The fungal-puppet lost its balance and lurched. Barra jumped away as it fell to the floor. Airborne, she twisted around and put her feet first, blind to where she was landing. In a frightening prescient flash, she saw herself face to face with the repulsive eyeless monster, and an instant later the flash became reality. Barra crashed into the monster and extended her claws deep into its flesh. His skin was like Umberwood bark, his breath like rotting wood. Clinging to his chest, Barra peered into his vacant sockets. A spark pricked up and down the length of her spine. Her fur hummed.

The eyeless thing's chest heaved and rumbled, a low growl issued forth, so low that it rattled Barra's bones. Unable to suppress the instinct, Barra bared her teeth, pointed incisors flashing with wet, her eyes filled with fury. She snarled and swept her tail beneath her in neat, menacing flicks.

Saliva rolled out over his parting lips, and he said, "*You* are mine."

Barra snapped her teeth and slashed at his face. She leapt from him, and flipped mid-air to hit the floor on all fours. Her ankle throbbed with adrenaline-dampened pain, and she ran, looking for her friends through a mess of dangling and reaching limbs.

"Over here!" Tory was at the edge of the concave wall with Plicks.

Barra raced around one fungal-puppet and between the rotten legs of another.

"Come on!" Plicks hollered, and unfurled his scruffs.

On the other side of the wall was an open area, branch-free into the visible distance. They were on the ledge of a ravine. Barra thought she'd done enough falling for a lifetime, but she didn't have a better idea. Plicks climbed up onto Tory like a backpack. Barra held onto Tory's waist and they jumped.

Chapter 16

Circling the Dream

The bups sailed through the air on warm drafts that blew up from the Root like giant gentle exhales. They were rising and falling at will, far from the reach of the rotting monsters. They were safe, but it couldn't last. Plicks couldn't float them forever.

Barra scanned the rootscape, worried that the eyeless thing would find them no matter where they touched down. Her forearm throbbed in time with the memory of his words, "*You are mine.*" Over and over again in her mind, the words repeated, until the muscle beneath the cut ached to the bone. She squeezed her eyes against the pain, and tried not to think about how far they were away from home.

"Over there!" Tory shouted. His eyes were least capable of seeing through the darkness, but he wasn't as distracted as the other two. He pointed to a large area isolated from the rest of the

Root by a roughly circular ridge. The ridge was an incomplete wall of bound boughs around a relatively level floor. As they floated over the cirque, Tory thought the bowl-shaped rootmass was well-insulated, the broken sections of ridge stuffed full of dangerous nettles. The whole cirque was washed with dim, diffuse light and Tory thought the flora within looked healthy opposed to everything else they'd seen.

Plicks glided them in closer, and they saw the old bindings that held the shape of the ridge together, and the sprays of metal threads where they hadn't. Many rings had passed since anyone or anything had cared for the construction, and Plicks took it as a good sign. He'd met enough inhabitants of the Root. He picked a large pad of moss and made his approach.

Barra jumped free even before Tory's feet touched down. She began prowling around, suspicious. Still perched on the Rugosic's shoulders, Plicks began gathering up his scruffs. Tory didn't seem to mind.

"Whaddya think?" Tory asked Barra in a hushed voice.

Barra was inspecting a group of flowers and plants. Sniffing at it guardedly, she said, "I'm not sure. This garden seems tended, doesn't it? Like someone's been here?"

Tory walked over to stand beside her. Plicks gathered his scruffs and hopped down to take a look for himself.

"Maybe..." Tory didn't want to admit that he agreed. "Maybe not. Either way, I can't picture one of those, those *things* living here."

Barra nodded. She purged her nostrils, and found her sense of smell returning. Sniffing around, she said, "Yeah. I think we're safe enough for now—"

Plicks interjected, his voice cracking, "Safe enough?" He paused. "What were those things?!"

"I don't know," Tory said. "I didn't get a great look at any of them." Feeling the back of his head, he winced. "I'll say this: I'm glad they're slow, because they're strong. What was that thing in the wall? It wasn't like the others. What did it say to you?" he asked Barra.

"I couldn't understand him," she lied. She turned away, hiding her wounded arm. "He just gurgled at me, that sick stuff pouring out of his mouth. He didn't have any eyes! Did you see that? But it was like he was staring right at me!" She shivered at the memory.

Plicks unloaded his thoughts, "What's going on down here, anyway? Everything is dead and empty, and covered with black ooze! And we were just tied up by a bunch of... of puppet things that probably wanted to kill us and serve us up as dinner for their eyeless master! I just wanna go home!"

"Hey, you're okay! *We're* okay," Tory said. "We got away from those things! Barra annihilated one! Did you see that? And now, we know we can outrun them, and we'll be able to avoid them by their smell. Right, Barra?"

Barra was distracted, but managed to say, "I can pick them out. No problem."

"So," Tory concluded, "let's just catch our breath for a bit." Smiling, he hit Plicks in the shoulder. "That's twice you saved us!"

"Ow," Plicks stumbled a bit, winced and rubbed his shoulder. Grimacing he added, "You're welcome?" The punch hadn't really hurt much. But it snapped him out of his hysterics a bit. He added, "Thanks again... for coming for me."

"You'd have done the same," Tory said.

Barra nodded, but then her stomach growled at her, changing the subject. She was eager to explore the cirque. She moved away from the boys. "There must be something to eat around here."

Tory didn't want to be separated again, and Plicks felt the same way. They nervously closed the gap between themselves and Barra, and stayed close as they joined the hunt. The cirque was even larger than it had seemed from above, and their search was slow. They still hadn't found food when Tory noticed something through a cluster of nettles that filled in one of the gaps in the wall.

"What is it?" Barra asked, worried.

"Not sure. Just curious," Tory said, reaching into the mess of twisted branches. His voice straining, he added, "Looks like... uh, you know. Those festival flowers..."

Plicks filled in the blank, "Hanging blood lilies."

Barra knew the flowers well. Her mother grew them in long strands for the New Ring festival. She thought about the sweet nectars and exotic fruits, the singing and dancing, and visiting with family and friends she only saw once every 312 buckles. She feared for the first time that they might not get back to the Loft.

She had to shake the thought from her mind before she could focus again on what they were doing.

"Can't quite..." Tory was still reaching, his tongue hanging out between his sharp incisors.

"Here." Barra stepped up. "There's a trick to it if they're really blood lilies."

Tory stepped aside and Barra got in close to take a look. The spherical bulbs were about the diameter of one of her hands. Each comprised of dark blue-green petals folded together tightly. They didn't look exactly like the blood lilies that Barra knew, but they were similar.

She ran her tail skillfully through the nettles. Examining the closest bulb, she closed her eyes to concentrate on the texture. Then she found the spot, a soft dimple in the shell, and she tapped it smartly.

Nothing happened.

Barra tapped the bulb again, and then she said, "Well, they might not be..." but before she could finish her sentence, the bulb popped open. The blue-green petals of the shell peeled back, and hundreds of thin orange and red tubes unfurled from inside. Every tube lit up, so that the flower resembled a floating ball of fire.

Going down the strand in both directions, the bulbs peeled open, fireballs appearing haphazardly through the brush. Each blood lily illuminated its own small sphere in the damp air, and Barra, Tory, and Plicks felt a connection to the Root for first time.

Plicks was the first to speak. "They're beautiful."

Barra enjoyed the lilies briefly before her smile faded. The lights might attract unwanted attention, especially if the eyeless thing's minions were looking for them. Probably a mistake to

have woken the lilies, but Barra tried not to dwell on it. No need to worry the boys about something that couldn't be undone. The lights wouldn't go out again for hours. "Yeah, they are nice," she said, trying to keep a positive tone.

Even without food, Barra's stomach had grown tired and so had she. She said, "I think we need to rest. I can't search anymore. Should we take turns keeping watch? Just to be safe?"

Tory said, "Yeah, I'll take the first."

Barra shook her head and started to argue, but Tory was insistent. Something in his eyes told Barra that he understood about the risk of the blood lilies. He raised his eyebrows and said for Plicks' benefit, "There's no way anything can sneak up on us with all those lilies burnin'." He winked at the fearful Kolalabat.

Plicks knew they were protecting him, tip-toeing around him. He felt embarrassed for how he'd been acting—he wanted to keep his chin up like Tory and Barra. Chewing on his lower lip, clicking his talons, he tried to think of something to say.

"Okay, so Tory has the first watch. I'll take the next," Barra said. She quickly counted the lilies knowing they would close back up at regular intervals, the reverse of how they'd opened. She said, "Wake me when there are sixteen left, or if you start to nod."

Tory agreed. Stretching his body in every conceivable direction, he bounced to get his blood moving. "Sleep well," he said and sauntered off.

"Come on, Plicks," Barra started off toward an inviting patch of ferns.

Always a natural with math, Plicks had only to glance at the lilies to know that the watch had been divided in half, instead of thirds. He felt like a burden. It was the same with his brothers and sisters. He was never sure what to do to help, or what he had to offer.

Barra saw Plicks staring blankly instead of following her, and she shouted, "Plicks!" Startled, he blinked several times, and then she continued, "Come on, worrywart. Tory's got it covered." She meant to be encouraging, but it was the last thing Plicks wanted to hear; that someone else was taking care of him again. After lifting and dropping a heavy sigh, he scuttled over to Barra.

The two had more than enough room to sleep comfortably on the patch together, but as Barra circled and flattened the ferns, Plicks stood apart. He released his scruffs and began arranging them on the floor of the Root. Barra liked sleeping alone, not having any siblings of her own, but was surprised to find that she wanted Plicks' company, wanted him close. She wouldn't have admitted it aloud, but she was scared. She was about to call him over, but as he settled into his scruffs, she decided not to bother him. Instead, she said, "Good night."

"Night," Plicks returned softly, looking out from beneath a blanket of fur. He didn't want to be a burden anymore. He wanted to apologize, but wasn't sure how. Tomorrow, he'd keep his head on straight. They were going to be okay. Pulling his furry scruff down over his face, he went to sleep.

Barra closed her eyes but stayed awake awhile longer. She thought about the eyeless monster. Her pulse quickened, and she had to stop herself from snarling. She had to think about something else if she wanted to sleep. She tried to occupy her mind with pragmatic thoughts. Food and water were important objectives. Knowing the layout of the cirque was another. After that? Well, that was tomorrow.

Eventually, her thoughts wandered to her father. He had left the trees long before Barra could've ever gone exploring with him. She envisioned them together adventuring in some exotic Loft abundant with curiosities. There were ancient dens with unique bindings, eccentric shapes, and strange rooms. She imagined a warm, safe place replete with fragrant blooms. Her father taught her the names of the flowers, and her breath fell into a regular rhythm, and she fell asleep.

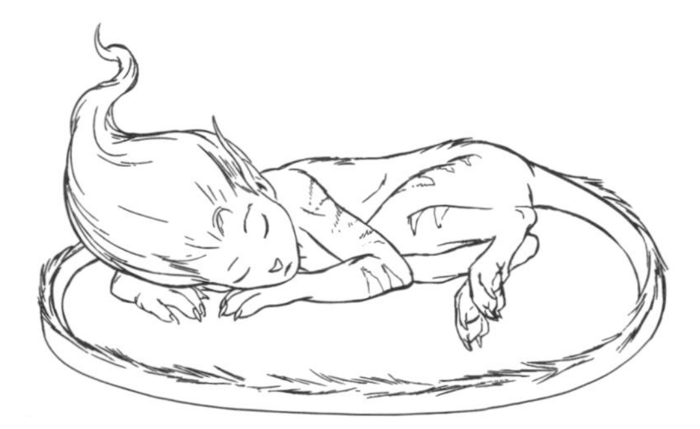

Barra's dream began like most dreams; it began in nothingness. And then…

A single seed appeared, and from that seed, a single sprout.

It grew tall and broad with countless roots and branches. Buds poked out from the bark and leaves unfurled. Petals burst and flowers were born.

A lush canopy expanded and created the sky. An intricate system of roots stretched and created the sea. New trees sprang to life in every direction. Vital shades of green painted the leaves, and radiant flowers illuminated the scene.

Barra sprinted over the boughs. Her veins pulsed and her lungs swelled. Her strong limbs carried her easily, as though at any moment, she might fly from the trees. Her tail rippled behind her, flexing and catching the rushing air. It swung behind her and kept her balanced.

Without slowing down, the treescape became abruptly static.

A Listlespur stood in front of her with his back turned. She knew it was her father, and he was staring at something far below them.

Dad? What is it? Barra's dreamself asked.

There's something down there, he said, curious.

That's the Fall… there's nothing down there but the end of branches, the end of life, Barra said.

Her father turned around, and said, No, beneath the Fall. See for yourself. It's the beginning…

Barra stepped up beside her father and stared down through the interwoven forever of boughs, leaves, and flowers. Deeper and deeper she looked until finally she saw a speck of darkness. The longer she looked the bigger it became. She was mesmerized. The black speck swallowed the trees, and she was stuck in place. It grew faster and faster, and made her feel like her whole world was falling into an abyss.

She turned to her father. We have to run! she screamed. But he was gone.

Running vertically at top speed, Barra tried to escape. But the darkness beneath her grew as fast as she climbed. She dug deep, and moved even faster. The darkness matched. The darkness gained.

Barra saw the sky. It was full of distant, bright purple sparks that pierced the thinning canopy above her. And the leaves parted, and she saw more of the red cloud that belted the Reach than she ever had before. And she knew that soon, there would be nothing left for her to climb. The darkness grew.

She ran even faster! And at the top of her home tree, she reached such a speed that she launched herself into the sky. She was free, floating and weightless. But the darkness was endless below her, the black swallowing everything.

And soon, there was nothing around her. Nothing to see. Nothing to smell, or taste. Barra commanded her arms and legs to grab something, to grab anything!

But there was nothing.

Nothing to hold.

Nothing to stop her fall.

Chapter 17

Three

In her dream, Barra plunged through nothingness until the big black became an ocean. She thrashed about helplessly, struggling to swim, but she couldn't find the surface. A voice echoed in the water, and a soft radiance followed it. She swam toward the light in fitful bursts and then broke through in a splash.

"Barra!"

She bolted up onto all fours, poised to strike. Water dripped from her whiskers and ears. She shook the remnants of her dream away, trying to make sense of things.

She heard laughter. It was Plicks. He rolled around, giggling fitfully, but Barra was still too lost to understand why. She saw Tory standing nearby holding a spongy-looking tuber as thick as his arm. Long, hair-like roots hung down in bunches from the tuber, dripping water from their ends.

Grinning widely, Tory asked, "Sleep well?" Barra looked a little like a drowned Kolalabat, at least around her face.

Brooding, Barra squinted and licked her piercing incisors, putting a point on her displeasure with each of them. "Sleeping was fine," Barra said. "It's the waking up part I could do without. Hey, that stuff tastes good!" she changed her attitude mid-sentence as she sampled the water on her lips.

"I know, right?" Tory handed her the tuber, and Plicks shuffled over to join them.

Sitting back on her haunches, Barra squeezed the root and droplets rained down. Thirsty, she licked at it while Plicks explained, "I couldn't sleep much, and neither could Tory, so we paired up for your shift and looked for food at the same time." He looked around and shrugged. "We didn't find much, but I found that perennating organ. The root filters all the salt, and—"

"Perennating?" Barra winced. "Plicks, this tastes great. Don't ruin it by teaching me about it." She regretted her words, as she watched Plicks' enthusiasm drain from him. He shuffled his feet, shoulders sagging.

Tory bailed her out. "I would've never found it on my own! He recognized the leaves sprouting from the floor bark over there."

The scenery had changed overnight. The cirque was better lit, though still dusky, and Barra could see much farther. The surrounding woods had opened up, new flowers had blossomed, and high above her, water was streaming over petals and leaves. The falling water filled the cirque with pitter-patter like a pleasant conversation among splashes, plops, and kerplunks.

Tory pointed to a small opening in the Root where bunches of long red leaves sprouted in ordered rows. He said, "Plicks spotted them right away, you should have seen him go! Dove in face first, talons clicking! Then he tricked the whole thing out at once. Pretty good, huh? I've had five already."

"Thank you," Barra said, making sure Plicks heard her sincerity. She drank again from the tuber, spilling more of the water on her face.

Plicks walked over to the remaining bunches. Scratching at the white tuft on his chest like a much older Kolalabat might, he said, "I've never seen them growing like this. Usually, they're farther apart. These taste better too. The sponges at home are just sorta bland."

"I *bet* they are." The unfamiliar voice was silky clear, and too close for comfort. The bups spun around, and Barra instinctively jumped out in front of her friends to protect them. But protect them from whom? There was no one there.

"Does the rotting thing know you're here?" the voice asked with passing curiosity.

Barra was sure she was staring right at the source, but she couldn't see anything there that could possibly talk. There came a sound like a Rattlebark moving slowly, like tree bark slapping softly against wood. Barra spoke over her shoulder to her friends, "I don't see anything."

"You're staring directly at me!" the voice exclaimed brightly. He went on, talking to himself out loud, "The rotting thing doesn't know you're *here*, but he knows you're here. Just like you know I'm *here*, but you don't know *where* I am. Interesting." He held the 'ng' for far too long, and then chuckled, a round, playful sound.

Standing where the owner of the voice should be was a tall broken bough thicker than Tory. That bough, where it leaned back into the bramble thickets, began to move. The stumped top bent around and down toward the bups. A twist of a knot curled in its bark and then puckered like lips preparing to kiss. The pucker whistled. The notes belonged to a song not one of them knew.

The bups were enthralled, unable to move.

Arms and legs unfurled from the animated bough, and three distinct tails snaked around its base. The tails rippled without rhythm as the whistling knot continued its hypnotizing dirge. The outline of an Arboreal-like body became clear as the woody camouflage dissolved into mottled, auburn fur.

Two molasses eyes opened beneath the knot of a mouth, and the whistling stopped. He winked one eye—apparently at Plicks—as a third eye opened between and beneath the other two. "I know where *you* are," he said.

Lowering itself head over heels to the ground, he put his hands on the floor and flipped over backwards in a flourish. His tails flowed up around him as he spun and stood up in one graceful motion. Melodramatic, poised, serious, the stranger said, "I'm proud to meet all of you." He closed his eyes—all three of them—and bowed slightly. His third eye opened first and took a shifty look around.

Unbowed the creature stood taller than Tory. Long flat fingers and toes like a Rattlebark's extended from his hands and feet, and fur similar to a Listlespur's covered his body. Similar, but not the same. His fur shifted often, blurring between patterns that hinted at familiar shapes. His somewhat flattened snout held many tiny sharp teeth. As creepy-looking as he was, Barra was relieved his eyes were finally above his mouth.

“I see you’ve helped yourselves to my garden?” he asked with a quirky twitch. He bounded over to the sprouted bunches where the tubers were growing. The bups circled, never taking their eyes off the strange creature.

Light from the small pool sparked in the rich molasses of his eyes, but the irises emitted their own light as well. The odd creature picked at the floor bark where Plicks had carefully dug up the spongy roots. Rather absentmindedly, he said, “Now that we’re all here, we should figure out where this is.”

Several heavy moments passed. The strange creature picked at his plants, meticulously rearranging tiny bits and licking his fingers. Feeling less threatened than she did at first, Barra looked to her friends to see if they felt the same. They shared a group shrug. Ending the silence, Barra shook her head while asking, “What are you?”

The creatures peeled back his lips and licked his teeth. With his head projected forward from his body, farther than Barra would have thought possible, he mirrored her shaking her head and said, “I’m Fizzit. What are you?” He pointed all three of his tails and a finger at her.

Barra squinted and leaned toward the Fizzit. She answered stiltedly, “I’m. A. Listlespur.” If he didn’t recognize a common Listlespur, she thought he might be challenged in other ways. When the Fizzit said nothing more, Barra settled back a bit. She tilted her head, deciding whether or not to trust the weird creature. Not able to make up her mind yet, she began introductions, “I’m Barra. This is…”

But the creature interjected, “Barra? Never heard of it.”

“No, *I’m* Barra,” she restated, pointing to herself, her patience worn thin from the journey.

He looked up from what he was doing, and observed Barra methodically. Each eye blinked, one after another in a circle. "No," he said clearly. With even greater impatience than Barra, he continued, "I'm positive this isn't *Barra*. I've been here a long time… if *you* were *here* I would have known it."

She wrinkled up her nose, unable to make heads or tails of his statement. "Well, who are you then?" she asked, a point on the end of the question.

"I told you already… not all of us are here, so we haven't all been introduced." He shrugged and went back to tending his plants.

"*You're* not all here," Tory said sarcastically under his breath, unable to stop himself from voicing the thought.

Plicks shot Tory a reproachful look, pleading for Tory not to rile the eccentric creature.

Barra decided she was done with pleasantries, and attempted to advance the conversation, "We fell, you know, from the Loft?" She pointed up. "The top of the Umberwood? We're trying to go home."

The stranger turned and sat, his tails dancing mysteriously behind him. His shiny teeth glistened as he spoke, "Aha! Now! Now, we're getting to somewhere. This must be the crossroads!" He saw how confused the bups were, and his face sagged, disappointed. Each eye focused on a different bup, and he said gently, "Come here. Sit with me." He even had three tones to his voice—an echo for each of them.

Tentatively, Barra and Tory made their way toward him. Plicks was apprehensive, but he joined the others where they sat across the small pool from Fizzit. Each of Fizzit's eyes followed a specific bup, though they traded from time to time. He braided

his tails masterfully and curled the result around his bottom, covering his feet.

"I didn't know this was the crossroads," Fizzit said. "I've been here for so long... so long. The pathwoods all went to no where—to the same no place—as far as I followed them." It was hard to tell to whom he was speaking exactly. He might have been talking to himself. His subtle echoes faded away, and then he said, "The pathwood home is the hardest to find sometimes. And sometimes it's the hardest to travel."

A broad silence followed, and Barra took it as an opportunity to speak again, "Well, we have a plan. We just need to get to the base of the trunk of the Umberwood, or any Great Tree really. We think we can climb from there."

"There are many ways from the crossroads." Fizzit shrugged. "That is the nature of its existence... going up is one direction. Going down is another." He spoke as though he was stating something obvious, trying hard not to be patronizing.

Barra was confused. She looked from Tory to Plicks, and neither seemed to understand more than she did. Trying to steer the conversation back to something she could use, she said, "Well, sure. There're lots of ways to go, but we want to go home. We have to go up. So, if you could help us find the—"

"You have many homes," Fizzit interrupted, toying with his braided tail. "One of them is at the end of every pathwood."

The conversation caught Tory's attention because he'd heard similar language used to describe the art of binding. Binders often described the process of shaping a branch as choosing a path for the growth. Allowing the intrinsic path to guide their choices, binders invariably produced better, healthier structures. But there were many paths, never just one, to the right binding.

But Tory didn't want to end up somewhere that became home because that's where he *happened* to be; he wanted to go to *his* home in the Loft. He tried to explain, "No, no. This is different. We're not exploring. We're not looking for a new place to live. We know where we want to go."

The stranger's three eyes blinked in unison, slowly, as he tilted his head. He whistled again to forestall the Rugosic. Smirking good-naturedly, he challenged, "Do you, *really*?" Then, to himself, he said, "Fascinating. I'm still finding my way… so many destinies. Each of us has so many destinies." Addressing Tory again, he asked, "How did you choose yours?"

"I…" Tory groped for a reasonable reply to what he thought was an unreasonable question. Assuming the stranger meant destination not destiny, Tory eventually settled on an answer. "I didn't have much to do with it. I was born there."

"Ahhh, that makes more sense," Fizzit said, nodding emphatically. One teasing eye winked at Tory. "You don't know where you're going. You don't know where you've been."

"Look, it's not that I don't appreciate the company, and the fresh water," Barra started in again, "But we've got to get back home. Can you help us?"

"You've left the nest. You should be proud. You can never go back," he stated, not without kindness.

Plicks heard those last words, and echoed in despair, "We can never go back."

Hearing the emptiness in his voice, Barra reached out with her tail, and put it around his shoulders. "Don't listen to *him*," she said. "He doesn't know anything. We're going home. I promise. We'll find a way."

The creature leaned over the pool, all his glinting eyes focused on Barra. "The way up is rotting and you know it. My brother's creeping vine is devouring it… it's eating at you too." One eye glanced subtly down at her forearm. She felt the gash pulse under his scrutiny, and placed her hand over it to hide it from view. Undeterred, he continued, "Sometimes you choose the pathwood, and sometimes it chooses you." Fizzit became preoccupied with his tail again.

Awkward silence stretched among them until Fizzit—satisfied with his tail—returned his roguish attention to the bups. "You've come a long way, but if you want to go home, to the home of your dreams, to a home bathed in light, you have to keep going. You have to look deeper." With that, the bizarre creature dunked his face into the pool.

Barra looked at her friends, uncomprehending. Fizzit's last words echoed the words of her dream-father, and goosebumps broke out beneath the fur all over Barra's skin. A tickling rush went up her spine.

Tory whispered, "What's he talking about? Choosing our own pathwood? Dreams and light?" He gestured around them. "It's darker here than the top of the Umberwood, than anywhere I've ever been."

But Barra wasn't listening. Her dream was coming back in vivid, oily patterns. That bright treescape full of light could be real. It felt right. Something was wrong with the Loft. She knew it. Her friends knew it too, even if they wouldn't admit it.

Her dream, her father, and this three-eyed oddity were linked to the solution, the way to the brighter world. She turned to her friends. "It's true. It *is* dark everywhere. But what if it doesn't have to be that way?" Plicks and Tory glared at her, incredulous, but they didn't interrupt. "You read the journal. There's, 'a growth threatening to drown us all in darkness.' Remember?"

The boys did remember. They'd had their own thoughts lately about the Loft, how even in their short lifetimes things had changed for the worse. They were hungry after they'd just eaten, thirsty right after a drink of water. Bindings weren't always working the way they used to work. And it was dimmer, wasn't it? Darker than usual? The flowers were growing faint.

Seeing that she had their attention, Barra went on, "What if the Creepervine and the Kudmoths are the problem? What if it all starts here at the Root?"

Tory shook his head, and Plicks was dumbfounded, his jaw hanging open. They looked at each other, grasping for truth or excuses. Neither was interested in doing anything other than going home.

Tory began carefully, "Listen, Barra, I know the journal is important to you, and I know we've seen some crazy things, but we have to get home. We'll tell the Council. We'll tell everyone! But we're going home."

Plicks was nodding in agreement, but then he furrowed his brow and gestured at Fizzit. "Doesn't he need air?"

His head was still submerged. In an elegant and unexpected flourish, his tail unbraided, and a tip waved to each of them. Fizzit was gesturing for them to join him. Without hesitation, Barra moved to the edge. She leaned over the pool and looked down at her dim reflection.

"Whoa, Barra," Tory said, letting a little frustration surface as he spoke, "*what* are you doing?"

"I'm just taking a look," she said, dismissing his concern. And with that, she took a deep breath, and pushed her face into the water. The water was warm, clear and bright, and she was blinded for several moments. When her vision adjusted, Barra was awed by how far down she could see. There was a forest beneath the surface, long fingers of roots stretching down all around her. Thickets more varied than they were in the Loft were woven together into dense walls. Intense floral bursts sprang up in abundance in every direction along with rough cylindrical tubes in groups of white, pink, and green. Dancing leaves waved to her and seemed to beckon her to join them.

Barra pulled her head out of the water. "You two have to see this!"

Tory and Plicks were dubious, and irritated. Water dripped from Barra's whiskers, and there was a wild glint in her eyes. Plicks plopped down onto his rump and began chewing at his lower lip. Tory stepped forward. "Are you out of your mind?!" He pointed at Plicks and said, "We need to go home." And then he gestured to include Barra as well, "We *all* need to go home. Now, come on. Let's leave this insane creature alone with his dreams—

thank you very much for the water and all that—and get to a trunk."

"Come on." Barra glared at Tory. "You don't think there's something wrong with the Loft? Look under the water. It's supposed to be like that." Tory only shook his head while Plicks clicked his talons. Disappointed, she begged them, "I'm not saying we're going for a swim. Just take a look."

Tory rolled his eyes. "If I look, can we go?" He was too tired to argue. He hoped if he gave in a little she'd be more willing to hear him out. Barra was always stubborn. He smiled halfheartedly at Plicks, and said, "I'm just going to take a look. Keep an eye on Crazy here for me." He dunked his head into the pool.

Plicks sat there chewing and clicking. In his heart, he agreed with Barra about the Great Trees, the Umberwood anyway. But they were only bups! He didn't care about Fizzit, his pool, or this place. He missed his family, and couldn't imagine anything else he'd rather see. Barra was staring at him, waiting, and he didn't care about that either. He wrinkled his nose and said, "I'll look, but then I'm going home, with or without you." He rolled himself toward the edge, got a good a grip, and poked his nose into the water. Taking a deep breath, he closed his eyes, and dunked his head. Barra did the same.

Under the surface, the bups found each other and looked around, fascinated. Even in the Mangrove Loft they'd never seen a watery world so diverse and vibrant. It was staggeringly beautiful. Far below them in the water, Barra saw a shape that reminded her of the tangerine creature she and Tory had tried to rescue. This one was sanguine, and it rose up through the water with elegant streaming tentacles. She stretched her neck and peered deeper, and thought she saw two more beside it, one azure and one the color of burnt wood.

Excited, Barra looked to her friends wondering if they saw the gelatinous glowing creatures swimming toward them. Instead of her friends, she found Fizzit. He still hadn't lifted his head to breathe. Through the water his irises shone jubilant amber.

Barra was spellbound. She didn't notice Fizzit's tails looming above her, one tail poised over each of them.

They would find a way home first if that's what her friends wanted, but Barra knew the answers were down there. Taking it all in, gazing at the underwater forest, Barra was resolute and confident. She was also ready to come up for air.

Before she could lift her head, Fizzit pushed her into the ocean.

He pushed all three into the sea.

Chapter 18

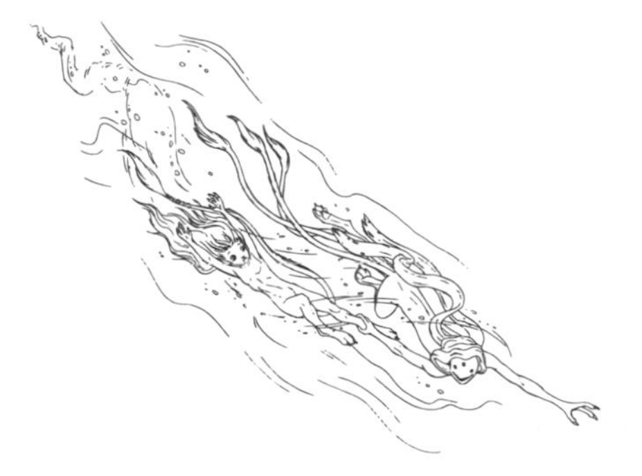

Suspension

Barra was frantic. She attacked the water, claws extended, like the ocean was an animal trying to drown her. Survival instinct oriented her to the surface, but even with her panic-wide eyes straining, the opening to the surface was impossible to distinguish, dark on dark. A close vine drew a line of hope back to the Root, but it was fragile, and it shredded and broke when she tugged at it. Whipping her tail around, she carved arcs into the water searching for a hold, but there was nothing. She was out of breath, her chest convulsing. Bubbles burst from her desperate swipes like small explosions.

The black fuzz of unconsciousness appeared at the edge of her vision, stark reality eaten by shadows. Her limbs felt heavy, her muscles seized, and Barra felt a new kind of fear—a certainty that she was powerless to direct her fate.

As Barra's eyes rolled back, something coiled around her legs and dragged her down hard. The jarring acceleration pried her vision open and kept her conscious. She looked down and saw three golden eyes gazing back at her. Fizzit smiled. He winked like he'd somehow known she'd look at him right then.

Fizzit flattened his tails into ribbons and used them to funnel the water into powerful jets. He swam faster and faster as he dragged Barra through the ocean, spinning contrails of fine bubbles behind them. Diving toward the colorful gelatinous creatures, he homed in on the sanguine one. Fizzit towed Barra into the blood-red creature without slowing down, released her, and then jetted away. The jelly's featureless, headless body opened up like a giant, floating mouth—four tentacles trailing behind it like slaver—and swallowed Barra's head, whole.

The jelly made distressed gestures with its tentacles, but Barra's vision was collapsing again, and she couldn't understand. She had to breathe. Nothing else mattered.

Barra drew a shuddering, quick breath.

The ocean water passed through the body of the jelly and became salty air. Barra's lungs were filled, but she gasped for more. She took fast, coarse breaths that burned her throat, but she barely noticed. Her heart fluttered and she quivered and shook. Shocked to be alive, Barra imagined herself suspended in the ocean with her head encased in red gelatin, and needed a moment to get her bearings. They floated in a narrow, deep trench defined by walls of tangled roots. Beneath them, as far as Barra could see, there was nothing but an endless band of blue, and she was awed by the dizzying effect of height and weightlessness.

Barra's chest ached. In fact, she was sore all over, but before another thought surfaced, terror struck. She screamed out Tory's name, and Plicks', but only incomprehensible cries emerged and foams of bubbles. Barra tried to wrench her head around to see more of the trench, and somehow, the red-colored jelly understood her flailing. With only a few graceful strokes, the jelly maneuvered them to bring Barra's friends into view.

Plicks was a mottled silver and purple sphere in the water. Air in the shape of mercuric worms slid around his fur, merged, and broke free into metallic globules. Plicks wasn't alone. A milky-blue jelly held onto him, tendrils belting his torso and flaps covering his mouth. Cloudy whorls formed and dissipated through the jelly's large flat wings. Plicks seemed okay, as okay as Barra anyway.

Tory was tangled up in the trench wall, and appeared unhurt. He'd also found a friend. The unique jelly creature palmed Tory's head with long glassy black fingers, each finger capped by a large orb. Many fingers jutted from the jelly's body in every direction so that Tory looked like he'd sprouted a new head of hair. The entire body of the jelly appeared cracked like fire-charred wood broken by thin lines of orange.

Barra breathed a sigh of relief. They were okay for the moment at least. She touched the sanguine jelly that hugged her face, and found Red's flesh was firm but pliable. Also, Red's translucent body seemed to sharpen Barra's vision under the water. Red's four most prominent tentacles spiraled around Barra's arms and legs, and held her fast. Many thinner tentacles like fine hairs were draped in a curtain around her as well. That curtain suddenly rippled to life as Red rotated them, and then accelerated toward Plicks.

Tory arrived just as Barra reached Plicks, and the three gesticulated to one another wildly. Barra trembled. She was exhilarated, and at the same time, exhausted and relieved. Communication was difficult with nothing but dramatic gestures to convey their thoughts, but the bups managed to share their awe. After some experimenting, the bups even discovered they could move.

The sea was full of distracting, blazing bright colors and shapes. Sweeping green ribbons and glowing maroon grasses beckoned dreamily, motivated by a subtle current. There were outlandish flowers with asymmetrical designs and unfamiliar textures. Barra thought she could almost feel the petals through her eyes. She thought about Fizzit forcing them into the water, and was furious with him, but it was difficult to stay angry in such a place—and he did save them too, didn't he?

Plicks needed a hug, but all he could do was flail his limbs. Somehow, Blue understood. His wings undulated, edges curling in a regular rhythm, and he guided the Kolalabat close to Barra. Uncomfortably close, actually. Barra winced and closed her eyes, but Blue opened his wings wide and hugged them all together. It took Plicks a moment to realize he was getting exactly what he wanted, and he shook all over, happy for the contact.

Tory laughed at the spectacle, bubbles exploding in tight, fuzzy bursts through Char's body. His laughter stopped short though, as Blue dashed over to give Tory a hug too.

As strange as the circumstances were, Barra trusted the jelly creatures. Still, she wanted to get back to the surface and breathe on her own. Her arm ached, and communication was frustrating without being able to talk. She gestured to the Root above, and shrugged.

Tory waved emphatically with his arms and legs in a caricature of swimming, trying to instigate some movement from Char. They drifted a bit, and rolled, but didn't get far. Mouthing words at Plicks, Tory tried to ask if he knew how to move, what with the hugs and all, but Plicks only shook his head.

It was Barra who first figured out enough to get moving. She moved her arms and legs slowly, and Red's tentacles responded. There was confusion, but soon they were engaged in a strange undersea dance. The boys picked up the cues and started swimming around awkwardly themselves.

Barra was a quick study, and she and Red began testing their skill. They swam in and out of the trench walls. Red took control at points, sweeping over slimy boughs, curling around sharp turns, and stopping and starting with brilliant eruptions of her fine tentacles.

Having figured out the movement, Barra turned her attention toward the Root. Before she could begin swimming toward it, she spied Fizzit. Her fur stood up, and she tried to swim toward him, but Red was unresponsive. Pushing and pulling, Barra tried to move, but Red only held her steady. Fizzit dashed away through the water. He split into three long chains of bubbles and dissolved, disappearing completely.

Barra sighed in disappointment. Fizzit was the only creature they'd met since the Fall that seemed to know anything about the Loft. Wishing her mother were there with her to see it all, she understood why her father wrote so much down; he must have wanted to share everything he explored. She took another long look for the three-eyed oddity, decided he was gone, and then joined her friends.

The throbbing pain of Barra's forearm abruptly sharpened. She examined the wound, trying not to draw attention to it. Dark slime seeped into the water. Red reached around the wounded arm with a writhing tentacle. She squeezed gently, and white suds formed over the slime. Barra felt the pain recede, and her heart went out with gratitude to Red, but there was something else; the tentacle that touched the slime had turned pale and blotchy. Despite the temporary relief, it was obvious to Barra for the first time that the wound wasn't healing.

Chapter 19

Undertow

Searching for an opening to the surface was more difficult than the bups would have guessed. Not only was the scenery outlandish and perhaps dangerous, but there were also pockets of air trapped up against the Root, and their reflections imitated holes, leading them astray. There were murky patches, too, obscuring the view, and when Barra reached into one, she had to snatch her hand back fast from the unexpected cold. They proceeded slowly.

For all the worry they could have felt, the search was joyful. The water was warm and they felt weightless in it. The underbelly of the Root was covered with hairy fronds, furry mosses, and colonies of exotic polyps. Although flowers meant light in the Loft, the ocean was full of leaves, petals, and grasses that were opaque, and shone no light of their own. Mysterious and new, if they weren't so homesick, they wouldn't have wanted to leave. Barra hoped they would return someday.

As they swam toward another possible opening, Barra and Red came to an abrupt stop. The sudden change demonstrated that Barra's control could be revoked on a whim, and Barra didn't like it. Her pulse raced, but she tried to stay calm and trust her sanguine friend. Tendrils danced around Barra as the three pairs of swimmers faced one another. Sudden flashes of color coursed through the creatures. White arcs, orange lines, and red bursts cast severe shadows in every direction. They were communicating, but the message was inscrutable to the bups. After a few rounds of flashes, they all descended together, away from the Root.

Barra was confused and frightened. She struggled against Red, but her resistance was futile. Thinking quickly, the Listlespur slung her tail around a close branch and coiled tightly, but Red was strong. She spiraled a tentacle around Barra's tail, and with gentle but powerful turns, unwound it from the branch. Barra was on the verge of alarm, but Red stroked her and shimmered faintly in what Barra believed must be an apology. Still, Barra felt the distance from her home and her mother grow, and no amount of calm was going to help the sadness she felt.

They accelerated, descending for several moments before punching into the trench wall. They darted in and out of the close spaces in the floating forest without slowing down. Instinct forced Barra to react as they went, and she felt like she was fighting her way through a crowd of Arboreals. Barra caught glimpses of blue and charcoal as they went, and wondered if Plicks and Tory were feeling the same.

And then, as suddenly as they'd entered the thicket, they shot free into open water.

Barra looked up, trying to gauge their depth, but she couldn't see the Root anymore. They were in another trench, except this one was roofed, the only opening beneath them. Tory and Plicks appeared. Hovering together, they exchanged questioning looks and gestures, but no answers. Barra wanted to know where they were going, what they were doing, but their companions were in control.

The woods around the bups were covered in swathes of manifold mosses with small flickering creatures bubbling through them. A white star-shaped flower at the end of a long stem probed near the bups and reeled away in a snap when Barra tried to touch it. The flower retreated all the way back to the floating ball of vines from which it grew. The large tangle of vines writhed. White flowers popped open and closed in cascades, and then the entire ball unraveled like a sentient knot undoing itself. The result was one impossibly long and slender sea-creature with hundreds of legs, each tipped with a flower blinking in rhythm. The abyssal creature didn't *swim*, it *crawled*. It travelled in water the way Barra travelled in trees. Then, entering the trench wall behind them, the creature wove itself into the branches

and disappeared. Barra blinked. If she hadn't just seen it, she wouldn't have believed it.

Barra's arm swelled full of pain from her quickened pulse. The Listlespur squeezed shut her eyes again because her irises were sore, unused to the abundant light. It was then that she noticed a subtle but strengthening current pulling them down. Her eyes fluttered open.

Far below, a great silvery rope of a whirlpool twisted out from the trench wall. Debris swelled around the length of it, sweeping in and out from its center. The whirlpool was as thick as a pathwood, and streaks of colors from the environment were warped around it. It carved an arc through the water as it travelled from wall to wall, tugging at the bups as it went. The bups' companions had to work to keep them steady until the whirlpool was gone.

Before any of them could breathe a sigh of relief though, the closest woods began to jitter. Barra's heart thudded in hear ears as she felt a new tug, much closer than the first. Abyssal animals of all shapes and sizes emerged out of the walls of branches. The sea creatures grouped together near the bups, and waited. It was becoming crowded, and the strength of the current was growing.

Red's tentacles rippled like they were heat gradients rising off Barra's back. They turned sideways together, angled away from the pull of the coming whirlpool. Blue was already horizontal, wings undulating, and Char was compressing and expanding in rapid waves to keep from being sucked away.

Another whirlpool came tearing through the far wall. The silvery rope spiraled toward them surrounded by debris, Abyssals shooting out from its turbulent core. The sea creatures came out fast, unharmed, and swam away. The gathered Abyssals suddenly flipped, and then flew toward the whirlpool one after another.

The bups followed.

They sped headlong toward the twister. Barra was too shocked to panic. She didn't blink as they swam toward the chaos. They didn't go straight in, they swam along it, spiraling around closer and faster until Barra was completely disoriented and they were sucked in.

The bups couldn't see each other as they hurtled through the ocean. Their companions dampened the spinning to keep them from getting sick, but the whirlpool was still a bouncy ride. Accelerating through the ocean—blurring colors and shadows all around—they turned sharply down.

They travelled down for longer than Barra cared to think about, and then the ride ended. The bups were thrown from the whirlpool. As the dizziness faded and the twister pulled away from them, Barra saw there were magnificent coral structures floating around them. No branches. No roots. The corals were connected to one another by nets of vegetation, and fine, looping strands of metals that looked like delicate, miniature trees. There were sagging flotillas of foliage too, sheltering sea creatures unlike anything Barra had ever seen.

They didn't get much time to admire the scenery because another whirlpool was already on its way toward them. More travelling Abyssals joined them and prepared to catch a ride. Same as before the bups didn't have much choice, the jellies caught the current and swam them in.

Deeper and deeper they wound down into the ocean. They passed through the webs of sea spiders, around porous metallic islands, and among migrating coral belts. The light grew brighter and the water warmer, and they tunneled ever closer to the center of Cerulean. They caught another intersecting whirlpool and continued uninterrupted until they were finally expelled into limitless blue.

Barra was rigid, tense and scared. Red felt her tension and gave her a gentle squeeze, slipped a tentacle around her arm, and offered some pain relief too. Barra's friends were receiving support too. Blue displayed a bright blaze for the Kolalabat to remind him to breathe, and color returned to his whiskers. Char was rolling Tory around like a ball to show him as much of the oceanic underworld as possible, and the Rugosic was beaming.

In the open water there were colorful far-off clouds, schools of Abyssals, and gargantuan silhouettes of creatures and structures the bups couldn't understand. A belt of floating corals extended flat in all directions over their heads drawing a line in the distance like a horizon.

Red was intent on swimming even farther down through the incredibly warm water, but Barra wasn't interested, not yet at least. After some effort, Barra managed to get Red to flip them over so that she could look up. Barra searched for a clear view through the orbiting coral, and as she watched, a natural break in the flow opened to her. The corals parted, and Barra's heart sank.

There was nothing to see, nothing Barra recognized. No branches, no trees. Nothing familiar, at all. There was no Root.

Not even a hint that the Great Forest existed. Nothing, but more water and the strange life and forms that inhabited it.

She didn't know where home was, but she did know that it was impossibly far away.

Chapter 20

The Drift

Swimming again, the bups and their jelly companions headed toward an enormous, pale-yellow drift that looked like a sponge made of bone. In actuality, the Drift was made of coral. As large as coral appeared floating in the near distance below them, it only seemed more massive as they approached. The bony surface was stippled with holes, Abyssals bustling in and out of the largest in seemingly endless streams. Each hole was an opening to a channel, and Barra imagined Abyssals travelling the entire length of the Drift from within. It reminded Barra of the Loft only much busier.

The Drift was caught in its own shadow, but the bups were gradually cresting the nearest craggy side. The mountainous surface was rimmed in light. As they came around, Barra saw the source of the white hot light and stared at it until her eyes hurt.

She'd never seen the Sun before.

Barra knew that she wasn't staring at the naked Sun, but that didn't make it any less inspiring. Instead, she was seeing the Sun through the Boil which created a much larger, diffuse false corona. Through the Boil, across the Void, and into the blinding the Sun according to the archives, but Barra didn't really know what that meant. She averted her eyes, but the impression left on her was as indelible as the image of her father.

But as soon as it dawned on her, what they were witnessing—maybe the first Arboreals ever, Barra thought—it was taken away. No matter how hard she resisted, Red swam on, carrying her up to a well-used opening above a prominent ledge in the bony coral.

They entered the Drift.

The channel the bups travelled through the Drift split and intersected other channels at countless angles. Barra's eyes relaxed in the dusky low light of the maze, but the channel *was* lit. Lined with reactive algae in shades of green, red, and brown, a fine circle of radiance burned into the wall of the channel wherever they were. The algae cooled slowly to dark behind them as they passed.

They were swift on their journey. They seemed to avoid the other Abyssals who were rushing through the channels, especially those who stopped to look. One seemed eager to follow, and they went even faster. Barra thought they must look pretty strange, as she tried to keep up mentally with their fast and winding course. When Barra's internal map failed she started stressing, but Red comforted her with a few soft squeezes.

There were so many kinds of Abyssals. Shelled, finned, serpentine, many-limbed, colorful, and stealthy, they passed them all in a whir. There were even other jelly creatures, and though they shimmered greetings to the bups' companions, they didn't stop. There were occasional chambers lush with polyps and grasses, and gardens of flowers in bunches. They echoed life in the boughs, but Barra couldn't identify any of them.

The channels narrowed and the bups and jellies were funneled into a single file line. Barra and Red took the lead. The radiant algae disappeared, replaced by rubbery, multi-fingered anemones. As the channel filled with anemones it became impossible to swim, but those same anemones began pushing the bups through. Finally, the bups and jellies were squished out onto the floor of a large cave, a cave filled mostly with air.

The round cave wall was stained by many circular bands that marked the stages of air replacing ocean, like the iridescent layers of a shell. The floor was grown full of slimy mosses and seaweed, and Barra squished some between her toes as she stood. The water came up to just below her waist. Red released Barra without warning, and shocked, Barra held her breath.

"Woo hoo! What a ride!" Tory exhaled, but then shrank away from his wet echo.

Barra was relieved to know she could breathe in the room, but still, she was scared. The jellies hovered on the surface of the pool, Red's tentacles dragging over the water sending out tiny waves.

Several tense moments passed, and then Tory grinned big. "I said, WOO HOO! What a ride!" The Rugosic splashed over to

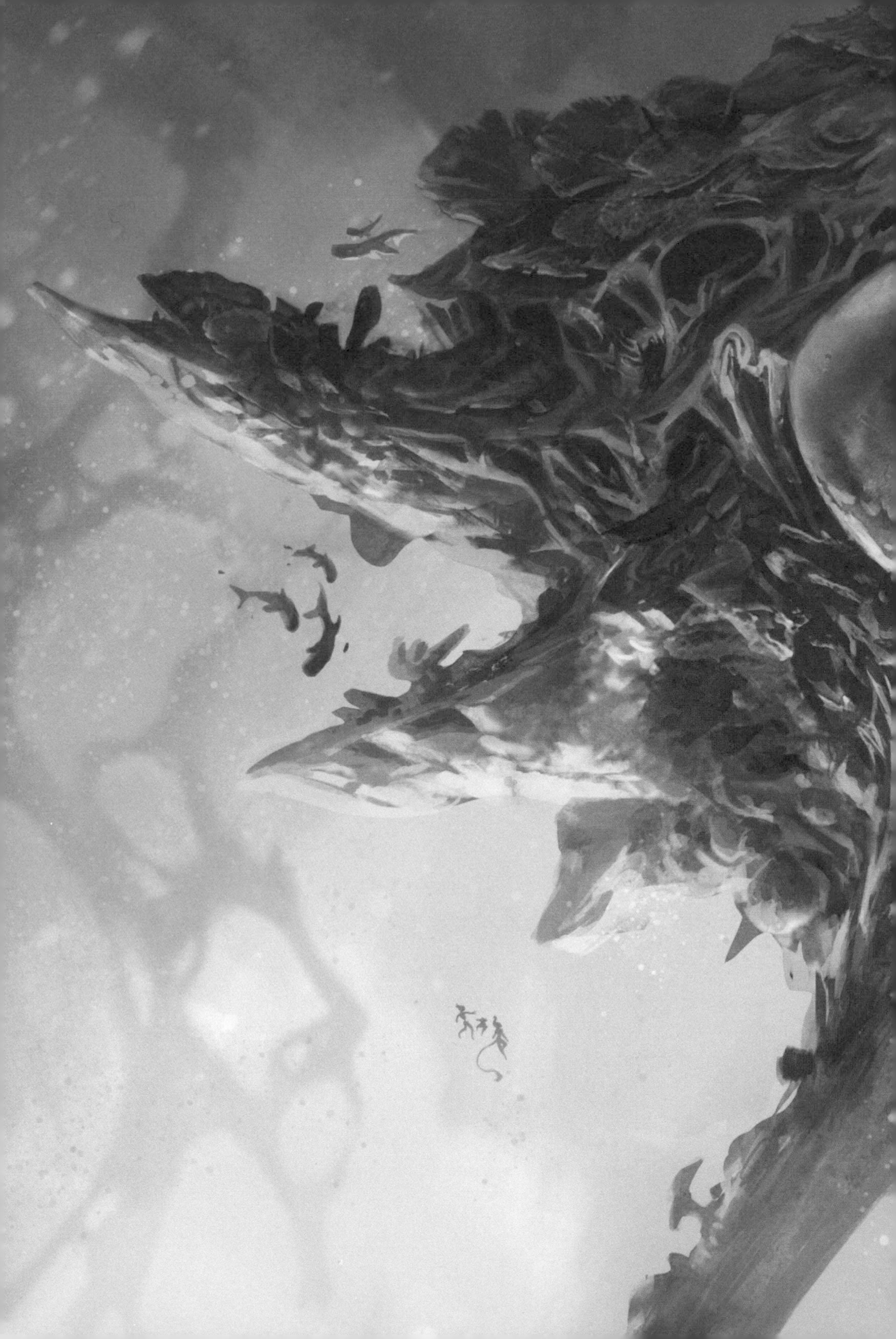

Plicks and picked him up in a spray of water. "We made it!" he exclaimed, shaking his waterlogged friend. He tossed him up and down a couple of times, and then hugged him and set him down.

Blue's cloudy whorls merged with the curling lip of his wings in a display that could only be interpreted as joy. He flapped at Plicks' cheek, and the Kolalabat thought it felt like he was getting licked. "Ew! Hey, uh, no thanks. No!" He said as he tried to fend off Blue, but his giggling only encouraged the affectionate jelly. "What are you?" he asked, but his words were almost inaudible. Defending against another lick, Plicks turned to Barra, "What are they?"

Red bobbed up and down like she wanted attention and Barra reached out to her. She touched the top of Red's bell-shaped body, and watched it spark beneath her fingers. Barra pulled away, unsure, but then Red pushed into her hand and began snuggling against it. As casually as she could, Barra switched to her other hand in order to keep her wounded arm hidden. She stroked the jelly and said, "I'm not sure. They seem really friendly." She smiled, and Red shimmered and vibrated. The jelly produced a soothing, gurgling sound, and Barra whispered to her, "You like that, huh? You like that, don't you, Red?"

Tory sloshed over to the wall, Char hovering close over his shoulder the whole way. Char projected his orbs out one at a time in a rapid cascade, stealing Tory's attention. Tory examined the jelly trying to figure out how it worked and what it meant. Char shriveled away from the inspection like he didn't enjoy the inspection. Having had enough, Char flashed his orbs out all at once, startling Tory who stumbled and splashed away. Tory eyed the jelly with suspicion. Char bobbed steadily, and seemed a bit smug. The Rugosic's lips turned up in a wry smile. "Okay, okay. Very funny. Hang around if you like. I'll get you back," he added with a wink

Running his fingers over the porous wall, Tory asked, "What is this place?"

"I'm not sure..." Barra's voice trailed off. The pool of water at her feet began to bubble and rise, waves breaking against the walls.

Barra sloshed backward, tail raised. Tripping through murk, Tory and Plicks quickly spun round and put their backs against the wall, never taking their eyes from the water. And there, at the center of the pool, emerged a sinuous, many-limbed creature. Drooping cobalt blue whiskers sprouted from the magnificent creature's snout as its head rose above the bups on a long arched back Sickled fangs shimmered wet against its lips, and a pair of deep set, cloudy blue eyes looked out from beneath a rigid brow. The shining eyes locked onto Barra and seemed to smile.

"Hellooo?" The great seabeast's voice did not project from her mouth which opened and closed in a rough imitation of speaking. Instead, her voice came from the entire length of her body vibrating. The sound reflected off the water and walls, filling the chamber, and somehow, it made the hollow space seem to grow.

Barra didn't know what to say. She was stunned.

Silvery runs of water rolled down the creature's slick ruddy-brown fur and trickled into the pool like dozens of miniature falls. Her eight arms fanned out from her back, four to a side, and were covered in shallow, tooth-rimmed cups. She stretched, her arms reaching, and practically divided the room in half. The submerged portion of her body slithered behind her, generating a steady flow of ripples.

Red, Blue, and Char exchanged flashes with each other, and with the glorious creature. The seabeast spoke again, drawing out each word, "You're quiet, aren't you? I suppose I should begin—I rarely have company. I'm Lootrinea. Welcome. It's been a long time since I've seen an Arboreal in the Drift. The Nebules tell me they found you drowning in the Top Water?"

"The Nebules?" Barra asked. A nervy prickle spread out from her cut, and she twitched.

"Your friends there. They were excited to find you. Only the most adventurous of their kind play near the Root. It's dangerous for them, Kudmoths feed on them like the Creeper feeds on light. Still, some stubborn ones like Red cannot be dissuaded." Lootrinea gestured to Red, not without pride.

Barra asked, "Why'd they bring us here? Are you their leader? An Elder or something?" She was curious, but her questions came out like accusations. She badly wanted to sctatch her arm.

"They brought you here because it is all that they know. I'm the only creature from the Trees living down here," Lootrinea said. "I'm not an Elder," she continued, "I'm merely a vestige of an old and forgotten way of life… tolerated because I'm quiet, useful because I know things no one else does. But I confess, I don't know you who you are."

"I'm Barra," the dripping Listlespur said as she shook water from her fur. Red hovered close, but as she was about to offer a soothing tentacle, Barra flinched away.

Tory saw Plicks chewing and clicking, and said, "That's Plicks. I'm Tory."

"It's a pleasure to meet you," Lootrinea said with kindness, but also with deference the bups were unused to receiving.

"You're from the Trees?" Barra was skeptical.

"Yes, but that was before I became an Aetherial, long ago," Lootrinea said. Plicks' eyes almost popped out of his head, and his legs wobbled. "My home Tree was the Mangrove. Which is your home Tree?"

Barra answered, "We're from the Umberwood." A wave of dizziness passed over her, but she wasn't sure if it was from her aching arm, or the awe that Lootrinea was an Aetherial. The bups stood there, mouths agape.

"The Umberwood. I used to know it well," she reflected. The water vibrated, and the walls echoed, and the stretched tones were sorrowful. Her mouth continued to move out of sync with her words.

"What do you mean, you used to know it?" Barra continued, stroking Red who had flown around her, and was now draped over her shoulders.

"It was so long ago, I can't say that I know it anymore, only that I knew it once," Lootrinea said. She rose up into a regal posture, her eyes distant. "Before Argus and his Creepervine. Before the cycle of light was broken." Lootrinea emitted a low, mournful howl and the chamber reflected it.

Char floated into Tory's arms. Blue hovered low and close to Plicks, and Red squeezed Barra, hugging the Listlespur until the howl quieted to nothing. The sorrowful note lingered in their bones the way an afterimage lingers in the eyes.

Lootrinea said, "I'm sure much has changed. But enough of that, the three of you look like hope to my old eyes. What is your story?"

The bups climbed over each other verbally to tell the tale. Lootrinea listened intently, even as they bickered about the details, and she gathered that the young Arboreals had been through a tremendous ordeal. As they described finding each other again after the fungal-puppets captured them, the Aetherial noticed the bups' energy ebbing. She interrupted, "Are you hungry?" Before they could respond, she plunged her suction-cupped limbs into the water. With a few deft grabs, she plucked a variety of slimy weeds and fronds, and even captured a few squirming slugs.

Plicks pushed his tongue out between his lips and grimaced, but he was too hungry to object. He leaned in to inspect the unusual food. His whiskers fluttering, he sampled the smells wafting from the fresh vegetables. When he caught the very edge of the first whiff, he recoiled in anticipation of something awful. He was wrong. The aroma was clean and sweet, and his mouth watered. The purple roots smelled like bolliberries crushed over creampods. Plicks ran a single extended talon along one of the roots, shaving a curl of slime from it. He sniffed the curl. Blue, who had been patient until then, smacked Plicks' hand so that the curl jumped into his mouth. Flabbergasted by the rush of flavor, Plicks barely snapped his tongue out fast enough to keep from drooling. The slimy residue tasted better than any nectar he'd ever had. He sucked on his talon, trying to extract more flavor until he realized he could simply eat a whole root, at which point he snatched up several.

Tory dove into the flowers and roots with both hands, but hesitated when he came to the slugs. They were similar to woodgrubs, only bigger and slimier. The food was so good—and he was so hungry—that he grabbed one, closed his eyes, and popped it in his mouth. The slug was bitter and salty on the outside, but crunched honey-sweet when chewed. The combination was a fast favorite, and soon his mouth was full of squishy juices.

Barra chose not to eat. Red tried to lure her into sampling something, but the Listlespur refused to bite. She was uncomfortable and hot, agitated. Her arm pulsed.

When the other bups had filled their bellies, Lootrinea returned the rest of the food to the water. Feeling safe and satiated, the after-meal groggy friends loosened up, and continued their story. The time that passed was elastic, and not one could guess how long it took to tell it all.

"He tried to drown us!" Tory said when they got to the part about Fizzit, frustrated with Barra's description of the three-eyed stranger.

"He saved us!" Barra yelled in Tory's face.

"Only after," Tory set himself up, "he tried to kill us!" he yelled. "You just couldn't leave it alone, could you? We needed to get home, but *you* needed us to look into the water?"

Lootrinea watched the back and forth with grave swings of her head. Plicks was biting his lip but shuffling between the two regardless, gaining courage as he went.

"Right," Barra said. "We shoulda left without ever seeing all this beauty. Shoulda just gone on walking through the fungus in the darkness. We were really getting somewhere then!" Barra was seething.

Tory shook his head. "You can't make this my fault." His voice was calm, uncharacteristically severe.

"It's my fault? My fault that the Loft is dying? My father's journal—"

"Your father?" Tory interrupted. "He didn't know what was going on, and neither do you."

His words stymied Barra, but only for a moment. She matched his serious calm. "What do you know?" she asked. "You haven't really cared about anything since your mom died."

Plicks finally stepped between them, "Whoa whoa. You don't mean that."

Barra was feverish, confused, and she snarled at Plicks, "Stay out of this!"

Her words hit Plicks hard in the gut, and knocked the wind out of him. His face burned with hurt. He didn't know what to say or do.

Tory put a hand on his shoulder, and said, "Come on, story-time's over. Sorry, Venress Lootrinea. We need a little break." The Rugosic turned his back on Barra and walked Plicks to the other side of the chamber.

Lootrinea said, "It's just Loo-tri-nea. And, no need to apologize."

Heaving out a tremendous sigh, Barra sagged like a wilting flower. Red floated in close, rubbed up against her cheek, and coiled a tentacle around her arm. The Nebule held her for several moments, and then shimmered something to Lootrinea. The Aetherial nodded.

Barra raised her head and opened her eyes, and said, "I'm sorry, too. I think... I think I'm... I don't know." Some instinct held her tongue. She didn't want to share more.

Lootrinea nodded, and vibrated, "You've been through a lot. Here." She reached into the shallow water and came up with several tiny yellow stones. "Tuck a few of these in your cheeks. They'll help you feel better, maybe even well enough to eat."

Barra accepted the little stones graciously enough, but didn't like that Lootrinea had noticed her lack of appetite. Putting it out of her mind, Barra tucked the stones into her cheek, and sat down on a thick lily pad.

The Aetherial splayed her arms. She tilted her head like she was listening to something far away. Casting her words out to her divided guests, she said, "Will you excuse me? I need to check on an old friend who's also recently come for a visit. You'll be safe here. I'll not be long."

Without a delay for objections, Lootrinea slid into the water and disappeared.

CHAPTER 21

Corresponding Shapes

Lootrinea swam through the channels of the Drift. The few Abyssals she passed kept their distance, but whether it was out of deference or distaste was unclear. Her journey ended at a room similar to her personal chamber, except that it was smaller. Tentacles pushed up against the short ceiling, she bellowed, and the whole room vibrated-fuzzy. Part of the wall seemed to bulge and flex, and then warped into the shape that Lootrinea knew well. Fizzit leaned against the curve of the wall as casual as picking flowers.

"They're so young, Fizzit. How can they save us?" Lootrinea seemed sad.

"Loo, Loo, who else? It's not just chance—although circumstance, perchance?—that found them circling the cirque, circumspect. I *may* purport to compose, but I maintain the

composition positioned them! And, I propose that—though I was poised to impose my proposition—given their condition, I merely acted to expedite their expedition home. They were already on their way, Loo!" He stopped and braided his tails.

Lootrinea was unimpressed with his excuses. "Well, you orchestrated all of this. What shall we do next?"

"Take them the rest of the way home, of course! So few confronted with the crossroads ever leave. We have to help them. Take them to the Roedtaw. He knows the way. The way it has to be… this way or that way…" he said. His multiple voices diverged, taking different words at the end of his thought. He stared, perplexed, at the knotted mess that his tail had become.

"But what about the bups? The Arboreals were never supposed to return to the sea. We made decisions... you were there," Lootrinea swayed as she spoke. Her hypnotic movement had no effect on Fizzit.

"I don't have to remember, Loo, I'm *still* there," he said with a hint of resentment. Then he added gravely, "The Great Trees are dying. When they're gone, the sea will follow. And all our homes will be gone." His eyes flashed as his tails untangled, and he smiled. "Well, there'll still be an *ocean*, of course. That's certain. That's a lot of water. I think that's nice, don't you?"

"Bups," Lootrinea didn't bother forming the word with her mouth. The word lingered between them, echoing off the water and the walls.

"Them? They certainly don't have any other agenda. They're untainted," Fizzit declared boldly.

Stabbing forward, Lootrinea put her snout a whisker's width from Fizzit's, and said, "One is infected!"

Unflappable, he responded, "That? That's nothing. A scratch."

"This is exactly the kind of thing we sought to protect ourselves from. If Argus finds a bridge into the ocean, the whole world is his. Is she part of your plan too? What's your game? Playing both sides?"

"*Both* sides? There are only two? That's a relief," Fizzit said. Though little space existed between them, Fizzit somehow managed to push even closer to Lootrinea and she retreated ever so slightly. All three of his eyes focused on her and he spoke without humor, "I'll do whatever I have to do, with or without your help. That scratch is compelling. It binds her to *her*. It may be the end of her... or her. I don't know..."

Lootrinea eased farther back from the three-eyed, three-tailed wonder and seemed to consult the room for answers. But it offered nothing more than the comforting sound of water licking at the walls. Fizzit was busy braiding and unbraiding his tails again, like he was solving a puzzle. She asked him, "The Roedtaw?"

"Yes," he shrugged.

She was skeptical. "He won't take the bups."

"He'll take them." Fizzit was confident.

"The golden kiss? But the gilded krill are so few. You'd kill them for your dimensionally challenged dreams?" Lootrinea asked, although it was clear she already knew the answer.

Fizzit blinked in a circular wave. "They won't be the only sacrifices."

Chapter 22

Legend

The wading pool lapped gently against the walls. The seagrasses swayed. The kelp stirred. Silent, tiny Abyssals appeared among the polyps and salty mosses only to disappear again without a trace. In a pocket of damp space, somewhere near the bottom of the Cerulean Ocean, three close and lonesome friends were lost.

Plicks was the first to wonder-wander away from the discomfort. Long ropes of light rolled and crisscrossed over the domed ceiling distracting him from the tension. Barra wasn't acting herself, but he knew she'd never admit to whatever was wrong. Instead of pressing her—and because he was nervous to disturb her—he studied the wall and its many bands of color. He stroked Blue who was floating close, half-in and half-out of the pool. Running a talon over the surface of the water, Plicks made thin waves and watched them travel all the way to Barra. The ripples broke against Tory too, and Plicks noticed an unusual color in the Rugosic's reflection. Veins of some fire-orange mineral had bonded to Tory's body. The veins were dull, but they were unmistakable. Startled by the change, Plicks tried to find the right words to ask Tory about it.

Seeing the perplexed expression directed at him, Tory guessed Plicks was about to suggest an apology. No way did Tory think he should be the one apologizing. Irritated, he asked, "What?"

Plicks' mouth hung open and he pointed at Tory. Again, Tory misunderstood. "Fine. You're right. I'll say something." Under his breath, he added, "It's not like she's gonna say anything." Before Plicks could stop him, Tory splashed over to Barra.

Barra stepped back, self-conscious that he'd see her arm or feel the heat of illness radiating from her. Tory stopped short, respecting what he interpreted as her need for space, and said,

"You shouldn't have yelled at him. You can be angry with me all you want, but you crossed a line when you snapped at Plicks."

She thought he was accusing her, like all of this was her fault. Tears pushed into her eyes, but she dammed them back. The pressure built in her head, and made it hard for her to respond. Barra would have apologized if she'd known how to say, *I'm sorry we might all die because of me.* The weight of it was too great for her to say out loud. The words plodded around stupidly in her head until she finally pushed them out. "I'm sorry." She kept her distance and turned away.

"This is our first spark of hope!" Tory said. "We shouldn't be barking at each other. We've just met an Aetherial! And she's gonna help us get home, right?" Char bobbed in agreement. Barra though, didn't seem to share their enthusiasm. Tory realized he'd forgotten something, and said, "I'm sorry, too."

Plicks had waded in closer. Happy his friends were sorting things out, he was still concerned about the new mineral deposits on Tory's skin. As he heard the apologies though, he became caught up in them. He reached out to offer his own, and unwittingly caused Barra to flinch away again. This time he didn't flinch back. He said, "My sisters and brothers are gonna be so jealous! An Aetherial, right? An Aetherial!"

Tory splashed, and Char darted around, excited. Tory said, "She's amazing! Almost makes this whole crazy adventure worth it!" Still, Barra appeared reserved.

"Come AWWNNN, Barra," Plicks pleaded. He slapped the water. "Tell me she isn't the most amazing thing you've ever seen!"

Barra didn't like the attention. The fever—if it was a fever—crawled beneath her fur, poking at her skin. Digging down deep into herself, she decided she had to show them—tell them. But just then, the water garden swelled, and Lootrinea swam back into the chamber, rising up majestically.

"Good news," said the Aetherial, shaking the room. "The Roedtaw will take you to the Root. There is a detour first, to the Boil, but nothing to worry about." The Nebules lit up, and Barra thought they recognized the name.

Gathering up his courage, Plicks asked, "What's a Roedtaw?"

Lootrinea said, "Some say he is a legend, but that word has many meanings. Perhaps, if you look at it from far away, there is only one meaning that matters; a legend is a key for understanding. If you see it that way, then yes, the Roedtaw is a legend, indeed."

The Aetherial prepared herself, shaking out her tentacles and getting comfortable. The Nebules signaled one another knowingly, and gathered in close. Lootrinea began, "Let me tell you the story of the Roedtaw..."

There was only the ocean. From the Great Void came a screaming rock filled with heat and fury. It scorched the sky, a tail of blue fire trailing behind it endlessly. It plunged into the ocean, but continued to burn as it arched toward the Cerulean sun. In its wake, billowing clouds of dust appeared and expanded; purple, red, and brown, orange, blue, and green. Like a fiery spear through the water it traveled fathoms without slowing or cooling. But the clouds that spilled from it were its body, and so it diminished, smaller and smaller. And though the furious spear did not intend to yield, the sun bore different ideas. Exploding out in a glorious ring of light, a million Nebules were born at once and they flew to intercept the fury.

Well, the angry head of the spear saw the wall, the silent tiny pieces of the Sun protecting their mother, and its fury shed. Layer after layer, jettisoned, as it tried to slow down. The Great Seeds were among the debris, so they say. And when the last layer tore free, what was left was a simple but gigantic creature, careening fast, still unable to stop. A single Nebule saw the truth of it, but instead of crying out, and gathering her brethren, she only gathered herself. She accelerated in bursts and reached a momentous speed. She swallowed the ocean and grew massive. She flew to meet the creature who couldn't stop. They collided, and from the cataclysm, the handle of the spear broke free and became the first branch of the root, the beginning of all the Great Trees. The head split open and became the first coral of the Drift, the origin of Abyssal life. And something new was born of both, of the courageous Nebule and the creature who carried the heart of fury: the Roedtaw.

When a star falls, the Roedtaw catches it. He carries the star back to the Sun where its body can be consumed by light and born again. That is his eternal journey. He bears the fallen home, forever traversing the Sea in honor of the sacrifice one made for all.

Everyone is on their way to the Roedtaw, even if they don't know it. The Roedtaw is there, ready and willing. And though his love is for those lost—for a kiss from the sun—his way is open to anyone.

The bups waited, not wanting to end the quiet. Not wanting to wake up from Lootrinea's story.

Lootrinea explained, "So you see, the Roedtaw can cross the whole of the ocean."

Barra held her arm close, the pain noticeably relieved by the little yellow stones. She could think again, and though it was a great relief, she knew it wasn't a cure. She said, "Thank you, really, but we need to go farther than the Root. Is there any way the Roedtaw or—do you know how we can get all the way back to the Loft? Back home?"

"The *Nebules* have offered to help you with that," answered the Aetherial.

"What? How?" Tory asked.

"Nebules are born from the sun. They travel through the Void to the Boil where they merge with the ocean and take shape. They can both swim *and* fly." Lootrinea let loose several long notes, and the Nebules flashed.

Without warning, Blue grabbed Plicks like they were about to swim, but instead, he flew the Kolalabat into the air. Plicks let out a startled whoop, and they skimmed along the surface of the water. Tory and Barra watched in eager anticipation of their own flights. The swooping pair splashed down together, and Plicks became catatonic. Tory went up to him, cheering, and seeing his expression, asked, "You okay, buddy?"

"Oh yeah, I'm okay. I was just *flying*," he said, and then he beamed brighter than Tory would have thought possible. The pieces all fell together for him, and he added, "We're going home. We're really going home!"

Barra stroked her sanguine companion, and Red returned her affection by pushing back into her hand. The Nebules could help them get home. It was true. Barra thought about the dangers, and she had to ask, "What about the Kudmoths?"

Somberly, Lootrinea said, "It's true, you'll have to find a way to protect the Nebules. One hasn't safely breached the Root since the Creeper broke the cycle." She added, lightness and pride returning to her voice, "But I don't think we can stop them from helping you. They're too stubborn, and they've developed a fondness for you. It's a kinship, as it should be."

Red wrapped around Barra and hugged her tight. She even managed to coil a tentacle around the wound, adding her own kind of relief to the mounting strength of the stones. Feeling more like herself with each passing moment, Barra asked, "Well then, when do we leave?"

Lootrinea said, "I'll take you to him now. But you'll need to pay him something precious for the ride."

Chapter 23

The Roedtaw

Lootrinea led the bups out of the Drift and into the warm, open sea. It was blinding. The bups Loft-attuned eyes had relaxed within the immense coral, and the bright ocean made them sore, even with the Nebules filtering.

They swam around the Drift, passing through the occasional crowds of Abyssals that hovered near the many, busy entrances. Large kelp forests grew from the Drift in places, but some were free-floating spheres. Lootrinea pointed to one swarming with krill. There were rare flashes of gold within the millions of silvery bodies, exactly the way the Aetherial had described them.

Lootrinea swept her arms back and accelerated away. She curled around deftly and snapped her mouth open and closed in a blink. Like a ribbon on the wind, she returned to the bups. She parted her lips, displaying a gilded krill jailed behind her teeth.

The small creature swam around frantically, and Lootrinea was careful not to crush it or swallow it. She gestured with her arms and curled into a bow. Barra knew it was their turn.

Tory and Char entered the swirling mass of krill, determined to be the first to grab a prize. Plicks and Blue flew in after, and the ball of crustaceans parted and collapsed around them.

They seemed able to forget how far they were away from home—more than Barra could, anyway. She felt alone, responsible for her friends, but unable to do anything more than follow the Aetherial and hope it worked out. She felt guilty. Fathoms away, she saw colonies of Nebules, voluminous and beautiful, and it seemed to her that their shapes held the answer to some great mystery, and if she looked long enough, she could solve it. Red pulled at Barra and dragged her back from her distant thoughts.

Tory and Plicks—try as they might—could not catch a golden krill. Eager to show them how it was done, Red tugged at Barra. The resilient Listlespur nodded that she was ready, and they spiraled into the swarm.

The trio tore through the ball, one futile attempt after another, but the krill were always out of reach. A few Abyssals hovered nearby spectating, and they seemed to laugh at the show of effort. Soon, Barra thought she'd never catch any krill, golden-shelled or otherwise.

Together, the bups paused and studied the swarm. Meanwhile, a pair of thick-shelled spectators swam into the ball. They were slow Abyssals with short fins and iridescent, stony scales. Their bodies were flat, and vertical, so that they looked like squat, flying walls. The pair swam into the krill and carved the swarm into two separate balls. They cut again and again, splitting the krill into smaller groups until they were managing less than a dozen. One gilded krill flashed among them. One of the Abyssals shot her neck out—much longer than Barra would have guessed—and snapped up a krill with her beak. She swam up to Tory, parted her beak enough to show the glint of the catch, and then she let it go.

Training session over, the bups divvied up the roles. Plicks was best at dividing and containing; he and Blue made themselves big and flat to corral the krill. They followed the system they'd seen, and soon Tory collected the first of the three they needed. Barra had hers soon after, but Plicks' took more effort. Tory and Barra weren't as adept at dividing and containing. Still, it wasn't long before Blue was allowing a gilded krill to pass through his skin into Plicks' mouth. Plicks clamped down, careful not to crush the squirmy thing. It felt like hundreds of tiny legs were running on his tongue, and he had to suppress the urge to let it go.

Lootrinea saw they were done and summoned them away from the re-forming swarm. The bups seemed to swim on endlessly, cresting one ridge after another along the outer surface of the Drift. Finally, they rounded a jagged outcropping and saw their first glimpse of the creature of legend, the one and only Roedtaw.

The gargantuan, lapis-colored Roedtaw was as thick as the trunk of a Great Tree. He was long, too, and Barra thought running from end to end would be exhausting. Though it

wasn't the Roedtaw's size that commanded Barra's attention, it was that the creature was hollow. Thousands of layers of fins spiraled around the inside of the giant from mouth to tail. The fins flapped in languid cascades, spinning the water into a tight sparkling vortex. There was a constant flow of debris and water funneled through the Roedtaw, though he floated idle.

Lootrinea led the bups to the front of the staggering creature where two curved black slits held his deep-set eyes in permanent shadow. The Roedtaw's true mouth yawned, the inner lip shrinking away from the outer all the way around the hollow. Dense brushes were exposed, bristles extending from behind both lips. An undulating black tongue pushed out like a tubeworm, and then retreated once again.

If not for the Nebules, the bups would have stayed floating there, maybe forever, the presence of the Roedtaw was so daunting. Barra decided he was beautiful. There was something else, too, something undeniable and magnificent about meeting a creature that was as old as the Great Trees—maybe older.

Lootrinea swam up to the Roedtaw's mouth, which had closed to a slit. She pushed her lips against him and kissed the golden krill in. There was a sucking force from the Roedtaw that tugged at her whiskers, and just like that, the krill was gone.

Each of the bups did the same.

A quaking grumble gorged up from the Roedtaw and shook the ocean. Barra's whole body seemed to vibrate. The grumble grew in pitch and volume, and then drew out long and low. The sound fluctuated, and then ended the way it started, like the end of a sonorous exhale. Barra was overcome by the sound, so broad and close, so gentle and safe. It cradled her very core. Tears formed, but she choked them back. As ancient as the Roedtaw was, she felt a connection to him and she was emboldened by it.

Looking over the bups, Lootrinea smiled knowingly at Barra. The young Listlespur met her gaze, confident and full of gratitude. Barra nodded, and as she did, Lootrinea witnessed a single tear form and then dissolve into Red as a fiery, brilliant ring.

Tory shook in happy disbelief. The Roedtaw was more than anything he'd ever dreamed.

Lootrinea waved to the Roedtaw, indicating they were ready. The Roedtaw's skin was an armor of ridged plates lying flush with his body. Veins of light blue minerals added cracks to the rough plates, and barnacles and seaweed added texture. The Roedtaw levered open a plate and the bups swam in behind it.

There was a shallow depression underneath the plate big enough to hold them all. When they were situated, bubbles began rising from Roedtaw's pores. The bubbles were held by a clear skin drawn across the opening like a nictitating membrane—Barra hadn't even noticed it happen. The bubbles pushed most of the water out of the space beneath the plate, creating a cavity of breathable air. The Nebules slid from the bups.

Emitting a few harmonious tones, Lootrinea spoke watery words of farewell and good luck before she floated away. The bups waved. The Aetherial had told them all she wouldn't be joining them, but nevertheless, Barra was uncomfortable watching her go.

"I don't understand why she couldn't come with us," Plicks said.

Tory sighed, and said, "I was thinking the same thing."

"'There's more to do than we can know.' That's what she said, right?" asked Barra.

"Yeah, but what does *that* mean?" Plicks asked as Blue flitted around him.

The Roedtaw bellowed, silencing the bups. The sound was powerful enough to reach every Abyssal in the sea, but languorous, uncaring whether he was heard or not. The Roedtaw spun up the whirlpool at his center, and accelerated away from the Drift.

There were bony hooks in the pocket flat against the Roedtaw's skin, and Barra reached for the closest to steady herself. Plicks did the same. They went faster and Barra could feel the Roedtaw's pulse as he whirled the water within his hollow. Inconceivable volumes of water passed through him continuously, and behind him, the tight twist stretched longer and longer. He roared yet again, hinting that the speed would increase even more, and Tory grabbed a hook.

They jetted toward the sun, carving a slender vacuum of space in the water that collapsed and exploded behind them. The Drift soon diminished to a speck and joined the rest of the world's details in a plane of far-off darkness, one object indistinguishable from the next. The water warmed as they travelled, and they passed other Drift-like corals, balled forests of vegetation, and immense flat ribbons of debris. The farther they went, the fewer they saw, and those that passed close, flew by in a blur.

Fascinated, the bups chatted about the Roedtaw. When they'd exhausted themselves, Barra remembered that she hadn't apologized to Plicks. The words poured out of her. "I'm sorry. I shouldn't have yelled at you."

Plicks' return was immediate and genuine, "I'm sorry too."

Tory was glad to hear it, but he had to ask, "I just don't understand what set you off like that. It's not like you. Are you all right?"

Barra had to be careful not to look at her arm. "I'm fine. I just need some sleep." She smiled, but the feverish heat was returning. "Now seems as good a time as any."

Tory didn't believe she was okay, but he didn't know what more he could say either. Barra was the most stubborn Listlespur that he knew.

There were bup-sized depressions in the pocket, and Barra slid down into one of them. Red snuggled in close, and intuitively covered Barra's cut. The Nebule eased the pain, but Barra wished she had more of Lootrinea's yellow stones. Those tucked in her cheeks had dissolved to almost nothing. The hypnotic hum of the Roedtaw was at least a comforting distraction. Barra focused on the sound and it lulled her to sleep.

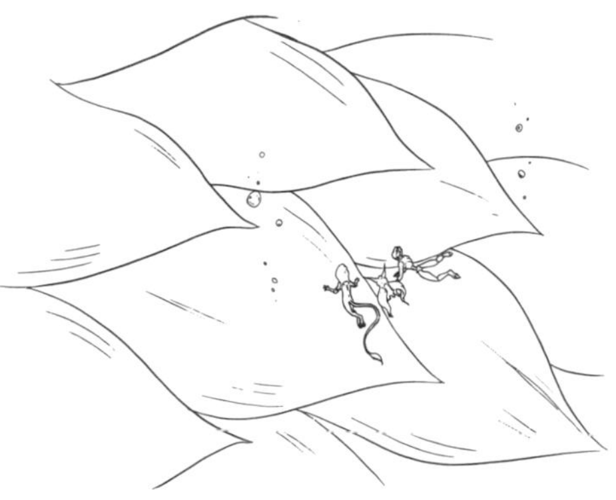

Barra dreamed of exploring with her father. He guided her from the darkness into the light, and back into the darkness again. Pieces of her body were cut and torn from her by an eyeless monster. The pieces fell into the monster's hands, and turned to ashes that he scattered over a crack in the Root. Barra bled into the sea, green and red, a poisonous cloud blocking out the Sun. There was distant laughter and she awoke.

Sweating, Barra sat up. Her fever was becoming more intense, but also, the ocean temperature had risen. The plates covering the Roedtaw were fanned open like a pinecone ready to seed, and they'd blackened too, so that the sun's light was partially blocked. Barra rolled over to see her friends.

Plicks was busy trying to explain to Blue that his scruffs were useful, but the Nebule wasn't getting it. Char bobbed and spun around Tory, who'd finally found the new lines of orange in his panoply. Tory's new color matched Char's cracked lines. Barra blinked away some feverish tears, but the lines were still there.

The Roedtaw bellowed out several stuttered notes.

Barra could feel them decelerating. The bups and the Nebules were squished into the front of the pocket from the force. When the pressure abated, she couldn't tell for sure if they were still moving or not, but the Roedtaw sounded out a boom that was a definitive end.

Red danced around, a surge of joy in her motion. The Nebule tugged in adoration at Barra. "*Come see!*" her body language seemed to beg. Giving in, Barra allowed herself to be dragged up to the tense, curved membrane that was the threshold between the air and the ocean. Pushing through the membrane, Red entered the water beyond with one tentacle still tethered to Barra.

Through the membrane, Barra watched Red burst into elaborate displays of light. The Nebule sparkled with tiny explosions. Waves of scarlet, rose, and vermillion blossomed through her skin.

Red was home.

Chapter 24

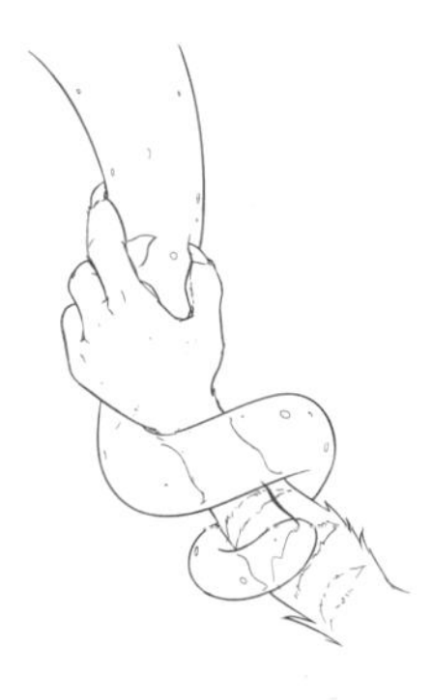

The Boil

Barra wondered what was out there. She followed Red's tentacle from where it was coiled around her arm to where it crossed the meniscus into the ocean. The wicked cut in her arm burned and wept. Normally, Barra would have already been out in the ocean with Red, but she hesitated. She saw Plicks and Tory waiting for her to act and gathered her spirit against her doubt and fear.

Red coiled and pulled, as though she couldn't leave Barra behind. For a moment, Barra saw her father in her weary mind's eye. He beckoned to her, his image bending through the meniscus and her imagination. Another impatient tug from Red broke the spell. The dreamy visage dissolved, and she remembered where she was. She flashed her friends her best *I-got-this* smile, held her breath, and jumped out.

The membrane stretched and resealed behind her, so that she emerged from the pocket with barely a bubble of air escaping with her. The ocean was hot, like crawling into a bowl of fireseeded broth. There was turbulence too as fast-rising bubbles collided with Barra. Flattening her tentacles into a shield, Red deflected the torrents and filtered the sun as she enveloped Barra again. The torrents hit Red and slid sideways around her before snaking up again in bent

ribbons. Reeling out all around the two were the thinner tentacles, rippling. They looked like they were falling fast, but really, they were swimming hard to keep from being pushed up and away from the Boil. Red kept them close to the Roedtaw. Barra thought Red's tentacles, transporting wrinkles of light away from them, were like tongues of fire made solid.

There was so much more to Cerulean than the Umberwood, than the whole of the Great Forest. Barra pushed her face deep into Red, and took a long inhale. The Root wasn't even visible from where they were. Beneath them, the Boil shifted and shimmered, the sun's light flickering madly as it bounced through the giant swathes of bubbles.

Suddenly, Barra realized they weren't alone. Countless scores of Nebules were gathered into roving clouds not far from her. Barra felt exactly how they looked: lost. The oceanic world was amazing, beyond anything she'd ever seen, and still she felt like she was missing something important. She wished her mother could see it. She wished her father was there.

Red folded one rippling tentacle, curled it up, and gently pressed it into Barra's side. Barra closed her eyes and allowed the warmth to soothe her. Her wound flared, and she decided she couldn't stay out longer. She heaved an overlong sigh into Red and their silhouette swelled. Determined more than ever to get home, Barra extended her tail back to the Roedtaw, and pulled. Red released her, and Barra returned to the pocket.

Tory and Plicks were beside themselves with wonder. They waited for details as Barra dripped, but she divulged nothing. Nervous about the answer but needing to know, Plicks finally asked, "Well? What's out there?"

"You have to see for yourselves," Barra said, and Tory was glad to see the intensity in her eyes. She looked alive again. Red poured back into the room, light shedding from her as she passed through the membrane. She was like liquid fire streaming into a pool at Barra's feet. In moments, she was thickening and molding into her be-tentacled self again, bell-shaped body and all. A renewed Red curled in and out of Barra's legs, happy and playful.

Eager, Char and Blue danced around for the boys' attention. They pushed through the meniscus, but Plicks and Tory hesitated. "Really, go. You have to see it," Barra said. "It's just... I don't know what to say. It's beautiful."

Narrowing his eyes skeptically, Plicks said, "There's nothing—"

"Hey, hey, let's go!" Tory interrupted. "Before they leave us behind!" The Rugosic gathered up Plicks and shoved him into the sea. Certain that Plicks was safe with Blue, Tory turned to Barra. "I don't know everything you're feeling, but I know that look. It's like every time I'm happy or excited about some random thing, that's when I miss her most. It makes me," he swallowed hard, "really sad that I can't share anything with her."

One of Char's orb-tipped fingers poked Tory. Smiling, Tory gathered his thoughts, and said, "It feels really lonely sometimes, but—"

"That's not what this is about," Barra responded weakly. Her skin pricked again, and she wanted to be alone to inspect her arm. Frustrated, she told him, "Just get out, already! You need to see the sun!"

Tory was sure Barra was sad about her father, but when he opened his mouth to say more, he had no words. He held Char's outstretched arm, and jumped out.

A feverish wave hit Barra, and she crouched low to keep her stomach from flip-flopping. Her arm was much worse. Soon, she wouldn't be able to hide it or her illness from anyone, much less her best friends. The yellow stones were gone, and Red's help was limited. Barra only hoped she could stave off the infection until they got back to the Umberwood.

The boys re-entered the room, speechless. Plicks fell onto his rump and tried unsuccessfully to combine sounds into words.

Tory grinned. "Incredible."

Plicks's eyes were like juicy berries. "Amazing!"

"The sun," Tory said.

"The ocean," Plicks said in an awed whisper.

"Seemed like it went on forever, didn't it? Did you see all those Nebules?" Tory asked.

Plicks' head was nodding like his neck was a spring. He turned to Barra, "Did you see all that?! Your father was right! Imagine all that light in the Loft!"

"Yeah. Yeah, I was just thinking that," Barra said. There was pressure building in her ears, and her own voice sounded muffled.

"What's the matter?" Tory asked, seeing her falter.

Barra pretended not to hear the question, and changed the focus of the conversation. "What do we do now?"

Plicks perked up. He didn't seem surprised that Barra forgot what Lootrinea told them about the Roedtaw and communicating with him through the bony hooks. With confidence, he reached for the closest and clung to it, white-knuckled. He pulled it hard. Once, twice, three times. He rubbed the patch of skin beneath the hook and then pulled one more time with his whole body.

The Roedtaw began winding up. Low, booming tones shook the bups, and Plicks urged the others, "Hold on!"

The Nebules and bups shrank into their shallow depressions, and held tight to their hooks. The Roedtaw made a gradual turn, end-over-end, forcing them all down, heavily. They couldn't have sat up even if they'd wanted to.

The Roedtaw bellowed. And for the first time in buckles, the bups ascended.

Chapter 25

Surfacing

The Roedtaw accelerated toward the Root. The great distance of the trip would take time despite their monumental speed. The Roedtaw's plates retracted and the space around the bups shrank. They chatted for a while, but Barra was in and out of sleep, leaving Tory and Plicks to get to know their Nebule friends better.

Blue slid over to nuzzle Barra, and then Tory, but soon returned to Plicks where he folded around the Kolalabat like a hug. Red was sleeping beside Barra, tentacles haphazard all around her. Barra brushed them away from her face several times. Half-awake, she yelled at Red, "Leave me alone!" Red crawled away, tucking herself into a corner, making herself as small as possible.

Plicks defended her, and said, "She just wants to be close to you."

"Well, she should keep her tentacles out of my face," Barra said, and then dozed back off again.

Char was playing with Tory, and both were ignoring Barra. The Nebule was almost exactly the same size as the pit stones the bups used in school, and Tory worked out a game, mimicking playing catch. Tory pretended that Char was incredibly heavy or light, and they performed tricks together. The motions looked natural at times, but then magical at others. "Plicks. Plicks! Watch this!" Tory exclaimed. He tossed Char between his feet and hands, which looked rubbery and silly. When Plicks looked, Char—sneaky as he apparently was—changed up the rules of the game. He stuck to Tory's hands like glue, and the two of them became an entangled mess.

Plicks laughed so hard that his scruffs popped out wild from his body. He tried to regather his scruffs, but he couldn't and he tumbled over into a giggling mess.

Char eventually stopped being difficult, and Tory said, "Thanks." His sarcasm palpable. The Nebule moved away and bobbed happily, proud of himself.

Tory noticed Barra's eyes were open, but glassed over. "Is she okay?" he asked.

Plicks leaned in close. "Barra?" She appeared catatonic, not speaking or moving a muscle. He pushed her. No response. He yelled in her face, and she snapped to attention.

"Hey!" she yelled back at him, "I'm trying to sleep!"

Plicks caught a whiff of the sour smell wafting from Barra. "What's wrong with you?"

"I'm fine!" Barra rejected Plicks' inspection, testily. "I just need some uninterrupted sleep." She dismissed his concerns with her bad arm.

"But you're burning…" Plicks trailed off, as he saw the cut. "What is that?!" he gasped, as Barra tried to hide her arm.

Tory interjected, "I thought you said it was only a scratch?" Barra tried to turn away, but there was no room in the cramped pocket. "Let me see," he demanded. He reached toward her, and since there was nowhere to go, she glared and hissed at him. Tory would not be intimidated. After a moment, Barra held out her arm.

Plicks wrinkled up his nose as Tory examined the gaping wound. Covered with a moist film, the cut sweat yellow fluids but no blood. Plicks was right. There was an awful smell effusing from it. What was worse, Tory thought he recognized the scent. It smelled like the eyeless thing's rotting puppets.

"How long's it been like this?" he asked.

"I don't know," Barra lied, not knowing why. Shaking her head, she added, "It's not as bad as it looks."

Plicks remembered seeing the cut when it happened. It didn't seem possible that small wound had become the festering mess on Barra's arm. He thought about it, and made the easy leap relating her cut to the one described in her father's journal. The cut they all believed killed her father. "Is that from the Creepervine?"

Barra tried to be strong, but she had to admit to herself that she was afraid. "It's not the same as my dad's. It can't be." Red slid in beside her and delicately threaded a tentacle into the gash.

White suds foamed over the area as the Nebule siphoned off part of the infection. The wound bled sick-brown and green into Red's body. The poisonous taint lingered as wispy threads worming through her sanguine color. Tory and Plicks were too focused on Barra to notice.

"See?" Barra said, delirious, "Kissed. All better…" and then her eyes rolled to the back of her head, and she passed out.

"Barra?" Plicks shook her gently. When she didn't respond he shook her and yelled, "Barra!?"

Tory intervened, holding Plicks back. He checked her breathing with a trembling hand. "She's breathing," he said through quivering lips.

Red touched Tory's shoulder, asking him to move aside. The Roedtaw's plates lowered again, and as Tory tried to reposition himself in the shrinking space he bumped his head hard. He got his wits back, and watched Red go to work.

The Nebule looped her tentacles around Barra's forearm and absorbed even more of the sickness. Having done as much as she could, Red curled up against Barra's side and rested.

"What're we gonna do?" Plicks whispered.

"I don't know," Tory answered gravely.

"But there wasn't anything... I mean, the journal. The way it ended? Remember how it ended?" Plicks said.

Tory remembered, and he didn't want to think about it. The plates continued to close, but he seemed almost not to notice. He said with firm belief, "Doctor Fenroar will know something. Someone must have treated Ven Swiftspur. We just have to stick to the plan and get home."

Plicks said, "We better get there soon. What if she doesn't wake up?!"

"I don't know," Tory said. "She has to wake up."

Moving in closer again, Plicks checked on Red. "What's happening to her?"

Tory shook his head. "I don't know. She's helping, I think."

The Roedtaw eased out a set of low tones, and the pocket shrank yet again. Taut fear stretched a look between the boys. The shallow depressions they'd been sleeping in suddenly seemed crucial; the only safe spaces if the plate kept closing. There was only room enough for one of them in any of the depressions. The Roedtaw projected a cyclical sound, a whooping, warning sound.

Plicks was shaking, and Tory assured him, "She'll be okay. Don't worry. Red will stay with her." He bundled Barra and Red into one of the depressions, and did his best to make them comfortable. "Come on, Plicks. We have to lie down or we're gonna get crushed." He didn't think the Roedtaw would hurt them, but he didn't feel like testing the theory.

They slid into the depressions and the Nebules joined them. The plate overhead had corresponding depressions so that if it closed completely neat oblong spaces would remain. Plicks was

pretty sure he'd fit. "I'm scared, Tory!" Plicks yelled over the whooping Roedtaw.

"I know! Me too!" Tory hollered back. He looked at Barra one last time to make sure she was secure and then he lay down. "At least she's not awake for this!" he called out. Plicks didn't hear him. The plate closed and the Roedtaw increased his volume. Plicks held Blue like a rolled up sheaf in his arms, and shut his eyes.

"What's happening?" Tory screamed over the wailing Roedtaw.

The violent sound of snapping wood answered his question; they collided with the Root. There was a thunderclap, an immense bough splintering as they breached. The Roedtaw came to rest half out of the ocean, leaning over the hole in the Root he'd just created.

Barra woke up, disoriented and shaky. She called out to her friends, but they didn't answer back. The Roedtaw bobbed slightly, and Barra's stomach floated and waffled, and she thought she'd be sick, but she managed to hold on. The tight space was bathed in sanguine light from the glowing Red, and Barra felt a regular, rhythmic pulse in the body of the Roedtaw, so she knew she wasn't alone.

The plate peeped open and a rush of new air flooded in.

"Tory!? Plicks!?" Barra yelled out.

"Here!"

"Barra!"

"What's going on?" Barra asked.

"Hold on!"

The plate opened farther, and upside down as they were, the bups had to scramble to keep from falling. But the angle was too severe, and the bone hooks were out of reach, and plunk, plunk, plunk, one after another they fell.

Chapter 26

Conflicted

"What was that?" Brace was haggard. She'd barely slept in buckles. Looking around the makeshift camp comprising slimy roots and mudmeal from sodden and rotting wood, it wasn't hard to believe that her sleep was disturbed. More than any other reason though, Brace hadn't slept well because the expedition still hadn't found her daughter.

The initial boom that disturbed Brace became a continuous rumbling rising up her limbs from the Root. She peered into the wood and tried to imagine the source. Splintering, breaking, quaking. A crash of boughs. And then silence.

It was an echo of the sound her heart had made when she'd discovered her daughter was gone. In the eerie silence, she recalled that moment and that feeling. She remembered her reaction when she'd first heard the news: she was alone. She couldn't have been more wrong. Word had travelled fast, and Arboreals from the Umberwood and all the neighboring Great Trees arrived to help.

Plicks' family and extended family had amassed at the Swiftspur den, and Brace welcomed them with open arms. There hadn't been room to accommodate them all, but Tory's father arrived with a binding force of his peers. It was a company of Rugosics, Nectarbadgers, and Haggidons. They opened up the Swiftspur den to make room for every Arboreal offering aid. Satchels of food had arrived, too. Bellbottoms, Listlespurs, and Rattlebarks had harvested and shuttled the packages to her place. The entire Umberwood had mobilized in spontaneous support of the Swiftspur, Mafic, and Battidash families.

The search parties that formed had been thorough and fast. Vallor was there too, and she led the trackers through the Middens, marking out the bups' route in great detail. They stumbled into the Creepervine, and Kudmoths too. They revealed these discoveries to the others, and though they'd continued searching for the bups, a new investigation was launched into the source of the creeping death.

Gammel's study had been laid open. His journal was read among numerous other sheaves, and his maps were gathered, reviewed, and revised. The encroaching fungus was dangerous

and broadly distributed. Jerrun was there when they'd learned about his dealings with Gammel, and his lies. The Arboreals didn't trust the withered Rattlebark after that, but they didn't shun him either. Jerrun became a shadow at the back of the crowd, known to everyone, but standing without their regard.

The trackers reported that the bups' trail ended at the Fall, and the families leaned on each other and held their heads. The Kudmoths and the Creepervine had taken their bups from them.

The dangers of descending through the Fall were discussed, alternatives negotiated. The myths and legends told them the Fall was the end of all things, but the Great Trees grew up from somewhere, out of something. There were sheaves, too, weathered leaves in the archives that described the Root in detail. Even if generations of Arboreals had forgotten, the sheaves had not. They had started to believe they could travel to the Root and return.

The archivists had pulled tomes from the disused corners of the reliquary, and they read, and they learned. A joining of passion and knowledge, a plan to find the lost bups had been born. Growing and maturing through discussions both heated and calculating, they figured a way to safely travel to the Root. With taboos and rules set aside, parachuting had suddenly become an obvious, deceptively simple, solution. Unspoken then, most of the gathered Arboreals had hoped the bups had figured the same.

An expedition was formed comprising thirty-one Arboreals of various species, and twenty-three Kolalabats—most, Plicks' blood relations—to glide them down. Among the thirty-one were Tory's father and his closest friends, binders all. Vallor Starch was there too, and even Jerrun. No one relished having the decrepit Elder along, but the silver-tongued Head of the Council had a unique knowledge of the archives, and so, he could not be reasonably denied.

As prepared as they could be, the expedition had launched from the last branch touched by the bups.

The plan worked.

They found the bups' trail at the Root. The relief was unanimous, palpable. They followed the tracks, made camp, and followed the tracks again. And the tracks led them to the fungal-puppets.

And they fought.

The monstrosities wouldn't stop them. Skirmishes became frequent, but the resolve of the expedition never faltered. They discovered evidence again and again, that the bups were alive.

So of course Brace wasn't sleeping when she heard the Root crack. She ran into Jerrun who was standing with Vallor on the periphery of camp trying to wrestle answers out of the darkness with his weak, cloudy eyes. She asked, "What was that? What could make a sound like that?"

"I don't know." Jerrun leaned hard on his staff, wringing it with both hands. The bottom of the staff had been sharpened to pierce the slime-coated Root.

Vallor spoke up, "We have to tread carefully. The fungal-puppets may have caused it, or if they didn't, they'll think we did. We should expect some opposition."

Mutterings spread through the Arboreals like a contagion. Three trackers were already dispatched to scout out the source of the disturbance. The rest were sharpening claws, teeth, and tails. A few Kolalabats were floating in with reports, but they were returning from unrelated tasks and gave no insight into the crash.

A Listlespur emerged from the fog as though she was fading into reality out of a dream. She was first to find the creature that had broken through the Root. Jaeden concluded her report to Brace, "No way of knowing how big it is. If you want to go, we should go now."

Brace hadn't known Jaeden long, but she trusted her. There was something in her eyes, an unwavering clarity of perspective—confidence, or perhaps stubbornness—and it reminded Brace of Gammel, and she needed that memory close, more now than ever before.

Brace locked eyes with Vallor, an urgent question on her face. Vallor said, "You don't even have to ask." The Haggidon's twin-toothed tails were restless behind her, and a mischievous smile played at her lips. Vallor seemed to thrive on the unknown. Brace nodded her thanks.

"Let's go," Vallor said, and they left Jerrun there without another word. The reporting Listlespur and a few other Arboreals rushed up to join them, and together they trekked to the site.

It wasn't long before they approached the site of the crash. The creature that broke through the Root ended unseen in the branches over their heads. It was lit ominously from beneath, the exposed portion already larger than any living creature Brace had ever known except for the Great Trees themselves. The plates that lines the beast started to open, bending or breaking any branches that were in the way.

There were voices. Brace heard them briefly, but they were clear enough. "Barra!"

Jaeden's arm flashed. She grabbed Brace by the wrist, and urged her to keep her voice under control.

One after another, three blurs fell out of the beast, and plopped into the water. Brace ripped free of Jaeden and dashed toward the broken Root. The others followed.

Three separate, brightly colored creatures followed the bups, and not knowing if they were a threat, Brace ran even faster. At the water, Brace stared through the pain of her vision adjusting to the light. Blurry shadows rose toward her, but couldn't make any sense of them. Whatever they were, they were coming up fast.

Brace jerked her head back to avoid being hit, and fell over as her daughter and her friends breached the surface and floated into the air.

Brace couldn't tell if the creatures were helping or harming at first, especially in the after-light blindness of the Root. The rippling, flying creatures were holding the bups by loops of tendrils and masks of flesh, and they came to hover beside Brace. She was rigid and ready to fight.

"Mom!" Barra yelled as Red peeled back from her mouth. The young Listlespur hit the Root with claws extended and ran for her mother. She pulled away from Red, and pounced onto her mother in an embrace that sent them both tumbling, end over end.

Brace hugged her back fiercely, and thought she'd never let her daughter go again. A Kolalabat dropped down beside them. He said, "The monsters are close. We have to go." Brace changed in an instant from mother to warrior. She nodded to the Kolalabat and gestured to both the visible and invisible Arboreal forces around them.

Tory and Plicks looked around bewildered, half-expecting their own families to appear out of the woods. They felt like they'd woken up from one crazy dream into another.

Addressing Barra firmly, Brace said, "We're leaving. Can you run?"

Barra grinned. "We can fly."

Chapter 27

Together in the Dark

Barra wasn't actually sure if they *could* fly, but Red swooped in and grabbed her before her mother had a chance to be shocked. Pride softened Brace's warlike expression as her daughter lifted off the ground. Brace signaled the group, and they started back toward the campsite. They moved like the crest of a wave through the wood.

The bups were flying, though their movements lacked the elegance they had under water. Barra had been mistaken believing the Nebules would know how to fly perfectly; they'd spent most of their lives underwater. There were bumps and scrapes, and collisions avoided by dizzy-luck, but they all made it back to camp.

The expedition was readying for a quick escape depending on what the scouting group found. Whispers blossomed among the Arboreals. The bups had arrived. Brace ran to her daughter and took her up in her arms again.

Time had stretched from extreme stress: the families hadn't been separated long, but they reunited as though rings had passed between them unmarked. They held onto each other while they tried to catch up. Were the bups okay? Had they been eating? What happened? Did the fungal-puppets harm them? Each new question was asked before the last was answered.

Barra edged away from the crowd. Brace scooped her up, knowing there was something wrong with her daughter, something more than fatigue. Brace carried her to an area the Weavers had made soft with twists of root hairs. Red followed, a tentacle tethered to Barra so that they were in constant contact. Brace was uncertain of the Nebule, and wished the creature would let her daughter alone, even if just for a short time.

Barra, tired as she was, noticed her mother's concern. "Don't worry, she's licking my wounds." She smiled wanly, her voice too thick to be convincing.

Brace didn't understand what her daughter meant, but knew there was something wrong with Barra's arm beneath the multiple loops of Red's tether. She laid Barra down, stroked her fur, and sang to her, and all the while Red swayed to the rhythm, but didn't let go. Sure her daughter was fast asleep, Brace leaned in, half-expecting the Nebule to react in protest. Red pulled away instead, clearing the way for inspection.

The smell wafted into Brace's nostrils. Even dampened as it was by a residue of sanguine jelly, the pungent scent at close range was enough to make her reel. Covering her nose, she examined the flesh which was open like an eyelet. Several worms of jaundiced fluid were trapped beneath the residue, wriggling and sliding around, bleeding trails in their wakes. Brace couldn't tell if the residue was helping or hurting. Suspect, she stared at Red.

There were two doctors with them, a Weaver named Searowe who could spin out a suture fast and clean with his eyes closed, and a Muskkat who went by Mareki. Methodical and keen of judgment, Mareki made sure the worst wounds were addressed first. Brace nodded toward nothing in particular at the periphery of the camp. A Listlespur emerged from the darkness, the same who had first reported the location of the towering creature that had broken through the Root.

"Get the doctors please?" she asked the slender, younger version of herself. Jaeden lowered her head in affirmation, and then bounded away.

Brace knew the doctors were busy—the fights against the fungal-puppets rarely ended well for the Arboreals. The diabolical creatures always came with greater numbers, and not being overly concerned with self-preservation, they could fight and keep fighting. Still, Brace needed the doctors to come for Barra. She needed them to tell her that her daughter was going to be okay.

Back at the center of the campsite, the rest of the expedition surrounded Plicks and Tory. They provided food, compassion, and more questions. The short version of the bups' story was relayed without embellishment—it didn't need any. The camp cheered, laughed, and cried as the story was told. Afterward, they asked about Argus and his minions; what had Tory seen, what had Plicks? Fizzit's description inspired confusion, awe, and suspicion. They ventured guesses about him in secretive whispers. Rumors began about the Nebules too. Arboreals familiar with the archives wondered if the jellies were related to the legendary creatures of the same name who had created the Aetherials. There was no way to know for sure.

Standing back, far away from the crowd, Jerrun leaned on his staff and listened. At the mention of Fizzit, he asked the mist, "What game are you playing?"

Behind him, an amber eye opened with no distinguishable head to hold it. "I explain myself to no one," said the stranger in a way that made his final word stick in Jerrun's ear like a barbed nettle. Then with a sudden change of tone, he added humorously, "If I explained myself we'd be here forever. I have that kind of time, but I don't think you do. Do you?"

The Head of Council didn't respond. He listened in on the expedition awhile longer, and then asked, "Is it already done then? The Creeper is in the water?" He seemed defeated.

"Not yet," Fizzit said. "We should talk." Jerrun, already sagging, managed to slump down even more. He turned around, limping around his staff. He joined Fizzit, and they disappeared into the mist.

Not one of the expedition noticed Jerrun's departure, or his uninvited guest. They were too preoccupied with Tory. The newly bonded minerals caused worry at first, but as his story unfolded, speculation consulted legend for answers. The Rugosics, Tory's father among them, thought about the ocean and the vast clouds of minerals, and wondered about their ancestors. The audience finally broke up, and Tory was alone with his father.

They had a few false starts, colliding with each other's words. "Thanks for being here," Tory said. He threw his arms around his Father and held on tight.

"I'm just so glad we found you." Tory's father hugged him back powerfully. He said, "I couldn't imagine..." The rough-skinned Rugosic held his son by the shoulders, "Let me look at you!" Tears glinted in his eyes. He sniffled, and then he said, "My bup!"

The outpouring of emotion overwhelmed Tory. His legs weakened and he just collapsed into his father's arms, allowing himself to be held. Char bobbed in, extending and retracting his small spheres in jubilant cascades. The Nebule kept at it until he finally got Tory's attention.

"Meet Char," Tory said. It was a personal introduction even though the Nebules had been announced to everyone. "Char, this is my father, Ven Luke Mafic," he said with pride. And the conversation gained momentum from there, words flowing smoothly, as though there hadn't been awkward rings of silence between them.

Plicks was bundled up into a ball and tossed around by his family. They hugged him and passed him on. The large collection of Kolalabats expressed their emotions easily, crying and laughing, hugging and petting. The boisterousness of Plicks' family usually made him anxious and embarrassed, but not now. He was glad for the unending chain of warmth and support. His feet never touched the ground as he went from greeting to greeting. Blue enjoyed it too, flying around behind Plicks, snuggling and being snuggled. He swooped in at times and stole some attention for himself.

While the rest of the camp was busy with Plicks and Tory, Jaeden returned to Brace with the doctors. The wound stumped both of them; they'd never seen anything like it. Red guided them through the examination. She demonstrated the wrap she provided for Barra, the way she wound her tentacle around the wound. Mareki was impressed, but solemn, respecting Brace's concern. The suds bubbled up on the wound and Red turned muddy. Searowe said he believed the Nebule was cleaning the wound, but not curing the infection. The doctors felt there was little more they could do. The sparse vegetation the Root provided was unfamiliar in terms of the herbs and remedies they knew. The consensus was to get Barra back to the Loft as soon as possible. The doctors were thanked and excused.

Brace became hardened by the news. She stroked her daughter's hair, and whispered, "Burbur. My sweet Burbur. We'll be home soon. I promise."

Jaeden appeared, forming out of seemingly distant branches. She stood, a mere tail's length away. "You'll have to tell me sometime how you got so good at that," Brace nodded, impressed. Stealth wasn't exactly practiced among Listlespurs anymore, at least not within the polite community of the Loft.

"Sometime," Jaeden said.

Brace wanted to know about Jaeden's Thread, too. Jaeden wore woven ropes around her forearms like a Rugosic but no curios had been sewn into them. When the expedition made it home, Brace looked forward an explanation. In the meantime, she said, "Right. What is it? Did you find Jerrun?"

"He's not in the camp." Jaeden's eyes were vivid orange with ash-gray rims, steady beacons against the dark.

"He was taken?" Brace was stunned.

"He wasn't ambushed. He left on his own," Jaeden said with a hint of intrigue, like she knew more but wasn't telling. She added, "I didn't follow his trail far, but it was like he knew where he was going."

"What do you mean?" Brace spoke tightly. She looked at her daughter. Wasn't there enough already to fear without Jerrun playing mysterious games? She reached down to Barra's forehead, and found that whatever Red was doing was at least relieving the fever.

"I mean there's something not right about that old Arboreal," Jaeden said, but then she shrugged. Disgusted, she went on, "Maybe it's just me, but this whole place stinks. I've got splashes of *them* in my nose. I'm scent-blind. It's making me twitchy."

"Well, we'll just leave him if he doesn't return before we break camp. I don't know how the rest will take it, but we're not waiting around for him." She spoke like there was acid on her tongue.

Jaeden bowed her head slightly to say farewell and then she vanished into the surrounding wood. Brace noted the glint in her fellow Listlespur's eye, the nervy twitch of a smile that had appeared when she'd suggested they leave Jerrun behind. Another question for Brace's list.

Brace nodded so that Jaeden would see, and pointed at Barra. She wanted her daughter guarded. Back in the main area of the camp, Brace began organizing the expedition to go home.

Chapter 28

Sacrifices

The pathwood back to the Loft was fraught and unknown. Even with all the accumulated knowledge, the expedition's plan to climb a Great Tree seemed much more daunting from the bottom. Routes had been built into the Trees many rings ago by Arboreals frequently traveling between Loft and Root. But the Trees were younger then, smaller. Worse than the prospect of the climb, as close as they were to the base of the Umberwood, Argus was closer. The eyeless wretch and his puppet minions seemed to be everywhere. While they debated climbing options, the scouting continued.

Kolalabats and Listlespurs returned regularly with information about the rootscape. They refined their understanding of the Root while keeping an eye out for the puppets. Everyone hoped a scout would return with news of a clandestine path, a secret way to the trunk. There was none. As the days passed, the creeping periphery seemed to grow closer and thicker, but Brace hoped it was just her imagination.

She made a round of the camp whenever she needed a break to think. She checked in on Barra—who was somewhat better, even if her arm wasn't—and then visited Plicks and Tory. There was a tight rope of emotion holding the families together. They'd been given a second chance, which doubled their fear of losing them. The families were jumpy and uncertain. Every shadow was a looming portent, the unseen threatening to swallow their young ones again. Brace did her rounds, kept her words short and encouraging, even though she shared their same fears.

Patrolling the outer fringes of the camp, Brace was intercepted by Jaeden, who reported, "Jerrun's back."

Brace was disappointed. "Well, at least I don't have to explain to the Council how I lost him," she said.

Jaeden was often terse, and quick to leave, so Brace thought it odd that the mysterious Listlespur was still standing there. She asked, "Was there something else?"

"He's addressing the camp… something about the bups or their companions? A threat to all of us," Jaeden said.

"What?!" Brace didn't wait for more explanation. She picked up her pace and found Jerrun already had everyone's attention at the center of camp. His tone was aggressive, his words condemning. His message was clear; the bups were infected.

With a strain of will, Brace composed herself and approached. "What's all this?"

"Ah, Brace, glad to see you could make it," Jerrun said. "I've spoken to Mareki and Searowe. When were you planning on telling the rest of us about your daughter's wound?"

Brace was caught completely off guard. She hadn't hidden anything from anyone. It hadn't occurred to her that a wounded bup was considered a threat. "It's hardly a secret, Jerrun. What's the problem?" she said impatiently.

"What's the problem?" Jerrun asked the crowd, suggesting Brace's question alone implied she was blind. "Problems, Brace, there are several." Jerrun turned his face up in disgust, "Your daughter has a gaping wound that smells like, well, everything in this place. It's full of rot, and we do not understand it, and you'd have us bring it to our Loft?"

Jerrun's barbed words worked their way into Brace's ears, stunning her. He sensed her weakness and continued, "Tory has strange new markings..."

Ven Mafic spoke up, unafraid, "They're harmless!"

"Maybe, Luke, maybe. But what if they're not?" Jerrun then implored the rest of the gathering, "We need to be sure for the sake of all of our families. As hard as it might be to hear, we didn't find the bups the same as they left." There was no response except the passive agreement of silence, and he turned again on Brace.

"We know the source of the darkness now. I assumed you, Brace, of all Arboreals, would be the first to want to put an end to it," Jerrun phrased the idea as though only a fool would think otherwise.

Brace was not a fool. Not so easily manipulated. "Our goal has always been to save the bups. We're only halfway there." She

waved to everyone. "We need to get home. With the bups, and everything we now know about the Root."

"We *can't* go back to the Loft," Jerrun hissed at Brace.

The crowd of Arboreals became restless. There were cries from the group. "You're mad!" they said. "We're going home!"

Jerrun implored the entire expedition, "Don't you see? None of us can go back. Not without carrying this… this rot right into our homes! Everyone will die!"

Brace was livid, "What are we even talking about?"

"Look around!" Jerrun leaned on his staff. "This Root? It's the land of the dead. And the Creepervine is just death's cold hand reaching up for our lives in the Loft. We can't let it succeed—"

"What would you have us do?! Attack what, exactly? The fungal-puppets?! We can't destroy them *all*." Brace was incredulous.

Jaeden slid into the enclave and walked right up to Brace. "The puppets are on the move."

The boughs began writhing all around them. Glowing eyes blinked on as the puppet horrors appeared out of the darkness. They were surrounded.

Chapter 29

Familiar Foes

All stories are merely moments strung together one after another into simple threads. The stories of grand adventures and great civilizations, the stories of uneventful days, and the stories of the Arboreals—each one of them, all stories, moments held together by the most fragile of strings. Usually, one precious moment gives birth to the next, so that every moment carries on the lineage, recognizable and easy to follow. But sometimes a moment seems to come from nothing. Sometimes, the ancestral tapestry is sown into knots, and new unfamiliar patterns grow. Where this present moment came from can be almost impossible to know, but this moment cannot lie, it can only make the thread harder to unravel. The rest of the times—perhaps, most of the times?—the causes are more obvious, and the effects, more immediate.

~ Excerpt: Fizzit's Leaves

The expedition was surrounded by Argus' minions. Their individual moments were collected, and exposed. Each Kolalabat, Listlespur, and Rugosic, every Nectarbadger and Weaver, every Rattlebark and Bellbottom was given a stretch of time to review the strings of their lives. Not one wondered how they'd arrived at that moment. Some felt regret and others pride, but each understood. It was a rare moment, the kind that grants absolute clarity. A moment from which no one can hide.

The moment of reflection collapsed. Time sped forward to catch up.

The circle broke. Brace alone stood her ground as the rest scattered. She bared her teeth and hissed vicious spittle. Growls and barks echoed back from the dark, the Arboreals responding to her call to stay. With control, she lowered herself to all fours, and punished the air with her tail. The sharp, staccato whipping made blood promises Brace intended to keep.

The monstrosities rushed the camp. They were held together by fungus and animated by vines like other puppets, but beyond that the similarities vanished. Where Brace expected dull claws and broken talons, sharpened and complete versions grew. More staggering than the physical differences, these puppets were coordinated. They worked together, closing off avenues of escape. They isolated the weakest Arboreals, and doubled up against the strong. In place of torpor, they had determination and awareness. They attacked from every direction.

The campsite exploded with howls, growls, and screams. A serpent-like puppet sprang at Brace, but she'd spied the intent in the creature's eyes and dodged easily. Brace lashed the beast to the ground, and then tore through its back with her claws. Yellow-green splashed into the air in bright spurts. The monstrosity wriggled, unable to stand up, and Brace shifted her attention to the only thing that mattered: her daughter.

She careened toward the wall of fungal-puppets. Crashing into the nearest, she tackled the monster while slashing at its vines, using her tail to tie up its limbs. They rolled to a stop, Brace landing on top. She sliced through each of its arms, and then, using its body like a spring board, she jumped up and dashed to where she'd left Barra sleeping.

Jerrun faded into the background at the first sign of the attack, hiding. As Brace left the area, he slunk after her using his robe as camouflage. His progress was slow, but he followed her scent.

Racing, Brace shivered as she heard a scream. The sound of it was so distorted by pain that it was almost impossible to imagine it came from any living creature. Her only solace was that the scream came from behind her. It wasn't Barra. Still, her heart reached back as she drove forward. She came up on the small resting area, and saw two hulking minions converging on her daughter.

Barra was already awake and alert. Red lashed out at the fungal-puppets, keeping them at bay. Waiting to reveal herself, Brace sampled the air and found Jaeden nearby. No words were exchanged, but their assault was coordinated, swift and lethal. Only severed limbs and mangled corpses remained.

"Mom," Barra jumped to her mother and embraced her. Red bobbed and flitted around, but never went far from Barra. Looking over her shoulder, Brace thanked Jaeden with a deep nod. Jaeden nodded back, and bowed into the darkness again.

Sounds of combat were ferocious and close. Barra's mother held her at arm's distance and asked, "Can you fly again? Or dive into the ocean? You have to get away! Someplace safe!"

"What about you!? And where are Tory and Plicks?" Barra said, high pitched with worry and fear. "Where are they?"

Brace thought back, trying to piece together what she'd seen. Plicks and Tory were caught in the fight, but she refused to tell her daughter that. She said calmly, "I'll find them, but I need to know you're safe in order to do that. Fly away with Red. Stealth, hide. I'll find you."

The ground rumbled before either could move. Wounds in the woods split open, and new scars were torn into the bark. A flood of dark liquid poured from the largest gaping rent. Vines appeared out of the treacle and climbed the nearby branches. A head emerged, sagging, eyeless, and heavy. Shoulders and torso followed, attached to a rising trunk of Creepervine that was riddled with thorns. Smaller vines continued to pour out around Argus' feet, along with more fungus and pooling darkness. He raised his head and peered at the Swiftspurs with empty sockets.

Brace imposed herself between the eyeless monster and her daughter, and Red flew in beside them, doing her best to look frightening. The Nebule puffed herself up, and sent flashes of color coursing through her body.

Argus raised his arms and the ooze all around them boiled. But instead of smoke or steam, Kudmoths rose from the bubbles. They gathered in the air and became a deadly extension of Argus' will.

"Get out of here!" Barra screamed at Red. Startled and unsure, Red didn't react until the Kudmoths swirled and darted toward her, and then she shifted away at a speed that defied vision. The Kudmoths followed her. Dodging and sliding through small spaces, Red began a series of daunting aerial maneuvers. She dispatched Kudmoths with flicks and sweeps of her tentacles, and even lassoed several at once. Shattered carapaces rained down onto the damp Root.

Argus leaned in closer. Drool slid out of his mouth and over his chin. If his face was capable of showing joy, it did then.

"Run!" Brace commanded her daughter. But Barra wouldn't listen. She only slid around her mother to an attack position. Argus unrolled a vine from the burgeoning grunge and flung it toward the pair. Brace dove toward her daughter, caught her and rolled away with her. When she stood up, she stared at her daughter with an irresistible blaze in her eyes, and yelled, "RUN!" She threw her daughter with all her strength, and turned to face the eyeless terror alone.

Barra reacted without thinking, righted herself mid-air, and landed, clinging to a far off branch. She turned in time to see her mother scooped up by her feet, and then thrashed from side to side. Barra screamed, but her mother was already breaking free, cutting through the vines that held her. Her mother dropped, scrambled away fast, but then turned to continue the fight. Barra's heart started again.

Turning to the sounds of distant combat, Barra had no idea where to go for help. She was stronger than she'd been in days, but still weak. Red flew down to meet her, the Kudmoths having broken off their attack. Barra knew they'd be back in greater numbers. She focused all of her will on Red and begged, "Find Tory and Plicks! Find them! Bring them here!" Red understood, and she flew away fast.

Never able to listen to her mother, Barra surged back into the fight where Brace was dodging endlessly. Barra stealthed and flanked Argus, but he knew she was coming. He swatted her aside with a vine before she could get too close. Barra recovered and jumped back in. They fought together, but they were on the defensive. Neither could seem to do any real damage.

Red reappeared with Char and Blue, carrying Tory and Plicks behind her. The Swiftspurs were faltering, and Barra hoped her friends hadn't arrived only to be pulled into the losing fight. Brace echoed her daughter's thoughts, and hollered, "We have to get out of here!"

Char dropped Tory close and he loped into the fray. He snagged an attacking vine out of the air and grappled it to the ground. Char pulsed around, pulling attention away from the busy Rugosic. Wary of the thorns, Tory struggled to bend the vine away. He twisted it around on itself, but despite his efforts,

a thorn struck him. It hit and caught in one of his new, smoky orange grooves where it ground itself to a nub. Tory snapped the vine, crunches sounding out inside it, and it fell to the Root, limp and lifeless.

Tory yelled out to Barra's mother, "The camp is almost under control. My dad'll be here soon!" He dove away from another grasping vine.

Blue swung down from above and dropped Plicks, who was a spinning ball of fur and talons. Plicks shredded a section of the attacking Creeper and left it wriggling uselessly on the floor of the Root.

Char caught a projecting vine, and stuck his many spheres to it as he rolled. He closed up, pulling the vine into a knot, and then he flashed. His light passed into the Creeper, and it seemed to thicken with the light, and Char pulsed even brighter. The Creeper kept siphoning off the energy. It became overfull and split down the middle, breaking open all the way down its length. And then, still knotted up, Char panicked and ignited in a powerful flash of blinding light. The vine erupted, bits splattering everywhere.

"What the...?" Barra whispered. But the fight was reengaged. She saw her mother lagging and yelled to Tory, "We can't wait for help!" She was spent too, barely able to get the words out.

Argus raised his arms again, and the sludge boiled once more. Kudmoths spawned from the slime, twice as many as the first time. Tory decided that was enough for him, and said, "Let's go!" The bups scattered with their Nebules. But Barra was opposite from the boys, closer to her mother, and she split off in her own direction.

"Toward the camp!" Plicks yelled to Barra. "Barra!" he hollered again. He was desperate to get her attention, but she was fast despite her weakness, and already too far. Yelling did, however, get him the attention of the Kudmoths.

Tory grabbed Plicks by the scruffs. “That’s done it! Come on!” They sped toward the camp.

Brace was last to leave. She feinted in to attack a few times to keep the ever-expanding reach of Argus occupied. Making sure the bups were clear, she lunged in one last time, and struck Argus across the face with her tail. She had to show him—had to prove to herself—that he wasn’t invincible. The Creeper curled in all around her, and she escaped. She was happy with herself for her parting shot, and didn’t notice that Barra had gone the opposite way from the main area of camp.

Ripping himself down from the Creepervine, Argus stood. Kudmoths swirled around him, buzzing, agitated. He gathered himself and trundled off after Barra. He gained speed as he went, Kudmoths billowing up behind him like he was kicking up angry dust.

Barra ran, Red beside her, but her adrenaline-powered retreat didn’t last long. Her strength was ebbing. Hampered by the throbbing in her arm, she began favoring it, and even her ankle—strained so long ago—was sore. She limped a bit, and then began walking upright. Red kept pulling and tugging at her, but Barra was too confused to understand. The exertion had made her dizzy hot, and it became hard for her to sort out where she was going. She swatted at her friend. “I’ll be alright, Red,” she said through gritted teeth, thinking Red was over-concerned.

Finally, Barra had to stop. Where was the main camp? She shouldn’t have had to run so far. What about Tory and Plicks? And her mom! Where was her mom?! Red wrapped a tentacle around her and pulled hard. Barra pulled back equally hard. “Knock it off!” She yanked the Nebule, and when Red released her, Barra stumbled and fell.

On her back, she realized just how bad off she was. She rolled over and saw a faint radiance. There was a narrow opening in the Root, barely visible, though it wasn't far. Red floated down beside Barra near her wound. Almost all the fur on the injured arm was gone. The exposed skin was vulnerable and soft. The Nebule encircled it. Red absorbed the dark ooze, but when she finished this time her healthy color did not return.

"Oh, Red, you don't look so good," Barra said, delirious. She felt a little better, but was still disoriented. She got up partially, and began hobbling toward the glow of the pool. She didn't see it, but a dark mound began moving to intercept her. Red saw it and tried to steer Barra away.

Only a short distance from the opening, the slithering mound blocked Barra. He stood hunched over, but with her fever-blurred vision Barra didn't recognize the Elder without his staff. When he spoke though, she knew it was Jerrun. "You're a very dangerous little girl."

Barra wasn't sure what he meant. She said, "I think I wandered out of the camp..."

"I'm sure you did, and this is an opportunity I might not have again. You're sick Barra, like your father was sick. And just like him you're a threat to everyone." Jerrun's voice was severe.

Perplexed, Barra stared at the old Rattlebark. She could hear his age in the crackling of his lungs as he breathed.

Maybe it was guilt, maybe it was arrogance—probably there was no good reason at all—but Jerrun was compelled to explain. "I told him not to explore the Middens. All Argus needs is the right medium, a way to contaminate the ocean and that's it, we're all dead. I swore an oath, I won't let it happen. I know how to deal with the recklessness of the Swiftspurs." His hands shot out so fast that Barra flinched only after his long slender fingers were holding her fast.

"Let me go!" she screamed at the top of her lungs. Red flogged the Elder with her tentacles, but Jerrun ignored the searing pain. He jumped onto Barra, his arms and legs finding her wrists and ankles with deceptive ease. He pinned her down and moved her hands together so that he could handcuff her with one hand. With his now free hand he grabbed her throat and squeezed.

Red threw herself over Jerrun's face and wrapped herself around him. Wherever she could find purchase, she pried at him. He released Barra's neck to swipe at the Nebule. Barra gasped a harsh breath that burned as it passed the rawness of her throat. She tried to scream, but she couldn't find her voice. She tried to strike Jerrun with her tail, but it was crushed beneath her and she couldn't prise him off.

Jerrun grabbed the tentacle that was noosed around his throat, and crushed it in his hand. Red flared in an instant, so bright it blinded both Barra and Jerrun. Fungus and Creeper in the area swelled, split open in sprays of yellow-green, and then shriveled away. Jerrun kept squeezing until his hand went all the way through, and the long dismembered piece of Red's tentacle fell to the Root. The pain was too much. Red released the Elder. Spinning around in the air, Red splattered droplets over the two tangled Arboreals.

Jerrun reached for Barra's neck again. "I accept the guilt… for the welfare of all the Arboreals of the Great Forest," he said like he was reciting a litany. He began to squeeze the life out of her again. "It was easier with your father. He willfully disobeyed me. Every attempt I made… I was trying to save him," he said, detached. "In the end, he was so sick, it only took a little push…"

Jerrun's grip loosened. Jaundiced white humors were exposed as his eyes rolled to the back of his head. He slumped over, and fell to the side of Barra. A Listlespur stood in his place. Whoever it was had saved her life, though Barra couldn't grasp it. The stranger's eyes glinted, orange and gray; Barra would never forget them. But the colors swirled together, and her vision blurred. Barra felt like she was spinning, and falling, and she blacked out.

Red held the stump of her injured tentacle curled up against her body. Jaeden scooped up the unconscious Barra. A clicking cacophony approached and Jaeden didn't need to sample the air to know what was coming. She broke out in a dead run for the campsite, and Red flew after.

Kudmoths filled the air like fast-rolling fog. They buzzed around the pool and the crumpled and robed mound of Jerrun. They collapsed into a tight stormy cloud, reached some collective decision, and then rolled toward the camp.

Soon after the Kudmoths left, Argus slid into the area. Without the stickiness of the fungus clinging to him, he was silent and almost graceful as he approached the tiny crack in the Root. Stopping by Jerrun's corpse, he stood tall and sniffed wetly several times. He crouched down low to the Root, folding into himself, shoulders between his knees. He sniffed again. He was unconcerned with Jerrun. There was something else that had his attention resting near the body.

It called to him; the mottled, discolored tentacle.

Reaching his hand out, Argus ran a grimy, gnarled finger along the twisted length of tentacle, scraping a sample onto his nail. He held the residue up to the holes where the flesh of his nose should have been. The amputated tentacle of the Nebule was different than any other he'd known. Different because the fungus was *alive* within it. The Nebule flesh was infected, something he'd been trying to do for as far back as he could remember. Here it was. A gift. Exactly what he'd always wanted.

He cradled the severed limb in his hands. He slid over to a nearby branch, and dunked the limb into an open scar. Turning it over and over in the sap, he coated it. Satisfied that the tentacle was protected against suddenly sparking to ash, he smiled. Ooze drooled from his face. He took three long strides, and faded away into the wood.

Hanging down from an overhead tangle of roots by two of his three tails, Fizzit lowered himself. At the extent of his tails, he flipped like he only weighed as much as a feather, and landed on his feet. He pulled back his hood and knelt beside Jerrun.

"It's like I said, old friend. Sacrifices."

Chapter 30

Surviving

The campsite was in disarray, but already pulling itself back together. Injured Arboreals were gathered for triage, some limping along while others were carried into the central clearing. There were mutterings about what had happened, and who was missing.

"Where'd all the lights go?" an injured Nectarbadger murmured. Searowe tapped out a small ribbon of gauze from a ball of silk in a pouch that crossed over his shoulder. His nails were long and curved with thin, hollow channels that he used to guide his thread. He was a master, capable of knitting almost anything if the right material was available. The Nectarbadger had a nasty gash in his head. The area of the injury was cleaned and treated, and the hair removed.

“Bite down on this,” Mareki placed a piece of bitter tasting bark in the Nectarbadger’s mouth. “Harder. Come on, now.” The hurt Arboreal’s teeth finally pierced the outer skin of the bark, and an anesthetic sap bled into his mouth. “Don’t spit it out. I know, I know. It tastes terrible. Just hold on.” Pinching the skin together with two long fingernails, Searowe tapped all the nails of his other hand in a flurry of motion. He sutured the gauze directly to his patient’s skin, doubled it and sewed it down again. He scrutinized his work. Mareki stood up, while Searowe finished evaluating, and said, “The bark will dissolve. Chew it until it’s all gone. It’ll help.”

Searowe, satisfied, stood up to join Mareki, but before they could move to the next patient, they heard a loud ruckus. It sounded like they’d found Brace and the bups. Mareki smiled, took a moment to breathe, and went back to work. A kind, compassionate expression softened his face, and he questioned the next patient, “Where does it hurt?”

“Where’s Barra? Where’s Red?” Brace said to no one as she looked over the camp. Some Arboreals were asking her questions, but she wasn’t listening. Luke Mafic gave her a status report, but she didn’t hear it. She grabbed Luke. “Where’s Barra? Have you seen Barra!?” Her body was tense like a coiled spring. Her voice stabbed the crowd and slayed their chatter.

“She’s not in the camp,” Luke said.

Brace’s eyes darted around, searching for the quickest path to Plicks and Tory. Making her own path, she pushed through the crowd.

The sudden quiet alerted Plicks. He kissed his mother, who’d been injured in the fight, and ran toward Barra’s mother. As he closed the distance, he said apologetically, “She was running off in the wrong direction when we left. You didn't see her?"

Brace's heart pounded. Not again. Not again.

A wave of voices drowned out her thoughts. Jaeden, Red, *and* Barra had just arrived. Released from her terror, Brace ran toward her daughter.

Tory looked down at Plicks, who was tearing up. Tory said, "It's not your fault. We didn't abandon Barra. We thought she was right behind us. Hey, everyone made it." Tory glanced up and saw Ven Battidash, Plicks' father, watching from where he sat with his wife. He had an expression of genuine gratitude on his face. Tory smiled, and Blue folded himself around Plicks. The nervous Kolalabat breathed a heavy sigh of relief, and went back to his mother.

Jaeden cradled Barra. Brace didn't know how to say thank you as she took her daughter. All she could do was cry and hold her close to her chest.

"Her throat is going to be raw, but I got there in time. She'll be alright." Jaeden's words were firm.

Brace shuddered with relief. She wiped the tears from her eyes, and her mettle returned. She spoke to Jaeden, "Spread the word. We break camp, now."

Chapter 31

Remembering the Fallen

The Arboreals were unsure how to care for their dead. They were at the Root. The tradition of committing loved ones to the Fall wasn't possible. The usual downy rope used to cocoon the body could not be found, and wouldn't have worked in the ocean. But they found delicate metallic threads in beautiful silvery sprays near the fissures into the sea, and braided them into heavy bands to bind and anchor the bodies. They spoke few words and cast the lost, one by one, into the sea. The effect on the gathered survivors was profound; they saw their loves carried into the light. But there was no time to dwell on the implications. They broke camp.

The company moved slowly over the Root. Barra slept, but not well, until she finally woke, screaming. More of a strangled "erp" than a scream, now that she was conscious. Looking around, testing her limbs, Barra discovered she was strapped to her mother's back. She felt like the scruffs on a Kolalabat. Her head was heavy and thick with fog, and her muscles were sick-sore.

Closing her eyes, Barra remembered the dream, her nightmare.

There were thousands of Nebules drifting together, lost in the ocean. Then they were caught in the Creepervine, the fungus strung between them like thick, dark webbing. Some of the Nebules were free, shooting through the water leaving trails. But black vine-fingers formed out of nothing and snatched them too. Barra was overcome with a terrible sadness, incapable of helping her entangled friends. They needed to be set free or they would dissolve into nothing. They needed to be free to survive. The webbing sucked the light from them in spirals of sparkling dust. There was an ache deep in her chest, but then—in only the way a dream can—everything changed without changing. Barra hovered above the Boil. The fungal webbing was gone. A vivid, multicolored fleet of Nebules circled happily. They churned like clouds of ink in a whirlpool. Then suddenly the fleet flew toward the Boil, a million heads of light burning trails of fire into the ocean. The hot streaks cooled but never caught up. The Nebules hit the Boil and became distorted. They rearranged into bursts and arcs. And the ache returned, sadness as vast as the ocean, and as heavy. But the dream changed. Barra stood with Red, stoking her fondly. They held each other, but faltered. Red withered in Barra's arms. One tentacle was only a blackened stub, but it gripped Barra's wounded arm like binding wire. Even as the rest of Red wilted, she squeezed the poisoned arm harder. Red grew thorns and bit into Barra's flesh. Dragging Barra behind her like a toy, Red flew. Through the Boil and into the void, they joined the other Nebules headed for the Sun. Barra couldn't breathe. She struggled against Red, begging for help. And then Red let her go. Alone and suffocating, Barra screamed.

She'd come back from the dream with the feeling—no, she thought, the *knowing*—that the sacrifices hadn't been enough. Despairingly, Barra dropped her head down to her mother's back, and let her body hang limply. Her dangling limbs were lazy, swaying to the rhythm of the walk.

Barra passed in and out of sleep. Her dreams blurred with memories into an incoherent mess of destiny. There was a need, something she knew she must do, something desperate she couldn't quite identify, consuming her thoughts. She was rushing toward fate—or fate was rushing toward her—and she felt powerless to do anything about it.

Barra shook the confusion from her head vigorously enough to call the attention of her mother. "You awake back there, baby?" she asked her daughter.

"Umph. Yeah. Sorta..." Barra's throat was raw, and her lungs heavy. She didn't feel ill anymore, but she didn't feel good either. Also, there was an inexplicable change in her vision. The Root seemed sharper and clearer. She thought the seeping radiant scars were emitting more light.

"Where's Red?" she asked, but right then, she found the Nebule coiled around her arm. Red wasn't very red anymore. She was muddy brown with dirty green streaks staining her from the inside out. Barra stroked her and Red loosened some. She stretched, and pushed her bell-shaped body into Barra's hand.

"She's been with you the whole time. Didn't leave your side even when we all stopped to rest," Brace spoke over her shoulder in a low voice. "Do you remember Tory and Plicks stopping to check on you?"

"Nah." Barra tried to think back, but everything was a blur. She remembered something about… "Jerrun!" She reached for her throat and touched it gingerly, testing it to see what was only a dream and what was real. She found pain and bruising.

"Jerrun? What about him?" Barra's mother was suspicious. "We haven't seen him since before the attack."

It was difficult for Barra to piece the memories together into a coherent picture. Jerrun, the head of the Council of Elders, had tried to kill her. She was positive. But what had happened next, she couldn't say with any certainty. There was Jerrun strangling her, a haunting image—she could still smell his rank breath—and then he was gone. Someone familiar took his place. It didn't make any sense. And there was something Jerrun had said, something about her father, something cruel. She couldn't remember. Barra clenched her jaw and snarled. She didn't know how she would do it, but she wanted to hurt Jerrun.

"What is it, dear? What about Jerrun?" Brace asked. She heard the snarling and was ready to hurt the scheming Elder if he'd done anything to harm her daughter.

Barra seethed. Pushing her words through gritted teeth, she said, "I hate him."

Brace stumbled a bit, startled by her daughter's tone. So much hatred. So absolute. It was no secret that Brace disliked Jerrun intensely, and no one trusted him anymore, but what had he done to her daughter? "Barra, sweetheart, what's going on?" Beneath her compassionate tone beat a war drum. Plicks swooped down, startling them. Brace reflexively prepared to strike, revved up to kill anything that threatened her daughter.

"A little warning next time?" Brace said as she shook her head at Plicks.

"Sorry, Venress Swiftspur." Plicks rushed past the apology, "My dad sent me. There's a problem up ahead. We're going to have to take another route."

Tory loped in, Char close at his side, a constant, elastic extension of Tory's movements. Char seemed innocuous enough, but after the attack the Arboreals of the expedition knew better. Brace felt better with them watching over Barra, Plicks and Blue too.

Brace stopped the caravan with a brief, rapid, percussion of her tail against the Root. She said to Plicks, "I guess I needed a break anyway." She released Barra from the straps and swung her around. Gently, she set her down.

After testing her limbs, Barra decided she was indeed feeling better. A few Arboreals arrived, jumping to Barra's mother with reports about the path ahead. Fast words and gestures indicated that the obstacles were serious. Barra tried to excuse herself without disrupting them, but her mother stopped her.

"How's the arm?" Brace asked, kneeling beside her daughter.

Red uncoiled to expose the wound. "It's okay, I guess," Barra said. She stared at it, more disappointment than in pain, and added, "I feel bad for what it's doing to Red."

Brace acknowledged the Nebule with a tentative pat, and then held Barra's hand. Barra's arm was bald from the wrist to the elbow. Some thinning had started above the elbow too. Her skin was scarred with ropey, viny, green lines that radiated from the open cut. It looked awful. Brace did her best to hide the thought. "It doesn't hurt?" she asked.

"Not really," Barra said, shrugging.

Brace said, "Well, whatever Red is doing, she wants to do it for you. I wish *I* could hug myself around you to make you feel better." She added as positively as she could, "I think it's helping. We just have to get you home." Indicating the other adults, she said, "We're going to be a little while. Will you be okay with your friends? Promise me you won't wander off."

Barra nodded. She seemed to have aged unnaturally. A terrible sense of loss tugged at Brace's heart; she hadn't been able to rescue her bup after all. She was gone. Brace had always known her daughter would grow up some day, even wanted her to grow up, but this was too soon, too fast.

Barra said, "We'll stay close. Don't worry. We know how dangerous it is."

Brace believed her. She nodded, stood up, and stepped away. But she didn't resume the meeting until she found Jaeden and asked for her to watch the bups.

Sitting with her friends, Barra said, "I'm so happy to see you! I don't remember everything from the fight, but I know you came to save us. Thank you." They passed hugs around, and she asked, "So, what's going on? I mean, why are we stopped?"

"The Root is grown together with thorny bushes and tangles of vine," Plicks said. "Some Creeper, some not. The scouts are trying to find a way around, or up and over."

Tory leaned in. "Your arm's getting worse," he said somberly.

"Yeah," Barra admitted. "But I *feel* better, thanks to Red."

Blue and Char inspected the sickly-looking Nebule. They cozied up to her, caressed her, and tried to cheer her up with little bobbing playful motions. It seemed to help.

Plicks looked down at his feet. "What're we gonna do?"

"What *can* we do?" Barra's hopelessness broke her words. The hiccup in her voice might have been mistaken for adolescence, but Tory knew better.

"Well, look at that. The hopelessly hopeful is admitting defeat. Giving in pretty easily, don't you think?" Tory said.

Barra shot Tory a look that she hoped would melt him. And then he clicked his tongue and added, "If I'd known it was this easy, I would have done it myself."

"Tory Mafic, when I get better I'm going to seriously hurt you," Barra said, trying to sound angry. But as she mimicked her mother—invoking Tory's whole name as though that somehow gave her power over him—she only sounded ridiculous. She felt embarrassed and in her stubborn way, she became petulant and cuffed Tory on the back of the head with her tail.

Tory yelped, acting hurt. He saw deep emotions behind Barra's emerald eyes. He hadn't annoyed her into being herself again on purpose; he'd just sort of stumbled into it, the way friends sometimes do. He flashed her a patronizing smile, one that said, *Gotcha!* And *that* was on purpose. Barra pounced on him—claws mostly retracted—and he soon regretted teasing her.

Then, the beating turned from playful to sincere. Barra let go of her frustration and gave into the moment. She roped the Rugosic to the ground with her tail around his throat, and unleashed a flurry of punches. Tory tried to call her off, "Okay, okay! Okay, already! I'm sorry!" The beating continued, and he growled at her.

Plicks had seen them fight before. He was waiting it out, patient until the growling started. He jumped up. He took a cautious step toward them, meaning to intervene if they kept going.

Barra held her punches for a moment, looking bewildered, and Tory took advantage of the lull. He yanked her tail from his throat and threw her off. He stood up and pushed her, a touch harder than he intended, and they squared off.

Barra's tail snapped in the air over her head. Bitter, she said, "I didn't give up."

"Good," Tory said. He checked his panoply for cracks. She'd done some damage, but nothing too severe.

"I'm not giving up." Her tail warnings became half-hearted, and her face turned grim. "I just don't know what to do."

Plicks told her, "You don't have to know what to do. This isn't your fault." The Nebules, who had cleared to the side when the fight started, were hovering close again.

Barra slumped down and said, "It's at least my fault that we're all stuck down here. If you hadn't followed—"

"Followed?" Tory interrupted. "We went with you to be with you, because we like you. Not because we think you're a good leader, and definitely not because you make the best decisions." He smiled.

A weight lifted from Barra's shoulders. She loved Plicks and Tory like brothers, but sometimes she treated them like subordinates. It had never occurred to her that each decision she'd made, they made *with* her, not *because* of her. They were in this together. Suggesting otherwise was an insult to them. She laughed at herself, and sighed.

Almost in unison, the three friends stepped closer to each other. Plicks asked, "So, what *are* we going to do?"

They exchanged whispers for a while, and Barra kept thinking about her arm. She knew the infection was spreading. It didn't seem like they were travelling fast enough to get her the help she needed. They thought about flying her up to the Loft with the Nebules, the way Lootrinea suggested, but convincing the adults to let them go it alone seemed impossible. Sneaking away could work, but none of them wanted to put their families through that again.

Barra became distracted as they talked. There was something she was forgetting, something she was missing. Her dreams kept swimming through her head, nagging at her to pay attention, but she couldn't make sense of the images. Red glided down beside her, obviously tired, and snuggled into her chest.

She stopped the boys, and asked, "Why did we visit the Boil? What was down there for us?"

They looked at her, confused. Tory said, "There was supposed to be something down there for us? I thought it was just part of the route? Lootrinea said it was the only way."

"Every time I close my eyes I see it. I dream about it. Something is supposed to happen there. We're supposed to be there."

The boys didn't know what to say.

"You've seen what the Nebules can do to the Creepervine, you know? The way they explode it. What if we could bring all of them up here?" Barra suggested.

It wasn't a terrible idea, Plicks thought, but still a look of consternation dragged over his face. He asked, "You're not even thinking about a cure, are you?"

Barra said, "My father wouldn't have given up. I know he tried everything to heal that wound. We have to assume the cure wasn't in the Loft." She was confident. "There might not be a cure to this infection, but there might be a cure to the Creepervine."

Plicks decided not to think about what that meant for Barra's future. He had to hold onto the hope that she was going to be okay.

Hanging his head low, Tory digested her statement. She was getting worse. She might not ever get better. How long did she have? There was no indication from her father's journal. Worse, they didn't even know for sure that the cut was what killed her father. Who could help them? Lootrinea, the Nebules, Fizzit? Tory would strangle the answers from that amber-eyed, three-tailed enigma if he saw him again.

Tory eventually nodded his head, and then slowly raised it. "What's the plan?" Char spun around once and cast out his spheres in a bright array.

Plicks stroked Blue. "It's okay, fella. We're going back to the Boil."

All they had to do was tell their parents.

Chapter 32

Diver Down

Barra crept up to her mother who was still in conversation with the other adults. Tory and Plicks were close beside Barra. She interrupted, "Mom?" Her voice startled everyone a bit. "We have an idea."

The idea was met with open minds. The adults had heard of the Nebules destroying the Creepervine even if they didn't understand it. How many Nebules would it take to defeat all of the Creeper? No one could guess. Nevertheless, the bups' idea soon became a serious option.

None of the adults wanted to allow the bups to go on their own. Unfortunately, they didn't have any other suggestions. Barra wasn't sure how they were going to return to the Boil, but she kept that to herself. In fact, she carefully steered the group away from questions about how they were going to travel, and how they were going to convince the Nebules to join them. Barra was working on the assumption that the system of whirlpools would get them down to the Boil, and that Red would help them recruit.

Brace noticed that there was no discussion about Barra's wound, but said nothing about it until the talks quieted. Stealing the opportunity, she reached for Barra and held her close. She stroked her daughter's fur and whispered in her ear, "You're strong. So much stronger than I ever was… stronger than I am."

Tears filled Barra's eyes and she let them fall silently. She allowed herself to be held. She allowed herself to be home.

Brace thought she would never let her daughter go again, loathed the idea. At least her daughter wouldn't be up against Argus again, even if she couldn't say the same for the rest of expedition. The pathwood ahead was treacherous and their odds were slim. Knowing her daughter was safe would give her the strength to carry on.

Red hovered nearby, a curled and blackened stub of a tentacle reminding Brace of how much the creature had done to protect her daughter. Brace reached out and stroked the Nebule; Red had not only gained her trust, but her affection. She realized she didn't know how Red had been injured, and felt sick for how little she knew about the creature.

"My little bup." Brace wiped away the wetness from the fur of Barra's cheeks, "Travelling to the Sun… your father would be so proud." She added, "Well, proud, but probably a little jealous, too."

Barra believed it. They laughed through their tears.

What remained of the expedition made their way together to a large fissure in the Root where the bups could begin their journey down again. There were hugs and kisses. They cast words like spells to keep their loved ones free from harm, to grant luck and speed and strength, and to ensure that they would all meet again.

While the bups were busy with the Nebules, Brace began unravelling her Thread, releasing the clasp that served as the point of both closure and growth.

Vallor quickly pulled her aside. "Brace? What're you doing?"

"I want to give this to my daughter." Brace was using every bit of composure she could muster to remain calm. "I want her to carry on my story. I want her to have me with her always... especially if..."

"You can't do that." Vallor's eyes shimmered brightly, welling up with tears of her own. "She'll never leave if you try to pass her your Thread. You know it's true."

The Battidashes were nearby and overheard. Luke was close too, and he was already following Brace's lead. Hearing Vallor's words though, they all agreed. No Threads could be passed. Their stories could not be their bups' burden, at least, not like this. Brace wrapped the loosened portion of the Thread doubly tight and nodded her gratitude to Vallor.

Threads secure, the mothers and fathers gathered strength from one another, and moved in close to their bups. They hugged the hugs of long goodbyes hoping their arms would never forget the shape of their loved ones. Then, they let go.

Red, Char, and Blue harnessed themselves to their charges and flew into the air. They hovered for a few more goodbyes, and then they broke the tension and descended into the water.

As the bups sank, Brace thought they looked frighteningly similar to something else she'd seen recently. The thought strangled her, robbed the strength from her legs, and crushed her heart as she remembered; they looked exactly like the fallen.

Chapter 33

Tides

The duration of that moment cannot be measured. The tension that held it, that it held, was so great that it stretched and distorted the flow of time until it became unrecognizable. It can be argued that that particular moment has not ended even yet, and will never end, for those who were there are still there in many ways.

Despite the urgency so many feel to capture a moment, sometimes the moment captures them and never lets them go. For the friends and foes gathered there, time was no longer theirs to spend.

~Excerpt: Fizzit's Leaves

The trio floated to the bottom of the oceanic trench. Red, Char, and Blue steered the bups into the submerged wood, swimming through the narrow passages easily. They navigated as though they had intimate knowledge of the entire Root. Barra thought they were heading for a whirlpool entry, but she didn't know for sure.

Emerging from the wood into open water, the bups half expected a viny ball of green serpents to come floating toward them. There was nothing. The water was still, lacking life. The only movement came from swaying vegetation. A faint vibration began, and developed into an unmistakable resonance. An enormous shadow passed below them as something enormous blocked out the sun.

It was the Roedtaw, and he bellowed as he ascended. He only just fit between the rough walls of the trench. As he came up beneath them, Barra swam up to one of his gigantic eyes, and smiled into the ancient, steel gray iris. The inner circle of its mouth parted from the outer ever so slightly, and Barra stretched down to it. She kissed its upper lip through Red's body. It wasn't the required golden kiss, but the Roedtaw wasn't there to collect a fare. Barra believed his arrival was a sign they were on the right course, doing the right thing. The Roedtaw opened up, ready for them.

The three slid in behind an open plate and felt the slow churning of the great beast begin to speed up as bubbles filled the small space. The Roedtaw swung around until they were pointed down. The last known surviving Olwone cycled up his internal whirlpool and began the voyage back to the Boil.

At the surface, sitting by the opening in the Root, Brace felt the first vibrations of the buckle. It still felt odd to her, so different from the sway high up in the Loft. It was surprising too how easily she'd lost track of time.

It wasn't the Buckle she had to fear.

Eyes shone out of the darkness. "The fungal-puppets are coming, Brace." The words came with echoes in different timbres. Lancing the shadows with her keen eyes, Brace tried to locate the source of the voices. Her nostrils flared and pulsed, but there was nothing. Behind the sound though, farther away in the converging branches, something else moved. It came fast in her direction. She stealthed reflexively and waited.

The pool was closing. Soon, she would be entombed in darkness. She steeled herself against attack, but whatever was out there didn't move like a monstrosity. In fact, the closer it came, the more familiar it looked.

"Brace!" Jaeden called. Brace was cautious, but she stepped away from the closing fissure and released her fur to become visible again. She was convinced something or someone was still hidden in the wood.

Jaeden dashed into the diminishing pocket of light and space. Out of breath, she went on, "The monsters… they're attacking again." Brace was listening, but still scanning the wood. "We have to go!" Jaeden told her.

Motionless, Brace spoke, "There's something else out there."

Jaeden spun around in a flash and crouched. After several seconds she whispered, "I don't see anything."

"He spoke to me," Brace said, but she began to doubt it. She couldn't see, hear, or smell anything, and her senses were acute.

Standing square to Brace, Jaeden said, "These woods play tricks, especially during the buckle." As more and more of the rootscape curled into itself, she added, "Time is short."

Brace frowned. She broke her vigilant stare into the wood to glimpse at the opening to the ocean. The exposed surface had dwindled to practically nothing, and then it was gone as though it had never been.

Her daughter was safe. All the bups were safe… safer than they would be here.

Brace nodded to Jaeden. They fled into the crooked tunnels formed by the mad growth of the Root and the unbound motion of the Buckle.

In the pocket behind the plate, the bups were silent. They had direction and purpose, but they also had Barra's worsening health. It was hard to know what they should say to each other.

Tory tried not to look, but it was hard not to wonder what the infection was doing to his friend. Her fever seemed to have broken, but the cut was open like an eye and as black as a pupil. The wriggling worms had disappeared, but the skin around the cut was bald and carved by jagged green lines. The entire arm looked like a withering flower. It was bad, but what was worse in Tory's mind was that Barra showed no concern for it.

Plicks was worried too, but tried his best not to focus on the festering arm. Instead, he focused on Red. The longer he observed the Nebule the more obvious it was she was getting worse. She was mottled auburn, and her severed tentacle was shredded at the edge, weeping liquid light that sparked to ash as it fell. He reached out to pet her, and she seemed to want the touch, but he could tell she was hurting. Despite her lethargy the Nebule tried to snuggle up against the Kolalabat and be playful. His chest ached for her. His eyes stung and his head felt swollen with emotions he had no words to describe. He stroked Red, tears sliding over his cheeks.

Too preoccupied to notice her friends, Barra thought about how to convince the Nebules to attack the Root. She didn't have any immediate solutions, and she wondered if the Roedtaw would stop at the Drift on the way down. She hoped Lootrinea would help.

Barra thought about her dreams, and began thinking of them as her guides. She believed in them, no matter how crazy that sounded. She only wished she could make more sense of them. It was like there were two separate threads spinning two different webs from the same central point. Each connection on a web was a vivid fragment of a dream, but when she tried to connect the webs to one another the image became too confusing to understand. The dream webs were similar but with important differences and Barra got lost between images.

The Nebules flashed brightly and gathered together. Barra's stomach flipped, and she sucked in a harsh breath. Her mother was in trouble. She didn't know how she knew it, but the entire expedition was under attack, she was certain of it. Char was spinning and extending and retracting spheres alarmingly. The boys watched intently, but didn't understand. Red flashed back sharply, and Char calmed down. Blue flowed about, clouds sliding over his back and belly. Adding a couple more subtle, softer flashes, Red seemed to offer a conciliatory message to the others. After a few more exchanges, the three Nebules bobbed together conclusively.

As the jellies returned to the bups, Barra's dreamy gossamers fell away, leaving only a single web behind. As she contemplated it, it became a single obvious thread. A thread with a severe and unavoidable end.

The camp was under attack. The expedition fought from behind their makeshift walls, walls that wouldn't protect them long against the fungal-puppets.

Brace and Jaeden met up with some Arboreals who had been outside the camp when the attack began. They were three Kolalabat scouts, a Nectarbadger, and a Listlespur. Brace and Jaeden made a total of seven. The fungal-puppets seemed only aware of the camp proper and Brace believed that gave her small squad the advantage. They separated into two groups. The Kolalas and Jaeden were going to drop in from above on the other side of the camp, just outside the best fortified wall. They could crush the fungal puppets against the defenders there. Brace would lead the rest of the Listlespurs into the fray from the near side. They could pick off the monstrosities one at a time, thin their numbers, and kill off their strong from within.

As much as the creatures resembled Arboreals, they weren't Arboreals. They didn't care when Jaeden's force ambushed them. They weren't surprised or confused. They just turned and fought without concern for their lives. It didn't matter to them when Brace and her crew silently snatched one after another from within the main group. They were neither demoralized nor frightened. They simply kept moving relentlessly forward into the camp.

Floating pairs of morbidly green eyes flickered in and out through the collapsed wood. A fog of flickering beasties rose from the Root and blackened the air. The Kudmoths had been there long before the attack began. They swarmed up and around the stealthed Listlespurs, making them visible as they flew into them.

Claws raked and screams tore the air.

Threads were severed and strings were snapped.

Arboreals and puppets fell, and at the Root, they weren't so different after all.

The Roedtaw wound his whirlpool faster and faster. The bups felt the smooth reverberation in the marrow of their bones. What small view was afforded by the opening of the plate was distorted by the deepening of the meniscus. There was no way to understand the blurred ocean outside. It wouldn't take them long to reach the Boil.

Barra's dream vision was finally clear. Still, she couldn't figure how to share the revelation with her friends. Red twisted around her. Barra knew intuitively that Red understood what had to be done.

Watching them, Plicks thought they looked like they were saying goodbye to each other. The thought upset him. "What's going on?"

"Nothing." Barra faced the Kolalabat, earnest and loving. "I'm just... I can't believe this is happening is all."

Plicks didn't believe her. He'd seen that look before, whenever one of his brothers or sisters left for a long trip, whenever a cousin from a distant Tree said farewell without knowing when or if they'd ever see each other again. The faces they wore were in anticipation of missing someone deeply. Seeing Barra wear that same face trapped the breath in his throat.

Red wrapped Barra and held her tight, one long tentacle in cords around her bald and cracking arm.

For the first time since their descent began, the Roedtaw slowed.

"Did you feel that?" Tory asked. "We've leveled out."

Plicks and Barra felt it, too. They'd arrived.

The expedition was surrounded. Between the efforts of the Kudmoths and the fungal-puppets, those Arboreals still alive were pressed in close, their backs against the only partially fortified wall of the camp. Brace was on the frontline, wounded like the rest, but standing fierce, Vallor at her side.

Argus's forces didn't push their advantage. They held their positions, a boundary of dark vines, flesh, and glowing eyes disguised by the fog of Kudmoths. The wall was intimidating and frightened everyone except Brace. She was busy trying to find a hole, a weak area that they could use to escape. Pounding the Root with her tail and hissing loudly, she tried to provoke them. They seemed not to notice her at all.

It wasn't the Buckle—that had ended before Brace arrived at the camp—but a new and similar vibration began travelling through the wood. Something was coming toward them. The wall their binders had built and fortified began shaking violently. The Arboreals shifted, terrified. They didn't know which way to turn. Their heads jerked left and right, pulled around by unseen strings.

Scars appeared in the quaking wall as thin cracks. Wounds yawned open and spilled dark green pus from their edges. The glowing poison flowed over the woven and bound branches, and pooled at the foot of the wall where it smoldered and blackened.

The newly-carved scars bulged. The dizzy attentions of the trapped Arboreals gathered, and focused on the culminating rattling of the wall. Stunned, they watched helplessly. Too terrible to turn their backs on it and run. Too alien to fight.

The wall that was set to shelter the small crew congealed into a single curved mass of rot, stench, and fungal ooze. The quaking became a soft rumble, and then disappeared. It was replaced by a squelching, wet sucking sound. The blackness that began in the pool at the base of the wall rose up through the noxious liquid until it swallowed the scars. No more light-emitting fluid spilled out, only slow, dark sap.

The largest scar in the wall swelled like a lung inhaling. Finger-like protrusions appeared and emerged one by one. They sharpened and lengthened, and then cut through the thin membrane of ooze that coated them. The dark skin peeled away, and hands were revealed, like two five-legged spiders. They moved precisely on their clawed fingertips, apparently searching for something. When they found a good place, the spidery hands pushed flat. They levered an eyeless, toothless head out of the muck, and a thin, hairless body followed.

Fully birthed, Argus perched in defiance of gravity, held to the wall only by the clawed tips of his fingers and toes. He leaned out and scanned the Arboreals with his sunken, empty orbitals. His face fixed over the top of the tightly packed group and onto the one creature that stood out. Brace didn't waver beneath his gaze; instead she put herself between the rotting monster and her friends. She pushed through the mesmerized Arboreals with peculiar ease.

Brace stood apart from the huddled and tattered remains of the expedition. She was prepared to face Argus alone, but glad to

spot Jaeden stalking along the top of the wall. Brace was careful not to blink, not to look in Jaeden's direction, cautious not to reveal her.

Brace turned away from Argus. She inspected her fur carefully, almost whimsically preoccupied with the cleanliness of each patch even though she was coated in grime. Finding an offensive spot of dirt, she licked her fur. She preened herself as though it were any other day, as though she were safe in the Loft.

The rest of the Arboreals tucked into that tiny pocket of space were so quiet, their silence so absolute, that the small sound of Brace's rough tongue scratching against her fur was cavernous like she was licking the inside of their ears. Argus heard the insult.

Argus leaned until his drooling face was close enough that Brace could feel the dampness of his breath on her fur. He roared a low rumbling note that shook the Root itself.

Brace's eyes moved first, and then her head followed in a silky pivot. Her whip of a tail raised up and flicked the air. Argus' roar continued as though he didn't need to breathe. Brace's nostrils flared and she hissed. She found a pure violence in herself so disturbing that she was at least as afraid of herself as she was of Argus.

There was a flash in her peripheral vision—Jaeden striking from above.

The pocket collapsed, and a churning mass of Arboreals and creepers took its place.

Anxiety flew into the bups' bellies like buzzing Kudmoths. Breath caught in their lungs and their nerves were taut like the strings of

an instrument pulled too tight, out of tune and ready to snap. The Nebules were worried too, and they spent their nervous energy by bouncing around, erratic.

The Roedtaw bellowed, and the bups felt the rush of blood to their feet as they slowed down. Barra concentrated on her vision to keep her steady. She reached out for Red.

Plicks said, "You're not planning on coming back with us, are you?"

Barra was afraid that if she shared her vision that she would fail to follow it through, so she lied, "We're just scared."

"I don't believe you." Plicks wasn't accusing Barra. He just wanted her to know that he knew.

Tory did nothing to mask his shock, and shot glances back and forth between his companions. Char nuzzled into Tory's hand. Suddenly, Tory was overwhelmed with the sense that he was the last to know some secret. He felt betrayed and hurt, and demanded, "What's that supposed to mean?!"

The Roedtaw stopped.

Barra felt the pressure of her friends, their caring voices. "What if an army isn't the answer? What if there is another way?

A better way?" Barra said. She locked eyes with Tory. She held up her arm, the severity of the infection plain to see. In the time they'd taken to descend her entire arm had shed, bald from shoulder to finger tips. Scarlet splotches had appeared around vivid green cracks in her skin. The original wound was black and seeping. "I'm not going to make it back."

Tory and Plicks shuffled uncomfortably, but before either could speak a word in protest, Barra and Red dove into the ocean.

Jaeden raked Argus viciously across the face and coiled her tail around his throat, squeezing. But Argus dropped to the ground and dragged her from his face with her claws still deeply embedded in his flesh. He threw her away. Brace didn't see how Jaeden landed or where. She lunged at the monster without looking back. Hissing and growling at each other they slashed and dodged as the battle exploded around them. They tumbled into bodies of puppets and Arboreals. Brace tried to avoid the others. Argus clutched, cleaved, and crushed anyone who got in his way.

Brace tried every trick she knew against the eyeless creature, but nothing phased him. He caught her by the scruff and held her up, his face out of range. She swung her tail around, and he grabbed it out of the air, unnaturally fast. Brace's tail was strong, armored by the story of her life. She levered herself around and unleashed a flurry of kicks. Reaching up, she clawed wildly at his flesh where he gripped her neck fur. Argus was unimpressed. He strangled her tail, his oozing flesh burning like acid through her braided protection.

He squeezed until her leathery skin bulged between his fingers.

She screamed and he split her tail in two.

Her Thread unraveled. Burnt, frayed ends splayed out, groping for attachments they could no longer find. The memories fell to the ground in a cascade of delicate sounds like raindrops on water-softened wood. Pain-blind, Brace heard the baubles fall even from within the cacophony.

Argus dropped her like a toy that bored him, and lifted his foot, threatening to crush her.

A sickle-shaped fang speared his lifted thigh with a thud, and another impaled his calf. Vallor Starch came lunging in, yanking Argus off balance with her twin tails. He stumbled, but didn't fall. Instead, he grabbed Vallor's tails, the tips still in his legs, and pulled her off her feet. Spinning around, he whipped her into a bough, and then against the Root, the Haggidon howling in pain, and then whimpering. Argus ripped the tail-tips out of his legs, reeled in the quivering Vallor, and held her up for a casual inspection.

Vallor looked for Brace, but she was gone. She felt relief, and smiled into the hideous, oozing face of Argus. He smiled back, and then he pulled her apart.

"Barra, wait!" Tory grabbed Char and threw him to the meniscus where he spread wide across the threshold. Tory jumped through, Char enveloped him, and they swam off after Barra.

Plicks and Blue followed quickly after.

Even with their Nebules shielding their eyes from the light, the bups were momentarily blinded. Out of the light emerged clouds of mingling colors. Huge families of Nebules congregated and swirled. There were thousands of them and when they saw the bups emerge from the Roedtaw, they slowed to stillness. They swayed as the current generated from the Boil swept huge volumes of bubbles around them. The Roedtaw blocked the rising bubbles for the bups, spreading open the curtain so that they barely had to swim to stay close.

Barra realized that the Roedtaw had gathered the Nebules from the entire ocean. She fought hard to understand how they could all know what to do, and then she saw them flashing subtly to one another. Red spoke to them, sharing a greeting. There was response from the entire cloud, a pulse of light that waved through them like a cheer through a crowded audience.

One dark shape moved from deep within the colonies, and Barra recognized the striding strokes of Lootrinea. The Aetherial swam out in front of the Nebules and greeted the bups though she only came as close as the mouth of the Roedtaw. Her slender sucker-cupped arms were spread widely around her, displayed like wings, and her body rippled all the way to the tip of her tail.

She folded her wings, flipped over majestically, and swam back into the cloud of variegated Nebules.

The burden fell to Barra and her dream. Only she could show them all what to do. She wasn't sure what would happen to her, to Red, or any of the Nebules willing to join her, but she was confident the Great Forest would thrive again and become the world of her father's journal. She knew he would be proud of her. She only wished he was there to see it.

Looking up one last time at the apparently endless darkness above, she wondered how it would all change if her plan worked. Barra took a deep breath and swam into the open water.

Brace writhed in agony. She might have blacked out for an instant or an eternity; she couldn't know. She saw eyes. Familiar orange and gray rims filled her vision. But the nerves of her tail ignited, confused and crying fire as she moved to see. Brace called out desperately, "Gammel!? Gammel!"

But it was Jaeden that hovered over her. She slapped Brace hard. "Get up!"

Violent efforts reported all around; breaking limbs, wood and bone, and flesh tearing. There were threats offered, and echoes of threats fulfilled. Brace reached up, and Jaeden hauled her to her feet.

Brace was dragged into the thicket. But soon her body remembered how to move, and they were running before she was truly conscious of it. As her senses returned, she stopped and whispered, "We can't leave them!"

"There's nothing you can do," Jaeden said.

Brace mistook the young warrior's calm for emotionless dismissal and yelled, "We're going back!" But Jaeden grabbed her by her mangled, shortened tail and sent a shock through her system that shut her down. A cold spike shot up her spine.

"You're done." Jaeden looked around suspiciously. "I promise I'll go back once we've got you someplace safe."

Unsure it was the right decision, but unable to ignore her injury, Brace gave up. Her head hung low and her shoulders fell.

Brace's taciturn agreement came too slow for Jaeden. She yanked the wounded Listlespur—by the arm this time—to start her running. Jaeden snarled, "They're coming!"

Barra wished she could tell Plicks and Tory that their support, being there with her, gave her the courage to do what had to be done. She didn't think she could thank them without breaking. She knew they were following, but she didn't turn around. She stared down into the Boil alone.

There was no other way. She gave Red the go ahead, and they swam as fast as they could into the cloud of Nebules. The gelatinous creatures gathered behind them in a lengthening tail of light and color.

Barra let the exhilaration of the moment wash over her. They swam faster and faster until the trio became three comets burning the ocean. Charging toward the Boil, a massive number of Nebules followed them. Flashes of communication rippled through the comets of Nebules. They drove toward the Boil. Barra felt one version of her dream becoming a reality. She hoped the jellies understood, truly knew what they were about to do. The

other versions of the dream faded, no longer possible now that she'd chosen a path.

They hit the Boil at blazing speed, and splashed through to the other side. For a moment, Barra thought they'd somehow stopped, as her sense of speed vanished completely. Red stretched to envelop even more of the young Listlespur until she was completely contained, safe from the heat and light.

The Sun, unbelievably large and unbelievably far away, distorted her perspective. It was quiet in the Void too. For the first time, Barra actually heard the light that pulsed through Red like a heartbeat. Or maybe it was her own heart that she heard. Their rhythm matched so that she couldn't tell which was the source and which was the echo. But the sun was too bright even for Red to block out and Barra had to close her eyes against it. Burned on her retinas was an image that promised never to leave her, no matter what darkness came.

The two friends fell out of synch. Red faltered. Barra felt heat on her arm. It was pleasant at first, but focused on the wound, the warmth soon turned to searing pain. Splitting her eyes open just a crack, Barra looked at her forearm through Red and saw her arm glowing white hot with blue vapors flying from it.

"I think we're safe," Jaeden whispered to Brace. They hadn't gone far, but they'd found a den sealed up tightly by the buckle. Managing to wriggle their way in, Jaeden busied herself trying to stymie Brace's oozing tail.

"You saved me. Thank you," Brace said, her voice weakened and breathy.

Jaeden watched her eyes roll back slightly and grabbed her up. She shook Brace. "Hey, hey. Stay with me." Brace was sitting on the floor of the den, and Jaeden scooted her around until she had her back propped against the overgrown wall. She didn't want her to pass out. Patting her shoulder, she said, "It wasn't me, it was Vallor."

"Vallor? Vallor! You, you have to go back for her," Brace said, but the words lacked her usual force.

"I will. As soon as you stop bleeding," Jaeden said through her teeth as she bit through some bitter bark and chewed on it.

Brace inhaled sharply and tried to focus. She grabbed some of the bark that Jaeden had torn from the walls and started chewing. "I don't need you to chew my bark for me," she said from the side of her mouth.

Removing a well-masticated chunk from her mouth, Jaeden flattened the mash into the pad of her paw and then spread it on Brace's tail. Brace winced, but didn't cry out. She added her own medicinal cud to Jaeden's and filled her mouth again.

Brace was faster with the bark than Jaeden, and continued adding to her tail until it was covered completely in a thick, rough paste. "Now go."

Jaeden thought it better to pretend to leave than stay and argue, but as she turned she saw fingers of Creepervine crawling in through the narrow gap of the entrance. Kudmoths flowed in, staying close to the vine.

One way in, one way out. Jaeden cursed herself. She'd buried them.

Brace still hadn't seen the danger when she heard Jaeden hiss. Spooked, she looked up, and the hope she'd clung to for so long flew from her. She held to one thought to give her courage to face the end: Barra—my daughter, my love—is safe, and far, far away.

Red spun Barra around so that she was looking away from the sun. The comet of Nebules surrounded them. They created a shield against the heat, and a pocket for Barra. Swimming toward Barra from the Boil was Fizzit. Coiled around Barra's scorched and withered arm, Red pulled the heat from the cauterized wound. She siphoned the blue vapors into her jelly body, absorbing the blackened, fungus-infested flesh. Barra watched the black and blue bleed into every molecule of Red's body, except where she still held Barra's arm. There, against the exposed skin, Red was the same deep red she had been when they first met.

Red let her go.

The diseased part of Red's body split from the healthy. Her darkened body flew toward the sun, at the head of the comet of Nebules. Fizzit caught the flailing Barra with his tails. He flipped and dragged her back toward the Boil. Barra struggled vigorously, angrily to turn around, to look at Red, to find her and call her back. Fizzit was unwavering. He flew against the flow of Nebules.

Fizzit looked back over his shoulder, "There's nothing you can do for her. This is what she wants."

Barra inhaled like she was coming up for air.

Fizzit curved around and fixed on Barra with all three of his richly glowing amber irises. "You should say goodbye."

Positioning Barra gently with his three tails, Fizzit held her so that she could see the sun. The Nebules closest to the sun crossed a threshold of distance or gravity, and streaked away, bright thin lines burned in their wake. The first Nebules hit the sun and their impacts created fiery rings and flares. The corona of the Sun came to life.

Barra thought about Red, not knowing how to say farewell. She looked down at her arm where the sanguine jelly coated it like a second skin. She flexed, and though there was still some soreness, her arm felt strong again.

She tried to find Red in the display of light. One after another, impact after impact, the explosions built. Watching the tiny impacts, she saw them stacking, creating bigger and more powerful waves. Nebules crashed into the sun by the thousands. Barra couldn't see her, but she imagined Red leading them in fearlessly. Tears welled up in her eyes. She hoped it was worth it, that they made a difference.

Fizzit said, "We can't stay." He pointed to the building intensity of light.

Barra nodded. Fizzit twirled her around, and they twisted their way back into the illuminated ocean.

Crouching and backing up, Jaeden imposed herself between the Kudmoths and Brace.

Brace refused to be a burden. She crawled forward on frayed nerves, wounded limbs, and courage. She joined in Jaeden's fearsome hissing. Out of habit, her muscles fired to raise and flick her tail, but the half that remained burned in protest, and her hiss broke into staccato inhale.

Jaeden risked a glance to her side. "I'm sorry for this."

Brace managed to smirk through her agony. "I'm not. I saw my daughter again. I know she's safe now."

Jaeden had hoped for something more encouraging, but knew that neither of them was likely to make it. Neither was rushing to die either, so they continued to threaten instead of charging into the fight.

Then, just as quickly as the Kudmoths had entered, the dark harbingers left. Jaeden crept carefully forward to investigate and noticed the Creepervine swelling. One arm of the vine burst and shocked Jaeden into jumping back to Brace. More arms exploded, and sprays of noxious green painted the walls.

The pair was stunned. A dim white light radiated from every break in the weeping vine. The glowing splashes faded, and the den was softly illuminated exclusively by the white light. It wasn't a bright light by any measure, but it wasn't dark.

Avoiding the splashes even though the poisonous radiance was gone, Brace and Jaeden approached the sliver of an entrance to the den. Jaeden went out first and then quickly poked her head back in. "You have to see this."

CHAPTER 34

The Rain

The Roedtaw held his plates open wide as he could as he carried the bups home. The underside of the Root was sparkling to life. Flashes burned across the sky, increasing the light with each burst. New bright colors and textures bloomed, and flowers overflowed with water.

Glowing waves overtook the Roedtaw from beneath. They rippled over the Olwone and continued to the Root. They diffused there, each impact bigger than the last. The enormous flotilla of interwoven Great Trees began to glow. The bups couldn't see from behind the plate, so they watched and wondered what the waves of light were doing to the Loft, and to their families.

They missed Red, Char, and Blue.

Plicks asked, "Do you think they'll come back?"

Barra looked at her arm. She ran her fingers over it. The sanguine jelly was fused to her and felt smoother than her own skin. "I don't know."

Tory asked, "Are you an Aetherial, now?" Curiosity didn't disguise the sadness in his voice. He felt sure he wouldn't see Char again.

Taking her time to think about it, Barra realized she had no idea. Plicks waited for her answer with mixed emotions. He was excited for her, that she might be an Aetherial, but not sure what it meant really. Barra thought that she should *know* whether or not she'd become an Aetherial. Not knowing probably meant she wasn't. "I'm not sure. I don't think so," she said somberly.

Tory seemed not to accept the answer. Plicks asked uncertainly, "Do you think our families are okay?"

"I hope so," Barra said, but her intuition was dead silent. A tear dropped down her cheek and traced her smile. It tasted like the ocean.

She wanted to return to her father's journal. Now she knew how it ended, and she could write the rest for him.

The fungus burned away from the Root, and the Creepervine receded into the few remaining places of shadow. Like wildfire, the sun's light was carried up the Great Trees. When the light reached the Loft it opened and spread out over the canopies. The radiance swelled until it extended out of the Reach and created a new sky, bright violet and alive.

The expedition was stunned, at first, unable to believe what was happening. The fungal-puppets fell mid-fight, crumpling to the Root as small mounds of rot. Their master's vines shriveled, weakened, and broke.

Luke Mafic said, "They did it." He looked around, found Kable, Plicks' father, and screamed, "They did it!"

Each Arboreal turned to the next, realizing what had happened. They erupted in bouts of joy and tears. They rejoiced for all the moments they had, and those they had yet to share together. They cheered, and they didn't stop cheering until they were too exhausted to continue.

The channels that carried the ocean to the boughs were cleansed of dark materials. The water rushed to the top of Cerulean's Great Trees, split into every branch and each flower, no matter how large or how small. For the first time in generations of rings, the rain fell. Prismatic droplets saturated the air and rolled down between leaves and petals, and over barks and needles. It came down in torrents. It appeared as showers and mists. It washed away the stifling darkness, and brought new life to all the Great Forest.

The rain came down.

And spirits rose.

Chapter 35

Red Tide

"Over here!" Barra yelled to her mother across a pathwood teeming with light and fresh growth.

Brace was still recovering, but she was hobbling around better each day. She'd already started weaving a new Thread around her lame tail. The new Thread was unique to the Forest; it began with Vallor's Thread. Brace had gathered the remains with reverence and sworn that she would carry Vallor's story as her own.

She fingered the new Thread while she admired the light of the Loft and the many changes it brought. There was even talk of making Brace an Elder, but for today, she was an explorer. She was on a journey through the Middens with her daughter, the way Gammel would have wanted. Her sense of balance was improving, but she still needed practice and couldn't imagine a better way to get it.

"There!" Barra said dramatically. She was pointing into an ancient, warped den that had newly opened up as the turgor of the upper boughs increased. "I've never seen that one before!" And then she bounded off.

Brace sighed as she faltered after Barra. "She's always been your daughter, Gammel." Her head turned up as she invoked his name, and she saw a spectracinthe flower sparkling down at her. Its lavender petals drew together, creating a chamber that filled with water and divided its own light into discrete bands of color. Gammel had given her the same flower the day they met. She remembered how he'd explained what the flower would look like if the Great Trees were healthy. He was right. It was beautiful.

"Mom!" Barra poked her head out from the old den. "Are you coming?" She gave her mom a playful, petulant look.

"Yes, yes," Brace said, shaking her head. She rolled her eyes and then tried to jump forward. Instead, she stumbled awkwardly. Catching herself, she swiped the spectracinthe and it burst open. Sugary water splashed all over her fur. She felt a little embarrassed as she noticed her daughter staring at her. "I'm fine. I'm fine. I'll be right there." Brace gathered herself up and moved with greater care toward Barra who was pretending not to worry.

As Brace shambled toward Barra, she held close to support branches, and as the boughs shook, one of the disturbed spectracinthe petals broke free from the flower. It floated gracefully on the air like it was floating down a river. It came to rest briefly now and again on various flowers and branches. Somehow, it always found the open spaces, slid through them quietly and continued to fall. Down through boughs, to the very bottom of the Middens. And then, fearlessly, it fell into the emptiness between the canopy and the Root. And it floated for a very long time. Long after Brace and Barra returned to their Nest and prepared for the Buckle and slumber, the petal was still falling.

Finally, deep into the night, into one of the few remaining dark corners of the Root, the vivid lavender petal came to rest on a slimy bed of rotting wood. The creature that lived there didn't notice the lively petal at all. He crushed it between his sooty toes and ground it carelessly into the grime. He moved to sit beside a radiant pool, a hole in the Root that was torn and jagged as though it had been forced open. Shredded branches were strewn as if a dervish of claws had cut through the branches.

The place was not so much a dark corner, or a shadowy den, as much as a hollow bored into the Great Umberwood by many rings of rotting.

The lithe creature held a shaking fist over the pool. Slowly, he opened muck-sodden fingers. In his palm rested a dozen jelly-covered seeds. Each was red with a smoky center curling within it. He pinched a single seed between two pincer-like claws and delicately submerged the seed in the water. Finally releasing the seed, he watched it float. It lay there suspended for a moment. But then it turned. It spun around and trembled. After a few desperate shakes the seed split into two.

A hollow, low rumble began. It rose in a steady crescendo until it became a self-satisfied, gloating laughter. As his mirth died to an arrogant chuckle, he cast the remaining seeds into the ocean.

Argus watched. The water turned red.

About the Author

Aaron Safronoff was born and raised in Michigan where he wrote his first novella, *Evening Breezes*. In his early twenties, he moved to California to attend culinary school. He fell in love with the Bay Area and has never considered leaving, although he did eventually leave the school.

During his ten years in the games industry, he worked at various levels and for several disciplines including quality assurance, production, and design. All the while he was writing a novel, short stories, plays, and poetry. His career in design introduced him to amazingly intelligent, fun, and creative people, many of whom he considers family today.

Safronoff self-published, *Spire*, in 2011, and won the Science Fiction Discovery Award for the same in the summer of 2012. By the end of that year he decided to drop everything and free fall into fiction. In the following three months he completed work on the sequel to *Spire*, *Fallen Spire*, edited *Evening Breezes*, and published both.

Today, Safronoff is co-founder and Chief Storyteller of Neoglyphic Entertainment and working on his fifth novel, the second book of the *Sunborn Rising* series. In his spare time, Safronoff enjoys reading a variety of authors, Philip K. Dick, Cormac McCarthy, and Joe Abercrombie among them. He enjoys living near the ocean, playing and watching hockey, and video games. He has a deep love of music and comedy.

Sunborn Rising:

This book, *Beneath the Fall*, is just one part of the Sunborn Rising world.

Immersive experiences across story, illustration, music, games, virtual reality and more await your discovery.

Continue the adventure at:

www.sunbornrising.com

Find us on:

Facebook

Instagram

Twitter

YouTube

Acknowledgments

Neoglyphic Entertainment would like to thank all of the wonderful artists and musicians who supported us throughout the development of this story and our company. Your indefatigable spirit and creativity shaped the world of Cerulean and the heart of this studio. We would not be who we are today, where we are today, if not for you.

We want to thank all of our families. Your belief in us fuels our efforts day and night, as we strive for the very best to make you proud. You are our first audience and we love you.

We'd like to thank all of our Sneak Peekers who contributed copious amounts of time and insightful criticism when we needed it most. You managed to see the potential even when the work was at its roughest, and inspired us to never stop in our pursuit of excellence.

We'd like to thank our advisers who represent so many facets of entertainment, art, and business. Your wisdom and expertise are our guiding lights as we explore new methods of development and creativity. Thank you for joining us on this adventure and imparting the confidence of your years of experience.

A huge thank you to our investors without whom we'd be a commune of starving artists instead of an entertainment company revolutionizing the way great stories are created and experienced. You are the power behind the vision. Thank you.

And a thank you to all of our
Sunborn Rising Fans!

NEOGLYPHIC
Entertainment

Neoglyphic Entertainment believes story is the heart of the human experience. Story inspires creativity, shapes minds, and catalyzes social change. Story connects us to one another, celebrating our greatest triumphs and exposing our deepest fears, establishing a common ground to learn, to understand, to be.

Stories are shared through written word, visual art, film, music, video games and more. Neoglyphic develops technology to cultivate story across all these art forms, and reduces the traditional risk and cost associated with entertainment production. We offer a storytelling platform to connect with fans, derive meaningful insights, and deliver immersive experiences.

Whether you're an author writing your first novel, or a studio creating a feature film, Neoglyphic will be your trusted partner to untether your imagination.

www.neoglyphic.com